J. D. PROFFITT

Fever
RUN

A NOVEL BASED ON
A TRUE STORY

Fever Run is a work of fiction, an entertainment, and even though painstaking care has been applied to historical detail, occasionally a fact has been stretched or a truth bent for the sake of story. Names, characters, places, and incidents are used fictitiously. Any resemblance to actual persons, living or dead, business establishments, events, or locales is coincidental.

To My Parents,

My Sons,

and My Siblings

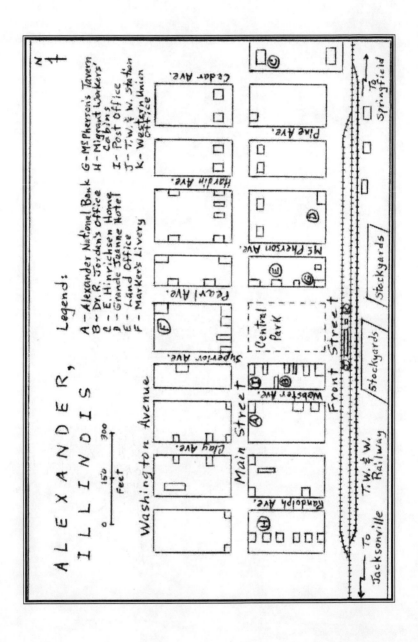

ALEXANDER, ILLINOIS

Legend:

A – Alexander National Bank
B – Dy. R. Jordan's office
C – E. Hinrichsen Home
D – Grande Jeanne Hotel
E – Land Office
F – Marker's Livery
G – McPherson's Tavern
H – Migrant Workers' Cabins
I – Post Office
J – T.W. & W. Station
K – Western Union office

Washington Avenue

Feet   0   150   300

Cedar Ave.
Pine Ave.
Hardin Ave.
McPherson Ave.
Pearl Ave.
Superior Ave.
Webster Ave.
Clay Ave.
Randolph Ave.

Main Street
Front Street

Central Park

To Springfield
To Jacksonville

T.W. & W. Railway

Stockyards
Stockyards
Stockyards

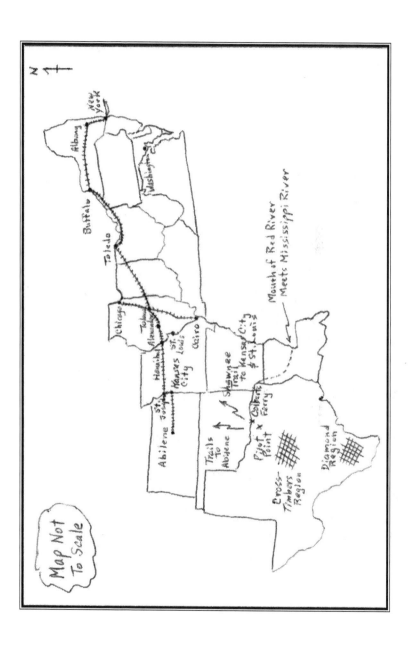

CHAPTER ONE

Abilene, Kansas
July 5, 1867

I lurched forward in my seat as the screams from the conductor and the squeals of locked iron wheels on hot iron rails blended into a cacophony of mind-numbing noise.

"Abileeeene...Abileeeene," he shrieked. "Abileeeene...Abileeeene. Next stop, Saliiiina, end of the line."

I shook the remnants of sleep from my aching head and rubbed my stubbled face with hands that had no feeling to them. As they slowly tingled back to life, my fingers gripped the overhead storage rack, and I pulled myself from the seat, stretching my tired frame. Out of habit, I reached down to straighten my holster, but it wasn't there as it used to be. The war was over, but the soldier in me lingered on.

Then I remembered where I was. I tried to move, but the thought of stepping out into the oppressive heat of the Kansas morning was enough to freeze me in my tracks.

"Don't forget your bag, Mr. Demsond," the conductor said. "I hope you have a pleasant stay. You're most likely to find Mr. McCoy right there in the station."

I tried to moisten my cotton mouth. "Thank you, Robert. If all goes well, I will quickly complete my business with Mr. McCoy and see you when I board again for the return trip to Wyandotte." I had no desire to stay in Abilene any longer than necessary.

"Suit yourself, Mr. Demsond," he said. "We'll make the turn-around up ahead in Salina, and then we'll be right back here at two p.m. sharp."

"Don't leave without me," I said with a laugh. He thanked me as I handed him a nice tip.

I took my worn alligator-skin bag from Robert and ambled to the rear of the empty car. I slowly stepped down onto the newly con-structed platform.

I was alone.

The small depot appeared to be a temporary structure that had been thrown together to house the telegraph office. Along with the sweet smell of freshly cut wood, I caught the scent of bacon in the air and remembered that I was hungry. There seemed to be some sort of eating establishment in the next building. I stood in place for a mo-ment, trying to decide which way to go.

In the background, Robert shouted "all aboard" to no one, and the small train slowly left the station. The platform was still empty. I stood alone in the heat of the Kansas sun, wishing that I was back home in Virginia.

But I had no home in Virginia...not even family...not now. The Yankees had seen to that. If the railroad had extended beyond Salina, I might have continued on westward...someday soon.

My reverie was interrupted by loud voices coming from within the railroad station structure. The tone wasn't friendly. My stomach growled. I thought about the bacon, but I found myself walking forward on the platform and entering the building.

Three men were arguing with another man who fit the description of Joseph McCoy, the man I came to see. The twenty-nine-year-old McCoy's close-set eyes and high cheekbones were distinctive. The three troublemakers had pushed him into a corner of the small building. The big man who was poking McCoy in the chest stopped and turned when I entered the room.

I didn't like him.

He glared at me with a scowl on his ugly face. "What do you want?" he said. Tobacco juice dripped from both sides of his mouth, and the stains covered the front of his dirty shirt.

I took a good look at his two friends. One of them wore an exposed firearm. I moved to be close to him. "I have some business to conduct with Mr. McCoy," I said.

The two smaller men looked to the big man to signal their next move. They didn't have to wait long, as he smashed his huge fist into McCoy's face.

Joseph McCoy was out cold before he hit the floor. I grabbed the pistol from the man next to me and tossed it into a nearby spittoon. The three of them bunched together as they tried to hit me at the same time. I tried to keep the smaller men between the big guy and me, but in doing so, I failed to see a good punch from the little left-hander.

He landed a solid blow just above my right eye. The blood came at once, blurring my vision. Things quickly went from bad to worse when the big man grabbed my shoulder and spun me around like a top. I was able to grab one of the smaller men to keep me from falling to the floor, and both of us immediately took glancing blows from the big fist that was swift and felt like a hammer.

I lost count of the blows that I was taking to the body, and just when I was sure that the end was near, I heard a rush of air and a sharp crack that put the big man on his knees. The second blow from the stout walnut cane landed high on the big man's back, sending him face-first into the wood flooring.

I broke the left-hander's nose with my first good punch, and he doubled over in pain, holding his face in his hands. Blood gushed through his closed fingers.

I pushed him to the floor.

The third man caught a bit of the last smack from the cane just before he dove headlong through the open window.

I was dizzy.

The cane-wielding stranger tossed me a large handkerchief. He stood there leaning against his weapon as I pressed the cloth against the cut above my eye.

A minute passed before we were able to get a good look at each other.

Another moment passed before either one of us could speak.

"I know you," he said. "You're the Rebel officer who rode with Jeb Stuart's Confederate cavalry!"

"And I know you," I said. "You're the Union agent who killed my three men at Burke's Station!"

CHAPTER TWO

Abilene, Kansas
July 5, 1867

The groans from the men on the floor broke the awkward silence, and I returned to the present after a brief glimpse of the past. The man who stood in front of me was Jason Alexander, a former agent of the War Department in Washington. We had fought against each other on several occasions during the war. I had pretty much forgotten about him...until now.

He stepped over to help Joseph McCoy before I could say another word. Alexander now had a wooden peg leg, and luckily for me, a solid walnut cane. I remembered him without both.

I left the building to get some water. I was surprised to find a new well with incredibly cold water. When I slowly returned with a full bucket, Alexander had moved McCoy to a chair near the door.

I gathered that Alexander knew McCoy. "What happened here?" Alexander said.

"I was going about my business, and before I knew it, these three guys were persuading me to get out of town," McCoy said. "I haven't seen any of them in Abilene before now. They must have just ridden in today."

"We'll turn them in to the local sheriff and let him find out who they are," I said.

Alexander and McCoy looked at me and shrugged. "There's no such thing here," McCoy said. "We don't even have a jail. I've yet to see a United States marshal show up in Abilene. People here fend for themselves."

"What do we do with these fellows?" I asked.

Jason Alexander nodded in their direction and said, "We send them on their way without their guns—and hope that they don't come back." He looked at me. "You might want to start carrying a gun again...Demsond, isn't it? That goes for you as well, Joseph. If we had enough hands at the farm in Illinois, I would get a couple of them out here to protect you."

"Yes, I'm John Demsond. I turned in my arms at the end of the war...not my idea, mind you," I said. I didn't see that Jason Alexander was carrying a gun, but then I remembered that he favored a Pocket Colt during the war, and I suspected that he still had one under his light coat.

"This isn't Virginia. This is Kansas," Alexander said. "And now you have some enemies."

He was right. Besides, if I strapped a pistol around my waist again, I might stop leaning to one side when I walked...but then again, I might want to use it. I'd have to think about it.

We helped McCoy to his tent, which was pitched next to a framework for a building with three levels. It stood like a stark apparition against the flat expanse of Kansas prairie. Only a few pieces of lumber were stacked near the structure, and there were no workers to be seen on this sizzling Friday morning.

A momentary breeze of hot air passed through the tent, flapping the canvas. We sat down in the chairs that surrounded a small table loaded with rough sketches of the building design. This was McCoy's construction project, and I was curious to find out more about it. But first, we had to make sure that McCoy was all right.

Jason Alexander and I exchanged glances once again. This time, I spoke up before he did. "What brings you to Abilene?"

"I was about to ask you the same question," he said.

We stared at each other some more.

Much to my amazement, McCoy seemed to revive quickly. He shook his head, rubbed his sore jaw, and looked at the both of us. "Are you two going to fight the War Between the States all over again, or what?"

"No, Joseph, I don't intend to fight the war all over again," Alexander said.

"Nor do I," I said, offering my hand to my former enemy.

He responded immediately, and we shook hands. Joseph McCoy nodded in approval and took another drink of water.

Jason Alexander placed his hand on Joseph McCoy's shoulder, and then he looked at me. "My father has a large farm in central Illinois, and we're anxious to receive shipments of Texas longhorn cattle from Abilene as soon as Joseph builds his hotel and stockyards. He has already sent men into Texas to inform the drovers that a new railhead has been established here in Abilene. I intend to help him get the word out to the buyers back east."

I rose from my chair and walked to the tent's entryway, looking out at the unfinished structure nearby. "I'm sorry to say that I am the bearer of some bad news for Mr. McCoy."

I turned to face him. "I am an employee of the Union Pacific Railroad, and even though this rail line that runs through Abilene is a separate entity at the moment, negotiations are under way for its acquisition by the company that I work for. The Union Pacific must approve any new spending during these talks, and Mr. McCoy's requests for funds to build the stockyards and a larger railroad station have been denied. I was sent here to deliver this message in person."

Joseph McCoy was visibly disturbed. "This makes no sense," he said. "The railroad stands to make a lot of money from these cattle shipments…and I mean a *lot* of money! I was in Wyandotte last week, and everything was in order."

Jason Alexander stabbed a plank on the floor of the tent with his cane. "The cattle in Texas number in the millions. It's impossible to drive them all through Missouri or along the Red River. We *must* open up the railway from Kansas. I'll leave for Wyandotte on the next train. Mr. Demsond, would you care to join me?"

"Please call me John, and I'll be happy to accompany you. Perhaps we can help them to see the business potential here."

"In the meantime, Joseph, go ahead with your construction," Alexander said. "J. T. Alexander and Company will cover your expenses."

"That's great, Jason," McCoy said. "I knew I could count on your help. I'm getting good prices on the construction lumber from the yards in Hannibal, Missouri, and on the hardwood flooring from Lenape, Kansas. In return for the upfront investment in my venture, I will give your father the first rights to purchase the best stock that arrive here in Abilene."

"Fair enough," Jason said.

CHAPTER THREE

— ≡✦≡ —

Union Pacific Railroad,
Eastern Division
July 5, 1867

Jason Alexander and I boarded the 2:00 p.m. train headed for Wyandotte, a town that was rapidly being consumed as part of the larger town of Kansas City, on the opposite side of the Missouri River. It was a small train with only two passenger cars, both of which were almost empty. The train would make a number of short stops before arriving in Wyandotte just before dark.

Robert took our bags, and we settled in for the ride.

"Alexander, I'm sorry about your leg," I said. "How did it happen, if I might ask?"

"Please call me Jason. It happened as a result of a fight with a member of the Knights of the Golden Circle just outside Washington. He stabbed me in the same place where he had shot me some days earlier. It was too much for the leg."

I thought about all of the battles that I'd been in, and I knew that I'd been blessed to escape injury...I had seen a lot of ugliness. "I must say that you move around on the leg quite well."

"It took a while to heal, but once I was fitted with the hickory peg, I didn't think about it much more. I can still ride about as well as I used to…but you don't want to see me try to jump," he said with a chuckle. "Did you make it all the way to the end of the fight?"

"Yes," I said, "after General Stuart was killed at Yellow Tavern in May of 1864, I spent a good part of the rest of my time riding with Colonel John Mosby's Forty-Third Virginia Cavalry. He actually disbanded the organization in April of 1865 rather than surrender it. That approach didn't sit well with some of the Union officers.

"They tried to hunt him down after Appomattox, even after President Johnson's pardon. He was arrested several times but always released afterward. Grant finally stepped in and ordered everyone to back off and leave him alone. Colonel Mosby now has a law practice in Warrenton, Virginia."

"Mosby captured me for a short time," Jason said. "He was taking a close look at my little Morgan named Dandy, but I managed to escape with him."

"He talked about that escape," I said. "Colonel Mosby said that it was one of the slickest getaways that he ever saw. I remember Mosby describing the whole incident in great detail."

During a dark and rainy night, Mosby accidentally found that he was riding with his captives on a narrow road alongside a slowly moving line of Union cavalry. Discovering this, Jason Alexander had somehow managed to move his horse into an open spot in the Union line even though his hands were tied to his saddle horn. I think Colonel Mosby actually admired Alexander for getting away from him. "He overlooked the possibility that you might be able to control the movements of your horse with your legs as you would when roping a steer back on your farm."

"If I'd had the time to think about all of the things that could've gone wrong, I probably wouldn't've done it."

"Yes," I said, having had many close calls of my own. "I understand."

The flat countryside continued to slide by the open window. The ride was comfortable on the newly laid tracks. "Once I was sure that Colonel Mosby was going to be left alone to live his life in peace, I started to work for a man by the name of Grenville Dodge. I purchased supplies for the restoration of the railroads and bridges that had been destroyed in the Confederacy during the war. I didn't particularly like the man, but I needed the job, and he recognized my ability to negotiate a good contract. I had worked in the very competitive medical supplies business prior to the war.

"Dodge had me do some work for Dr. Thomas Durant of the Union Pacific Railroad last spring. One thing led to another, and before long, I was working for Doc on a full-time basis. This went well until late last year when we had a disagreement over bookkeeping practices. Since then, I've been running small-time errands such as this one."

Jason Alexander listened intently to the brief description of my recent work. "I've been reading about the feud that Dr. Durant is having with the Ames brothers and their Boston friends," he said. "Didn't the Union Pacific board of directors remove Durant from the position of president?"

"Yes, that happened in November," I said. "The Ames brothers view me as one of Durant's people, so I'm afraid that my future at the Union Pacific appears rather bleak at the moment. I'm doing my best, hoping that they'll keep me on." I was quite sure that they would not keep me on much longer. I'd pretty much decided to head for California at the first opportunity.

"I understand." He was quiet for a moment. "Whom should we talk with in Wyandotte?"

"A new general superintendent by the name of Anderson just replaced General W. W. Wright in May. We can ask to see Mr.

Anderson, but we'll probably end up with the division superintendent, George Noble, and that's just fine since he's the one who runs things. His office is located at the end of the line. We can spend the night at the Union Railroad Hotel right next door."

As the train moved slowly from station to station, Jason Alexander went on to explain that he left Washington and returned home after his leg injury in 1863. He continued to do a bit of work for the War Department, but he spent the majority of his time working the large family farm, which shipped about forty railroad carloads of cattle to the East every week.

Any animosity that might have been present when the two of us first met a short time ago had disappeared by the time we reached Wyandotte. We were both looking at the future and letting go of the past. I found clean-cut, fair-haired Jason Alexander to be of upright character, and I believed that I could now call him a friend.

CHAPTER FOUR

——— ❈✦❈ ———

Wyandotte, Kansas
July 6, 1867

By the time we completed our 160-mile trip to Wyandotte on Friday night, the office of the division superintendent was closed. Such was also the case on Saturday morning, so we extended our stay at the Union Railroad Hotel for two more nights. Mrs. Rogers, the owner, made us feel very much at home. We weren't invited to the executive suites on the top floor, but I found that my room was more than adequate for sleeping.

I needed the time to rest my battered body. Jason Alexander passed the hours in the hotel lobby reading. A series of thunderstorms provided a much-needed respite from the summer heat, so by the time we sat down for supper in the hotel's small dining room at 7:00 p.m. on Saturday night, it was quite pleasant. Modern gas lighting brightened the room, which was filled with pictures of railroad men and locomotives. I discovered that Jason knew a lot about trains.

The menu was essentially beef and potatoes and apple pie. The beer was fresh, and the large, padded leather chairs were very comfortable. The dining room was crowded.

"Your eye looks better." Jason Alexander was melancholy. "You know what's funny? I sometimes reach down to scratch an itch on the part of my leg that isn't there any longer. Apparently, my mind isn't easily convinced that it's gone."

"Some of the men I knew who lost limbs told me the same thing," I said. "You told me that the guy who did it was from the KGC. I recall that Colonel Mosby really didn't think much of that group. Even though they supported the Confederate cause, he thought they should've gone ahead and joined the Partisan Rangers."

"Well, there were plenty of folks who didn't think too highly of the Partisan Rangers either...even people on your own side," he said. "I recall that your General Lee wasn't fond of them. From personal experience, I know that Secretary Stanton didn't like them. He considered both the KGC and the Partisan Rangers to be guerrilla combatants, and he suggested that they be hung as soon as they were captured rather than taken as prisoners of war."

"I'll have to admit that some of the Partisan Rangers were nothing more than outlaws, but that wasn't the case with Mosby. He hated the mindless bureaucracy and lethargy of the military. His operations were all built around the element of surprise, and they would've failed if he'd had to wait for approval or allow time for his plans to be leaked to the enemy.

"And now that you've brought up Secretary Stanton," I continued as the steaks arrived, "I've read about the problems that he's having in Washington, claiming that President Johnson doesn't have the right to remove him from the War Department. It seems to me that President Johnson has the right to appoint his own cabinet."

"I won't argue that point," Jason said. "However, President Johnson cannot be allowed to act as if the rebellion never happened."

"That's true, Jason," I said. "But this nation will never come together again if the soldiers of the Confederacy aren't fully pardoned as I believe Abraham Lincoln would have wanted it."

"I was fortunate enough to spend some time with President Lincoln," Jason said. An awkward moment followed as he regained his composure. "His loss was such a waste...and you're right about the direction that he would've taken had he not been killed. In fact, he very well might have removed Stanton from office just as President Johnson is doing."

We continued to eat in silence. In the distance I could hear the tunes from a piano and soft rumbles of thunder. I found them to be a pleasant combination.

Jason and I ate slowly.

After a while, I spoke up again. "I believe that this venture of Joseph McCoy's is just what a part of the South, namely Texas, needs to get its feet back on the ground again. Moving these longhorns out of Texas will stimulate the economy in many ways—and just at the right time. You were right to encourage him to move forward, and I will help you in any way that I can."

"I'm troubled that the railroad hasn't approved the construction of the Abilene stockyards," he said. "The financial benefits are obvious, so there must be something else going on here, and that's what bothers me. Do you think it's just a misunderstanding?"

"No," I said.

CHAPTER FIVE

—— ⌖ ——

Hannibal and St. Joseph Railroad
July 8, 1867

The Monday morning meeting with George Noble, division super-intendent of the Union Pacific Railroad, Eastern Division, was very short. He wasn't in the mood to spend much time with us. He voiced his displeasure with my suggestion that he reconsider his company's agreement with the Union Pacific, my employer.

I assured him that I was only suggesting that he investigate the matter and evaluate the situation based on its own merits. Noble warned us that we would be wasting our time trying to see Adna Anderson, the new general superintendent, because he was out of town.

Before we left the building, I was able to send a message to the Union Pacific office in New York to report that I had met with Joseph McCoy in Abilene and informed him that the railroad would not build the stockyards there.

Since we were heading in the same general direction, Jason and I decided to continue traveling together for a bit longer. We crossed the Missouri River to Kansas City on a ferryboat and took the fifty-mile ride north to Cameron on the Kansas City and Cameron Railroad. From there, we were able to board the noon eastbound train on the Hannibal and St. Joseph Railroad.

We sat in the second of three passenger cars on the crowded train. The land was flat and barren except for the small settlements around the train stations that were scattered along the way to Hannibal.

"We'll be there in about three hours," Jason said. After looking out the open window for a moment, he added, "If you have the time, I'd like for you to spend a few days on our farm."

"I'd like that," I said. I could stay in touch with my boss at the railroad by way of the telegraph. Unless it was an emergency, I needn't be in any hurry to get to my next destination.

The clacking of the train's wheels changed from intrusive noise to a calming rhythm as we moved along the rails. While Jason stretched out in his seat and napped, I decided to catch up on the news in several papers that I had collected over the past few days. Eventually, I picked up the *Wyandotte Commercial Gazette*. There was a lengthy article about the promising future of Wyandotte, Kansas, and Kansas City, Missouri.

The writer indicated that there were three distinct routes between these twin cities and New York City. The shortest route was 1,358 miles in length. This route included the path that we had taken to connect with the Hannibal and St. Joseph Railroad at Cameron and then further connecting to the Toledo, Wabash, and Western Railway, the Fort Wayne and Pittsburg Railroad, and the Pennsylvania Railroad via Allentown.

The writer claimed that only an additional thirty miles would be added to this route if the city of Chicago was included. I found this rather hard to believe. The third path also included Chicago, along with Buffalo and Albany on a number of different railroads that had been recently brought under the control of the New York Central

Railroad; this one was 125 miles longer than the shortest route, but it included the capital of the state of New York.

In addition to providing this information, the writer put forth a strong argument indicating that it would be the combination of Wyandotte and Kansas City that would replace St. Louis as the gateway to the west because of its superior location.

I was just about to finish the article when a gentleman in the seat across the aisle spoke to me. "I couldn't help but notice that you were reading the article about the development of Kansas City. My name is Kirkland Armour, and I would be interested in your thoughts." The man was well dressed. His hair was cut short, and his full moustache was neatly trimmed.

I introduced myself. We shook hands. "I'd have to agree that the cities seem to offer a lot of promise for the future," I said.

He nodded. "The whole thing will be called Kansas City in the not-too-distant future. My brothers and I are looking to expand our business to this area in order to be closer to our product, which is beef, or meatpacking, to be more specific. We're currently getting established in Chicago and Milwaukee...great meatpacking towns."

He pointed to the man sitting next to him. "Simeon and I have been looking over the Kansas City area for the past few days. I think my visit to the editor of the *Wyandotte Commercial Gazette* may have prompted the story that you've been reading."

He paused to give me a chance to speak, and when I didn't say anything, he continued. "The population of many cities of the North has increased by about twenty percent since the end of the war, and the availability of beef has decreased by ten percent. I don't think it's possible to get enough beef on the hoof to these markets. The meat must be packed. Are you a cattleman?"

I put the paper down. "No, I'm not," I said.

"I didn't think so. You and your brother don't look like cattlemen."

I didn't correct him. "What makes you say that?"

He rubbed his chin and laughed. "It probably comes from spending way too much time with cattlemen...and some of them don't dress that well."

I had to laugh at that comment. "I work for the railroad," I said.

"Well, second only to cattlemen, I spend too much time with railroad men," he said.

I laughed again. I liked the man and made a mental note to watch for news about his forays into the meatpacking industry. I had a feeling that he was going to be successful.

Our conversation continued all the way to Hannibal, moving to many other topics ranging from politics to the weather. The thunderstorms had moved along with us.

CHAPTER SIX

⇥⇤

Hannibal, Missouri
July 8, 1867

Jason Alexander popped up in his seat as the train approached the station in Hannibal. "I envy your ability to sleep on the train," I said.

"I wouldn't really call it *sleep*," he said. "It's more like occasional napping." He stood up and stretched. We were of similar height and build, a bit under six foot, medium frame, 160 pounds. Apparently, to some, we looked a bit like brothers. "I have some business to conduct here in Hannibal, but it shouldn't take too long. Do you mind riding along on a cattle train?"

"Not at all," I said, "as long as we get separate cars."

"That's the plan," he said and laughed. "Our agent should be here with the cattle that he purchased for us from Sol Wagoner in the Blossom Prairie of Texas...about one thousand head."

We walked from the train station to the holding pens near the Missouri River crossing. "Hannibal has really grown. There are about ten thousand people here now. I can't imagine what's going to happen to this place when the cattle start rolling in here from *both* St. Louis and Abilene."

I immediately noticed the beginnings of a bridge that was being constructed for a railroad crossing. Having purchased materials for bridge construction for Grenville Dodge, I was able to estimate that it would take two years to complete this project. Jason noticed my interest. "It will be quite a chore to ferry the cattle from Abilene across the river until the bridge is built, but we'll just have to handle it. Currently, most of the cattle come up from St. Louis on the barges, and they are directly offloaded on the Illinois side."

As we neared the holding pens, I could tell that Jason was becoming disturbed. "They aren't here," he said. Some cattle were in the pens, so I wasn't sure how he could tell. He seemed to sense my quandary. "Sol's longhorns are speckled."

We walked into the stockyard manager's office. "Jed, this is John Demsond, a friend of mine." We shook hands. "I'm surprised to see that William Halsell hasn't arrived with my longhorns," Jason said.

"I know you left word that he'd be here by now, but he hasn't shown up. And to make matters worse, no one on the trail to St. Louis has seen him."

Jason turned to me. "These cattle were being driven up through Indian Territory and areas in Missouri infested with robbers. This marked our first attempt to bring a substantial herd of longhorns into Illinois. William went down to Sol's ranch in the spring to close an ongoing deal and to scout out a return path for future use. He brought a few of Sol's longhorns back to Illinois with him at that time so we could get a better look at them and try out the meat."

"How many men are with him?" I asked.

"I'm sure that Sol provided enough riders to assist William with this herd. They were to stay with him until the cattle were loaded onto the barges at St. Louis for the ride to Hannibal. We'll spend the night here and see if he shows up with the longhorns tomorrow."

⌘　⌘　⌘

I learned a lot more about the hazards associated with attempting to drive cattle out of Texas as I sat with Jason at supper that night. "Roving bands of outlaws and Indians will steal the cattle outright or demand a tax of some sort to permit passage. Many prefer the latter course, as they will encounter the same problems as the drovers if they try to move the cattle farther by themselves. Some of the bandits will just stampede the herd in order to break it up into smaller groups that they can butcher or run off with.

"I've even heard of them holding the stolen cattle close by and then offering to help the drovers find them for a price, pocketing a nice profit for little effort. In some cases, the agents are in on the swindle as well.

"As you might imagine, the condition of the cattle upon arrival in St. Louis can be so bad that they are worth only about one to two dollars a head. In our case, we sent William to purchase the herd directly from the rancher at about four dollars a head, which allows him to select the cattle and make sure that they are well fed and watered along the trail."

"But you accept the risk of them not arriving," I said.

"Yes, but if they arrive near dead, it may not be possible to fatten them up for sale to the meat packers," Jason said, "and the meat packers are paying as much as forty dollars a head."

I had to be sure that I'd heard him correctly. "So if you pay four dollars a head to buy the longhorns, and spend another two dollars or so to fatten them up and ship them to the meat packer, you can make thirty-four dollars a head?"

"Yes," he said. "It gets better than that if we can get them into the New York market because we should be able to sell them for anywhere from eighty dollars to one hundred and forty dollars a head there."

I dropped my fork.

CHAPTER SEVEN

***

Albany, New York
July 10, 1867

There were no written invitations. All communication was conducted via word-of-mouth with messengers carrying both the invitations and the responses. They used code names to hide their identities from others, and even though such precautions weren't really necessary for this private gathering, they used them anyway. Trust was sacrosanct, but these were businesspeople. Some had military backgrounds. Some were very wealthy. All of them coveted power and carried hidden agendas.

No trail would ever lead back to the twelve people who sat in the great room of this elaborate cabin nestled in the hills of upstate New York. The large wagon wheel platforms that were hanging from massive overhead beams were filled with rings of large unlighted candles. The tall windows welcomed the midday sunshine. Some of the guests had been here before, but many had not. They all knew the rules.

Raven stood before the others and spoke first. "The recent developments that have brought us here today are disturbing, but nothing is insurmountable." He made eye contact with each individual member of the small group seated in the circle of chairs. "I've already acquired resources in the primary areas of concern to us. These people will not hesitate to take actions as necessary. And even though I anticipate favorable results, I also expect to be able to call upon each one of you if I need your immediate assistance."

Most of the heads in the circle nodded in approval. Badger stood up. "I'm afraid that you may have grossly underestimated this threat. The weak laws forbidding the importation of Texas cattle imposed by Governor Crawford in Kansas and a few others in neighboring states are not enough. You need to do more."

"Those are strong words, Badger, and I don't like strong words," Raven said, raising his voice. "The fact is that these laws place a great burden on the drovers. It forces them to drive their cattle miles out of their way in order to avoid the forbidden areas so they can get them to market during the best months of the year."

Badger remained standing. "The numbers in Texas are overwhelming. There are so many cattle that they don't even count them. We mustn't put undue faith in this effort of yours. I strongly suggest that we place our attentions elsewhere."

"Nonsense!" This time it was Bear who rose from his chair. "We cannot allow this Confederate vermin to spoil our fine tables. I will not permit it under any circumstances."

"Well spoken, Bear," Raven said. "I believe that your sentiments represent the majority here." Raven glared at Badger. An uneasy silence filled the room. Badger slowly sat down.

The big, hairy Bear remained standing. "I will return to the area as soon as we are done here," he said. "I will personally see to it that our enemies are discouraged from pursuing their dreams. I have plenty of men, and they aren't afraid to use a gun like some people I know." He dropped into his chair with a loud thud that shook the room.

Mink was the only woman in the group. Her threadbare clothing denied the notion that she was one of the wealthiest women in the country. She didn't spend her money on clothing.

Mink remained seated. "I believe that I have traveled even a greater distance than Bear to attend this meeting, and I don't intend to leave until I'm convinced that this august group will stop at nothing to end this threat. I have loaned millions of dollars to those who have established the current means of commerce, which is quite profitable, but it is a delicate balance that can be upset with a large increase in supply. This *cannot* happen. Have I made myself clear?"

"Trust me, it won't," Raven said, looking at Badger.

Badger shrugged.

After this heated discussion, a few lesser items of business were handled very calmly and very quickly before the group dispersed. Badger was the first one to depart. He didn't say a word to anyone on his way out.

Badger sat in his carriage in the distance, watching the others leave. "These people just don't understand what's going on here," he muttered to himself. After a while, he motioned for his driver to depart.

"Albany, sir?"

"Of course," Badger said with a laugh.

CHAPTER EIGHT

———— ✦ ————

Toledo, Wabash, and Western Railway
July 12, 1867

We waited until Friday to leave Hannibal. Jason left word that he was to be wired immediately if William Halsell arrived with the herd. "I need to talk this situation over with my father," he said. "Under normal circumstances, he'd send someone to check on William, but we're short of help right now, and the task requires that one of our best people be sent."

We crossed the river and boarded the Toledo, Wabash, and Western Railway for the trip to Alexander, Illinois. Jason said that the town was named after his father. After we settled in for the ride, Jason continued. "We're in the process of expanding our operation to a farm near a little town by the name of Tolono, which is located about one hundred miles east of Alexander where the Illinois Central Railroad crosses the tracks of the TW&W Railway. The Illinois Central carries freight from Cairo to Chicago. My father just purchased twenty thousand acres right outside of Tolono, and we are enlarging the stockyards at both railroad stations in town.

"We can send our cattle on to the New York market as we've always done, or we can offload our cattle at the TW&W Station in Tolono, and then we have the choice of moving them out to the land to fatten up, or if they're ready for market, we can move them over to the Illinois Central Station for the trip to Chicago," he said. "We're counting on the ability to bring thousands of longhorns from Abilene each year.

"The Tolono location in Champaign County also gives us the option of continuing to bring the cattle from the Red River to Cairo on the Mississippi, and shipping directly from there on the Illinois Central. My father calls our extensive pastures located near the stock-yard railheads in Alexander and Tolono our two points of presence. He plans to build many more such places in the future. His vision is grandiose."

"It sounds like a pretty good plan to me on the surface," I said, "but how will you keep the prices from falling when the supply of cattle is greatly increased?"

"That's a very good question, and, as you might expect, you're certainly not the first to raise it. Actually, we expect the demand to greatly increase in lockstep with the increase in supply due to the rapid expansion of the meatpacking industry. A gentleman by the name of Gustavus Swift is a family friend, and he is building a huge plant in Chicago. He and others are experimenting with ice-packed railroad cars that would allow the meat to be shipped long distances from the processing plant. Many more people will be able to buy meat."

"While you were napping on the trip to Hannibal, I spoke with a man named Kirkland Armour," I said. "He and his brother, Simeon, were looking into a meat processing plant in Kansas City."

"I caught bits and pieces of your conversation with him," Jason said. "He thought I was your brother and not a cattleman...and you didn't set him straight."

"He was so far off the mark that I didn't know how to begin to correct him," I said.

Jason laughed. "The Armours compete with the Swifts, but I think the industry can handle both of them, and probably many more. As far as the J. T. Alexander and Company is concerned, they're all welcome…and the sooner, the better."

The ride along the raised tracks of the TW&W provided a great view of the lush prairie lands as they passed by the open windows of the comfortable passenger car. We slowly moved from town to town, stopping at each one along the way. Jason seemed to know all of the station agents.

"The train will spend some extra time in Jacksonville up ahead," he said. "Arnold Station is the only other one between there and Alexander."

"I sure hope I'm not imposing upon your family."

"Not at all," he said with a laugh. "We have plenty of room in the big house, and if it's full of guests for some reason, as it sometimes is, I'm sure there will be space in one of the bunkhouses."

Actually, I was quite anxious to see the place.

CHAPTER NINE

✦

Alexander, Illinois
July 10, 1867

The town of Alexander was larger than I imagined it would be. It was a busy place on this late afternoon. Our train stopped on the main set of tracks, which ran along the south side of the station. There were two sets of very long sidetracks; one ran along the north side of the train station, and another was located south of the main track—this one was currently occupied by a train with men busily loading up its cattle cars...a whole bunch of cattle cars.

Jason noticed the attention that I was giving to the process. "We load cattle at this station on Monday, Wednesday, and Friday. It's mostly our stock, but there are a growing number of smaller stock raisers in the area. After that train pulls out of the station, you'll be able to see the large stockyard complex that lies to the south. I like to tease Mr. H., Edward Hinrichsen, about his bad design in laying out the town ten years ago. He should have placed the stockyards on the north side of town so the prevailing winds of the summer would blow the smell *away* from the town. He claims that the smell of money takes on many different forms."

"That's funny," I said.

"Mr. H. has a great sense of humor," Jason said. "He's also an astute businessman. He buys and sells wheat and corn when he's not busy working for the railroad. We won't see as much of him as we used to because he was just promoted to the position of general stock agent for the TW&W Railway. His territory runs from Quincy, Illinois, to Buffalo, New York. We'll miss him around here. He's always been at the center of this community." I was looking forward to meeting Edward Hinrichsen.

"I'll introduce you to Mr. H.'s replacement," Jason said, just before we walked into the station building.

A large man with a thick moustache was sitting behind a small desk. "John, I'd like you to meet Henry Fitch, our new station agent. He comes to us all the way from Rochester, New York. Henry, this is John Demsond, a friend of mine."

"It's a pleasure to meet you, Mr. Fitch," I said, offering my hand.

Henry Fitch remained seated and extended his hand. "Likewise," he said. His limp handshake was annoying.

A few moments of uneasy silence passed, and then Jason asked about Edward Hinrichsen. "The last I heard he was working on some kind of a problem in Toledo," the station agent said. "Of course, I have more to do here than to keep track of him."

Jason started to turn toward the door, but then he stopped abruptly. "Did I receive a wire from Hannibal?" After the war, the public was permitted to use the telegraph service owned by the railroad but contracted to a company named Western Union, which had recently moved its headquarters from Rochester to New York City. Eventually, the company intended to build out its own entirely private telegraph service across the nation.

"No, you didn't receive anything," he said, "but now that you mention it, your friend here received a telegram from the Union Pacific Railroad." Fitch had an odd smirk on his face.

Henry Fitch lifted the wire from a small stack sitting atop his desk. After doing so, he returned the railroad spike that he was using for a paperweight to the top of the pile. "Mr. Demsond, I need you to sign the ledger indicating that you've received the message."

I did so. I read the telegram as we walked outside. I read it a second time to make sure that it said what I thought it said.

Jason took note of the change in my countenance. "Bad news?"

"I've been fired," I said.

CHAPTER TEN

* ⋙✦⋘ *

McPherson's Tavern
July 10, 1867

Jason and I remained in town for a while before we left for the farm. "We bounce back and forth between *farm* and *ranch* when we describe the place—actually it's more of a farm these days because our corn-growing operation is bigger than the stock-raising part," he said as we entered the double doors of McPherson's Tavern, located on the southeast corner of the town square, across the street from the central park.

I immediately noticed the elaborate oaken bar extending across the length of the north side of the building. An impressive mirror reached almost the full length behind the bar, making the place look much larger than it was. Jason raised two fingers to the bartender, and then we took seats at a table on the right. A pleasant-looking young lady promptly brought the drinks to our table.

Raising his glass, Jason said, "I always like to buy a man his first drink after he loses his last job. Here's to your future…I think it's a bright one."

"Thanks," I said and laughed. "I feel better already. I suspected that I might take the fall along with Doc Durant. They considered me to be one of *his people*—I was nothing of the sort."

Just then, two men joined us. The small fellow in the stylish suit of clothing spoke first. "Jason, it's good to see you. May Robert and I join you?" The other man, who was dressed more casually, was about our size.

"Certainly," Jason said. "I'd like you to meet my friend John Demsond. John, this is William Orear, our banker, and this is Robert Keenan, owner of the Grande Jeanne Hotel, which is on the next block east of here."

We shook hands. "What brings you to our fair town, Mr. Demsond?" the well-dressed banker asked.

Jason spoke up right away in a firm tone. "John is visiting our family."

"Wonderful," Robert Keenan joined in. "I hope that you will enjoy your stay. I love to meet visitors...even if they don't stay in my hotel."

Jason ordered four beers and changed the topic. "Do you know if James McCoy is in town?"

"He borrowed some money a couple of weeks ago for that place out west in Dickinson County, Kansas...the place he and his brother are building," William Orear said. "I suppose he took the cash out there."

"That's where we just came from," Jason said, "and he wasn't with Joseph."

"They usually stay at the Grande Jeanne when they're in town," Robert Keenan said, "but I suppose you could check at the migrant workers' cabins down at the west end, just to be sure."

"No need," Jason said. "They'd be filled up this time of the year, and I doubt that he'd be keeping a room in any of the boarding houses around town."

"That's all he might be able to afford at some point," the banker said, "but let's hope that the venture in Kansas works out well for all of us." William Orear had a lot at stake, for he had loaned the McCoy brothers money from both of his banks, the Alexander National Bank and the Jacksonville National Bank.

"We'll certainly know by this time next year," Jason said.

After they departed, we sat in silence for a while. I was thinking about my need to look for a new job...after moving to California. I surmised that Jason was worrying about William Halsell...or something else.

"John, do you think about the war much?"

"Only when I can't avoid it," I said. "It took me a while to learn how to sleep again. During the war, I could sleep better on a horse than on my back."

"I have my leg back when I dream," Jason said. "I like that."

We finished our beers. Jason stood up and motioned for me to follow as he headed for the door. "We keep some horses and a buggy at Marker's Livery at the end of Pearl Avenue. Let's walk down there and head on out to the farm."

CHAPTER ELEVEN

———— ⇥✦⇤ ————

John S. Alexander Farm
July 10, 1867

The farm was located just to the northwest of town. The route was staked out with telegraph poles. "When I returned from Washington in the fall of 1863, I set up a telegraph line from our place to the train station in town, making it easy for me to keep in touch with the War Department while I finished some tasks for them." He pointed ahead. "We ran it right into the cupola that sits on the top of the second story of the big house. It's my father's favorite spot—he likes to sit up there with what he calls his *looking glass* and watch over the cattle. He quickly learned the telegraph code and spent some time conversing with Mr. H. each day."

"I suspect that Mr. Fitch doesn't think much of the arrangement," I said.

Jason nodded. "He hasn't said a word about it as yet, but we know it's probably coming. If he's a wise man, he'll keep his thoughts to himself. My father is slow to anger, but Fitch should walk softly."

A long lane ran north from the new Jacksonville Road, which ran alongside the railroad. The old Jacksonville Road was a bit farther to the north, and another lane from the farm connected to it. I noticed cattle and horses in areas partitioned off with a combination of wooden fences and thick Osage orange hedgerows. The cattle were shorthorns, and the horses were Morgans. There were also broad fields of corn about knee-high in growth. As we grew closer, I could see that there were three large barns and several good-size bunkhouses, but the center of attraction was certainly the big house.

The marvelous structure was a combination of log, frame, and stone. It reminded me of a house that was nestled among a grove of poplars near the Appomattox Court House in Virginia. I'd stayed there for a night after carrying a message from Colonel Mosby to General Lee.

The intricate, diamond-notched corners of John T. Alexander's home immediately caught my eye. The stonework was extensive, promising marvelous fireplaces within. In the months that were to come, I would find that this home served as a good representation of its builder—strong and reliable, but at the same time, warm and comforting.

I particularly liked the broad porch that surrounded the perimeter of the home and the small balconies that extended from each of the double doors adorning the second-floor rooms. It was a showplace but at the same time quite functional. I was anxious to go inside.

But the anticipation of that moment was trumped by the arrival of Jeanine Alexander. She rode up on her buckskin named Star with a hat hanging behind dark brown hair, which flowed like silk with the gentle breeze. It was obvious that she was an excellent rider. Our eyes met, and we smiled.

"Jason, aren't you going to introduce me to our visitor?" she asked.

"I will, if you give me a moment," he joked. "John, this is my little sister, Jeanine. Jeanine, this is my friend John Demsond."

She reached down from atop her mount and extended a gloved hand. "Funny you never mentioned *him* before," she said to her brother. Her handshake was firm. "I trust you'll be staying for supper."

"He will," Jason offered. "In fact, he'll be staying with us for a few days."

I couldn't take my eyes off her.

"Good," she said, and then, in one swift motion, she turned her horse back in the direction from which she had come and rode off in a cloud of dust. Moments later, when I turned to speak to Jason, I discovered that he was halfway to the house.

I caught up with him just as he stepped up onto the porch. "She's quite a young lady, isn't she?" he said, keeping his eyes straight ahead.

Before I could answer, a man rose from a wicker chair on the porch to greet Jason. I was introduced to the local justice of the peace, Owen Luby. He looked me over very carefully, but he didn't say a word. He was waiting to provide a ride back to town for General Murray McConnell, who was meeting with John T. Alexander. General McConnell, who served with Abraham Lincoln in the Blackhawk War, had a law practice in Jacksonville, and he was a newly elected member of the state legislature.

I chatted with Jason Alexander and Justice Luby for a bit before John T. Alexander and the general joined us. Mr. Alexander welcomed me to his farm with a pleasant greeting. He was tall and thin and full of energy. General McConnell was aloof and anxious to depart.

Just inside the home, I met Mary Alexander, Jason's mother. I recognized the Kentucky accent immediately. She was a gracious hostess who promised a wonderful supper in short order. I was shown to my guest room on the second floor and offered a bit of time to freshen up before the meal.

I stepped out on the small balcony that extended from my room. I could see a long way because the land was so flat. There was a small creek that snaked its way from the west edge of town out past the east side of the large barn. I leaned out over the balcony railing and looked back up at the cupola. I could imagine how much more one could see from up there.

It wasn't long before we sat down to eat. The dining room walls were lined with highly polished English walnut. The room easily swallowed the large oak table and its twelve chairs. Jason acknowledged that his favorites were on the table this evening; I was also quite happy to see the ham and beans, corn bread, carrots, and apple pie.

A local couple, Sebastian and Gertrude Kumle, were also guests for the gathering. Mr. Kumle, who was identified as a leading member of the Catholic farming community, offered up a short prayer before we dined.

"Our youngest son, Jerome, is in Champaign County this week," Mary Alexander said, looking at me. She had a wonderful smile. "I hope you'll be here long enough to meet him."

"Actually, my schedule is somewhat flexible at the moment," I said.

"You're welcome to stay as long as you like," John T. Alexander said. His soft brown eyes were closely set above high cheekbones. "Over the years, we've found that our visitors provide us with the best source of news." He looked at Jeanine. "But we'll refrain from asking too many questions this evening." Jeanine shrugged and forced a smile.

It was quiet for a while as everyone enjoyed the delicious food. If this was a typical meal, I wasn't going to be in any hurry to leave. I decided to satisfy the obvious curiosity about me by giving them some information about my background. "My family came from England and settled in the Shenandoah Valley, and my grandfather fought in the Revolutionary War. My father and mother were killed in the War Between the States when our home was destroyed in a

Union raid. I was off fighting with the Confederacy in a different location at the time."

"I'm sorry," Jeanine said. The others nodded in silence. Their sympathy was genuine.

"My parents could have saved themselves and much of their property from Sheridan's forces if they had just run up a Union flag, as some of their neighbors did. But my parents were forthright people. They didn't own any slaves, but they believed in defending Virginia. For them, as for most of the people in the South, it was a matter of defending their state's right to decide how they wanted things to be. It was part of our freedom."

They nodded. I felt comfortable amongst these people. "I decided to leave Virginia behind, and start a new life elsewhere...I'm going to California."

"Yes, a new life elsewhere...Gertrude and I met shortly after we both arrived in America in 1850," Sebastian Kumle said. "Edward Hinrichsen had sent word back to Germany about the great opportunity here, and many of us took advantage of it. We've been able to buy over 300 acres of good land. We raise some cattle and horses, but our specialty is the swine."

"Your specialty is the Norman trotting and saddle horses," Jeanine said.

Sebastian acknowledged the compliment with a nod. "Even the Kentuckians know it," Gertrude said, "but they'd never admit it. And when it comes to horses, you're making quite a statement of your own, young lady."

"That's true...she has a little Kentuckian blood in her, you know," Mary Alexander said as she rose from the table to assist her kitchen helper. The two apple pies that they brought to the table disappeared quickly with cups of excellent coffee.

Afterward, we passed through the double doors that opened to the great room with its high ceiling that exposed more English walnut-lined walls standing behind a second-story catwalk. The stonework of the massive fireplace seemed to climb right up into the sky. Nice furniture, a thick rug, and a dazzling chandelier added to the comfortable feeling.

John T. Alexander offered us a fine cigar, but only Sebastian Kumle accepted one. The aroma from their smokes filled the air, and I was somewhat tempted to join in, but I wanted to stay away from that stuff, even though it reminded me of the smells from back home.

Mary Alexander and Gertrude Kumle went off on their own to look at some new dress material that Mary had recently purchased. Jeanine sat down next to her father.

Everyone waited for John T. Alexander to start the conversation. "How'd you like the steak, Mr. Demsond?"

"Please call me John, Mr. Alexander," I said. "The steak was delicious."

John T. Alexander leaned back into the tufted, green leather of his couch and smiled. "It was Texas longhorn," he said.

I immediately understood the significance of what he'd just told me. The others watched for my reaction. "I'm not one who believed the stories from the New York papers about the evils of the Texas beef." The articles claimed that the meat tasted bad and would make you very sick.

"What are we going to do about William?" Sebastian said. "Pardon me for bringing up business, Mr. Demsond."

"That's quite all right," I said. "Jason has informed me about the problem."

Everyone was quiet, awaiting John T. Alexander's response. "Someone will have to ride down there and find out what happened. I don't see any other way to take care of the matter."

"I'll go, Father," Jason said.

"No, I need for you to go to Tolono and give Jerome a hand. Things aren't moving along as fast as I would hope to see them going. We need some cooperation between the two railroad station agents there, and I think you can best handle that. Jerome can get a little hotheaded."

John T. Alexander rubbed the back of his neck as he searched for a solution.

"I'll go," I heard myself say.

CHAPTER TWELVE

Phil Sheridan
Mississippi River
July 23, 1867

When Jason jumped in and immediately approved of my suggestion, the others caved in quickly, and things began to happen in rapid succession. After Jason and Jeanine conversed for a short time about which horse I should take with me on my journey, they decided upon Sting, a feisty three-year-old Morgan with a chestnut brown coat and a dark mane and tail. I was quite familiar with horses, and I knew that they had given me one of their best.

Jason loaned me his Henry Repeater. I assumed it was the same one that I saw him use so effectively at Burke's Station less than five years ago. If I'd raced after Agent Alexander as three of my men did, I would probably have been killed as they were. The long gun holstered nicely on one side of the leather carrier that flopped across the saddle horn; the other side of the apparatus had a place for a spare pistol. He gave me a couple of Colt Model 1860 Army revolvers and ten packs of Johnson and Dow .44-caliber cartridges. I began to wonder what I was getting into.

John T. Alexander gave me some gold coins and a money belt that fit under my clothes. "This is the way we carry money," he said. "It must remain with you at all times."

I was able to leave the farm on Friday with a rough map describing William Halsell's expected path to and from Texas, and a signed contract indicating that I was in the employ of J. T. Alexander and Company.

The TW&W Railway carried Sting and me to Hannibal. On Saturday we boarded the *Phil Sheridan* steamboat, providing an interesting moment for a former Confederate. Union General Phil Sheridan killed many people in the South.

Phil Sheridan was a packet boat that was used to carry freight as well as people. It was one of a fleet of sixteen such boats owned by the Northwestern Union Packet Company, which served the upper Mississippi River, going north from Cairo, Illinois.

A large picture of General Sheridan on horseback emblazoned both of the side-wheel covers, and the impressive pilothouse cupola was a showplace in itself. Once I found a home for Sting in the boat's horse corral, I moved up to the observation deck near the pilothouse. A nice breeze accompanied the panoramic view, and I quickly decided to spend as much of my time as possible upon this deck for the short ride to St. Louis, William Halsell's expected arrival point.

Before long, I struck up a conversation with a gentleman who turned out to be a steamboat construction engineer. "I work out of a small town on the Monongahela River by the name of California, Pennsylvania." I thought he was joking about the name at first. "It's a little town south of Pittsburgh," he said. "We've built close to a hundred steamboats there. This particular boat, the *Phil Sheridan*, was constructed by one of our competitors in Cincinnati. It's a seven-hundred-and-twenty-eight-tonner."

I guessed that there were about fifty people on the boat, and most of the cargo consisted of milk cows and bags of grain. The engineer continued. "I'm heading down to Cairo to meet one of the owners of Dunlevy and Company. Their newest boat, the *Dubuque*, a six-hundred-and-five-tonner, suffered some damage on her starboard side in May when she hit the Rock Island bridge pier. If I help them out, I figure they might offer me a better job."

Eventually, he tendered the question I knew was coming. "What about you?"

"I'm looking for a missing man," I said.

"Are you a lawman?"

"No, I'm working under contract for a large farmer in Illinois named John T. Alexander," I said. "One of his men is late returning with a herd of Texas longhorns."

"You look like a lawman," he said. "I'm not from this area, but I've sure heard of Mr. Alexander. Supposedly, he and a fellow by the name of Strawn fed the East during the war. They're Union heroes, you know."

I didn't know, but I was sure that he was right.

We watched another large steamboat pass by as it worked its way up the river. "The fellow you're looking for may be skinned alive or swinging from a tree if he was trying to bring longhorns through Indian Territory and Missouri." He studied the wake of the passing sternwheeler. "They say the longhorn meat is tough and tasteless."

"Those who say it are those who wish it was so," I said. "I've eaten it, and it tastes just fine." I was beginning to understand the significance of John T. Alexander's venture into Texas beef. My experience with the intricacies of the relationship between supply and demand was enough to help me understand the turmoil that the introduction of the longhorns would create in the marketplace. Mr. Alexander was taking a great risk. My father would have said that he was "upsetting the applecart."

The steamboat engineer eventually drifted off to find someone more interesting to talk to. However, his words of warning about the dangers that may lie ahead lingered long after he was gone. I had some time to stop and think about what I was doing. The self-examination wasn't encouraging—what I was doing made absolutely no sense at all.

You look like a lawman.

CHAPTER THIRTEEN

——❈——

St. Louis, Missouri
July 23, 1867

Just before the *Phil Sheridan* reached the landing in St. Louis, I moved back to the area where the horses were held in order to saddle Sting. A short time later, I led him through the gangway and onto the gangplank. I took one last look at the steamboat that was named after the man who had killed my father and mother.

When we walked to the end of the pier, I was shocked to see Jeanine Alexander standing there. She had her father's high cheekbones and the twinkle of her mother's eyes. Her hands were planted on her hips, and the sheepish grin of perfect lips invited my response.

"What in the world are you doing here?"

"I was going to ask *you* the same question," she said. "I thought you would be well on your way to Texas by now." She walked over to Sting and rubbed his nose.

Jeanine was dressed in fashionable buckskin with fringe running along the length of the arms and legs. She carried a holstered pistol that I immediately recognized as a Confederate favorite, the Colt Model 1862 police revolver. It was a small Colt but still a heavy pistol for a young lady to carry. I was beginning to expect that I was in store for a lot more surprises yet to come.

"I hope you're here to deliver a message," I said, doubting that this was the case.

"John Demsond, you know full well why I'm here," she said. "I'm riding down to Texas with you. It's not safe for you to be on the trail alone."

I shook my head in disbelief. There was no way to respond to her statement. I removed my flop hat and scratched the top of my head. "Does your family know that you're here?"

"I left them a note." She pulled a carrot from her back pocket and fed it to Sting. Jeanine anticipated what I was about to say. "I'm going on with or without you. Halsell's not here...I've asked around," she said. "I can ride and I can shoot. You could do far worse for company."

This was going to be awkward, but I knew that I wasn't going to be able to change her mind. "I'm not going to slow down if you can't keep up with me," I said.

"You took the words right out of my mouth," she said. Jeanine's hard eyes softened a bit. "I won't be a burden to you. I'm here to help."

"So you say," I said. "It looks like you're ready to ride, and we've got some daylight, so let's get going."

"Star is right over there," she said, pointing to a nearby hitching rail.

"We'll stop by the Western Union office before we leave town and get a message off to your family," I said. "They've got to be worried about you."

"Good idea," Jeanine said, "but we're riding off before a response comes back."

Suddenly, my life had gone from bad to worse.

I was going to Texas with my boss's daughter.

CHAPTER FOURTEEN

Shawnee Trail
July 14, 1867

The rough map that I carried with me was extremely important because of the many routes to Texas. As we rode through the heat on this Sunday, Jeanine and I followed what was commonly known as the Shawnee Trail. It extended from St. Louis in a southeasterly direction down to the corner of the state of Missouri, and then it turned more southerly all the way through the Indian Territory to the Red River, which defined the northern border of Texas.

"How did you get to St. Louis so quickly?" I asked.

"There are many ways to go," she said. "You took the long way."

Jeanine and I didn't talk much. She knew that I wasn't happy with the situation, and she didn't try to start a friendly conversation. She was a good rider on a strong horse. We made good time.

We spent the night at a small inn about thirty miles from St. Louis. The innkeeper was surprised when we asked for separate rooms. I didn't bother trying to explain anything.

Our journey through Missouri passed quickly. I was surprised to find a well-armed band of men at the Missouri border. Some of the men appeared to be former cavalry riders for both the Union and the Confederacy.

One of the men recognized me. "Are my eyes playing tricks on me, or is it Captain John Demsond?" Other heads turned. Their eyes quickly passed from me to Jeanine.

"It's been a while, Tanner," I said. Tanner Biggs was an occasional rider with Mosby's Partisan Rangers. He came along for the contraband, and Mosby didn't like him. "You're a long way from Virginia."

"I might say the same for you, Demsond," he said. His eyes were fixed on Jeanine. "You're traveling light these days." The others laughed.

I didn't introduce Jeanine. "I'm going to see some friends in Texas," I said.

He flashed a toothless smile. "Don't bring any longhorns back with you, or we'll have to take them off your hands...along with anything else that might interest us." The others laughed again.

He was starting to annoy me. "Why would you do that?"

"Because we're a rough bunch of bastards, and we do what we damn well please," he said. The others nodded their ugly heads in approval, laughing even more loudly than before. Among them were the three men who had assailed Joseph McCoy in Abilene. They didn't recognize me. I pulled my flop hat down a bit farther. I didn't want a shootout.

Tanner Biggs and his friends were looking for trouble. I could see empty bottles of liquor that had been dropped at the feet of their mounts. It wouldn't take much to set them off.

I couldn't tell which one of them was the leader, but I guessed that it was the stout fellow on the gray mare standing under the nearby shade tree. His red beard bounced gently atop his broad chest as he munched on an apple. He seemed to be watching me very carefully, ignoring Jeanine, unlike the others.

"I'll take your warning under advisement, Tanner." I touched the brim of my hat, and we rode off.

I could hear Tanner Biggs continuing his chatter in the distance. "You best do better than that, Demsond. We'll kill every longhorn that tries to enter this state."

We hurried off.

"You travel with nice company," Jeanine said.

"Are you talking about now, or the in the past?" I said.

She muttered something, and we rode on, picking up our pace.

After we'd traveled a safe distance from the troublemakers, I asked Jeanine if she'd noticed the man in the background.

She smiled. "I saw old Red Beard back there."

I was at a loss for words for a moment. "I thought you might have missed that."

"You thought wrong," she said.

We rode on.

⌘　⌘　⌘

We did encounter a few large herds of longhorns moving in the direction of St. Louis as we advanced along the trail. We warned the drovers about the problem facing them at the Missouri border. Most of the trail bosses knew nothing about William Halsell, but one of them, a man by the name of John Adare, whom we met near the Canadian River, seemed to remember a note posted at the Texas Ranger station at Pilot Point, just southwest of the Red River crossing. "It had something to do with some longhorns purchased from Sol Wagoner in the Blossom Prairie," he said.

We rode on. I was still turning Adare's comment over in my mind when Jeanine's Morgan snorted a warning, and Jeanine pointed to a huge cloud of dust just beyond the next ridge. The thunderous noise followed immediately, leaving no doubt that we were riding headlong into a stampede. I was disappointed that Sting hadn't noticed the danger, but I'd already observed that the three-year-old gelding was easily distracted.

We had little time to respond as the leaders were already coming over the top of the hill. We had few options—all of them bad. Just then, two riders quickly appeared with the cattle as they came over the rise. They were trying to turn the herd. Instinctively, Sting and Star wanted to join them. We didn't hold them back.

Our trained horses were all business now. Sting knew exactly what to do, and I was along for the ride. I grabbed my hat and fanned it out like the cowboys were doing. Their attention was entirely focused upon the massive lead bull. He was stubborn and determined to move forward. His eyes were red with rage as he jabbed with sharp horns that spanned seven feet from tip to tip.

A churning sea of menacing horns pierced the air like cavalry sabers. As the lead bull slowly began to give in, Sting moved up into his path to convince him to continue the turn. The bull swiped at him with a spear that would have ripped him apart, but Sting was aware of the threat and maintained just enough safe distance.

The other cattle followed the lead bull without hesitation as he was reluctantly turned to the right. As we pushed the longhorns back across the top of the hill, I was shocked to see the full size of the herd for the first time—well over two thousand head! Another dozen riders were trying to contain the herd as it bunched up and surged forward. We continued to drive the leaders all the way to the back of the herd, and then the cowboys at the rear turned them again, bringing the herd into a large circle.

The longhorns ran around in this circle for a while as it was made smaller and smaller by the skilled cowboys, and then the cattle slowed to a walk before coming to a complete stop. I pulled back on Sting, and we paused for a much-needed rest. A smile came across

Jeanine's dirt-covered face. A wisp of her hair was hanging down across her face, and she blew it away with a touch of elegance.

Three of the cowboys rode up to join us. "Those are mighty fine horses that you have there," a tall cowboy said.

"Thanks," Jeanine said.

My heart was still pounding from the adventure. "Sting just taught me a thing or two," I said. If I hadn't given him his head, I probably would have ridden him right into a horn that might have taken his life.

All of us reached for our canteens. We were exhausted.

I saw the cowboys looking at the intertwined JTA brand that Sting and Star bore. "I work for John T. Alexander. This is his daughter."

They tipped their sweat-stained hats. "A fine cattleman, Mr. Alexander." This time it was the smaller man who spoke. Tobacco juice dribbled down both sides of his mouth. "I'm surprised that the man would have his daughter runnin' about in such places."

Jeanine shrugged.

They looked at me. I shrugged.

"You might wanna keep an eye out for runnin' cattle down the trail." It was the smaller man again.

"For certain," I said. I gave them a short explanation about the missing Halsell.

They couldn't help us.

⌘　⌘　⌘

That night we camped at a trading post south of the Canadian River. We needed to spend the night near such places because we were now riding along the edge of the Shawnee Hills, dangerous Indian country. We ate with some men from Wise County in the Cross-Timbers region of Texas. They were moving a herd of longhorns northward to Kansas.

Joseph Martin, Alexander Brandon, Tom Mahaffy, and Edward Cumby would take their cattle as far north as necessary to avoid the ruffians in Kansas and Missouri. I told them about the work going on in Abilene, and they were very excited to hear this.

"Ed, would you be willing to ride back and spread the word about the new railhead in Abilene?" Mahaffy said. "We'll see that your cattle are cared for." It was common for several drovers to combine their herds for a long drive and sort them out when they reached their destination.

"I suppose I can do that," Cumby said. "I'll ride with you folks for a while if you don't mind."

"We'd be glad to have you join us," Jeanine said.

Now I had two people to keep an eye on.

CHAPTER FIFTEEN

✦ ⚊✦⚊ ✦

Red River
July 16, 1867

We made good time moving southward. Edward Cumby helped us to avoid the problem areas where the Indians and the outlaws were likely to be lurking. We camped at Allen Wright's flour mill and cotton gin near Boggy Depot in southern Indian Territory on Monday night. He told us that people came as far as a hundred miles to get their wheat ground at his mill. It was also a common stopping point for the cattlemen. Talking to Allen Wright was as good as reading a newspaper. "People in these parts expect me to have the latest information about almost everything," he said. I could tell that he enjoyed this role.

"I'm quite sure that this fellow, Halsell, stopped by here on his way to Texas," Wright said. "That would have been about two or three weeks ago...although I do seem to lose track of time more these days. He was riding alone...very dangerous." Jeanine looked at me and nodded.

"But you didn't see him come back?" I said.

"No," he said, twisting his face in sympathetic dismay, "I would've remembered that."

I told Allen Wright about our encounter at the Missouri border. "These men were armed and dangerous. Why are they trying to keep out the longhorns?"

"Many of the stock raisers in Missouri claim that the longhorns carry a disease that kills their cattle," he said. "Some people say that the story is made up by the northerners in order to maintain the high price for their beef. No one seems to know for sure. I expect that the men you encountered were in it for the money."

Jeanine was mysteriously silent. I chose not to press the matter at the moment, but I was curious about his reference to a disease. She knew something about this, but I didn't want to question her until we were alone.

Nonetheless, the conversation lingered with me as the three of us rode to the Red River on this Tuesday morning. We crossed at Colbert's Ferry and found time to cool our horses in the muddy water for a while before we started off again. We had noticed that Jeanine also needed the rest. I was sure that this was her longest trip on horseback. If we'd had much farther to go, I was sure that she would begin to slow us down, but I had to admit that she'd hung in there with us so far...although I was going to keep that observation to myself.

It was another thirty miles to Pilot Point in Denton County, Texas. Edward Cumby informed us that he would be departing our company at that location and heading westward.

It was easy to spot the large cottonwood tree that stood out among the other trees in the grove at the top of the hill where Pilot Point was located. This landmark had been clearly identified on the map that I carried.

"I hope you find the man," Cumby said as he waved good-bye.

Jeanine and I watched him ride off. "That man probably kept us from stumbling into some trouble," Jeanine said.

"We'd been all right," I said, knowing that she was probably right.

We found the note that we were looking for at the Texas Ranger station. It was signed by John Bump, but the ranger wasn't there. Jeanine sat down in a chair to rest, and I walked next door to the general store.

There wasn't much to Pilot Point at the moment, but there was new construction under way, and its location guaranteed a good deal of future growth.

The general store's owner, James Walcott, was aware of the note. "Ranger Bump told me to inform any interested party that he would be at Sol Wagoner's place in Red River County. That's a good day's ride east of here. You best spend the night here and head out in the morning."

"I'm sorry, I can't do that," I said. "I need to get there as soon as I can."

"Suit yourself," he said. "There's a lot of cattle rustling going on around here, so you might want to be careful out there. You could get yourself shot for just sneezing too loud. People are jumpy."

CHAPTER SIXTEEN

—→ ⚞✦⚟ ←—

Sol Wagoner's Ranch
Northeast Texas
July 17, 1867

After spending the night in a copse of birch trees near a small creek, we rode under the sign that marked the entryway to Sol Wagoner's large ranch. "The Lazy W" was artfully burned into the large wooden block that was attached to a massive crossbeam held high in the air by two long, vertical beams. The prairie was thick with tall wire grass with a narrow leaf. The grass was standing about three feet high in places where the cattle hadn't grazed for a while.

It wasn't long before we rode through areas where the grass had been burned out recently. They'd done this to bring out the new green shoots. I could see some buildings less than a mile ahead. No riders were in sight.

As we approached the main house, I could see some shorthorn and longhorn cattle mixed together in a holding pen. It appeared that Sol Wagoner was hoping to mix the breeds in an attempt to gain improved offspring.

Many believed that the Texas longhorns were actually a mix between the cattle brought in by the Spaniards late in the seventeenth
century and those introduced by the English early in the nineteenth
century. The longhorns had long legs and lanky bodies, and their
legs and feet were formed for speed. It took a good rider on a good
horse to outrun a longhorn.

It was early morning, but it was already hot. Sting and Star wanted some water, so we tied them up at the hitching post near the large
trough in front of the impressive house. Three other saddled horses
were drinking there. I noticed that the two bays carried the Lazy W
brand. The other horse was a palomino.

Before we could reach the first step to the front porch, a sandy-
haired cowboy wearing full leather chaps and worn spurs opened the
door with a burst of energy. "Who are you here to see...my pappy,
or John Bump?"

"Both," I said. "My name is John Demsond. I work for John T.
Alexander. This is his daughter, Jeanine Alexander."

The man was about my age. He extended his hand. "We've been
expecting someone from Illinois to show up about now...but I'll have
to admit that we didn't expect John T. Alexander's daughter. I'm
Daniel Wagoner. Come on inside."

He led me to Solomon Wagoner's office. I shook the man's large
hand as Daniel introduced us. His father was introduced as "Sol,"
and his large frame made his desk look small.

Ranger John Bump returned a book to a shelf in Sol Wagoner's
library before greeting us. "Is it just the two of you?"

"Yes, Mr. Alexander was shorthanded, so I...we rode here alone."

Ranger Bump shook his head in disbelief, but he remained quiet.

"I understand that problem," Sol Wagoner said. "There aren't
enough men to go around these days...we lost so many good ones
in the war." He pointed to the chairs, and the five of us sat down

to talk. The men were in a very serious mood, so I wasn't expecting good news.

Everyone waited for Sol Wagoner to begin. "William Halsell arrived here in plenty of time to get the cattle back to Illinois in the first week of July, which is what I understood your father wanted," he said, looking at Jeanine. "But your man wanted to be involved in picking his own herd, and that took some time—even longer than he thought it would. I've got a lot of land here. Halsell didn't seem to be in any sort of a hurry.

"We generally apply a trail-rode brand to the cattle as an extra precaution, just in case there is a need to mix them in with another owner's cattle somewhere along the drive, but he wasn't interested in that. We went back and forth about this for a couple of days." It was obvious that Sol Wagoner had been displeased with William Halsell.

"My father finally gave in on the branding issue, and then Halsell questioned the number of cowboys that we were going to provide him," Daniel Wagoner said, shaking his head. "He thought we were sending too many...can you believe that?"

"On the morning that he was ready to move out, he decided to take a route directly north instead of going back west a bit to cross the Red River at Colbert's Ferry like everyone else does," Sol Wagoner said. "We warned him that this was a bad idea because of the rocky, tree-covered terrain that he would encounter when going in that direction. There's fifteen miles of it to go through before you even get to the Red River, and it's worse beyond there. No one takes that route."

Ranger Bump stood up and stretched his muscular frame. "And the savages and outlaws are another problem," he added. "I just received word of an Indian attack west of here at Elm Creek. Three young men were killed and cattle were taken. Reports are that the braves were headed this way. And if this wasn't enough, a cattle thief named Joel Collins is said to be working the area just north of the Red River."

"A wise man will stick to the common cattle trails instead of going off in some other direction," Sol Wagoner said. He rose from his chair and walked to the large window facing northward. "I didn't want to see my men riding off into such danger, but I was bound to provide the help for the buyer...especially a buyer like John T. Alexander." He turned to look at Jeanine. "I won't be happy if any harm has come to them...and you can pass that along to your father."

"I understand," she said. This was a bad situation, and Jeanine recognized that there was no point trying to defend Halsell. "We appreciate your help."

"I posted the note at Pilot Point when some cattle were found by the men from Elm Creek who were chasing the Indians," Ranger Bump said. "Now that I've talked to Sol, I'm sure that it was some of the cattle William Halsell purchased from him."

"What do you think we should do?" I asked.

"Who is *we*?" It was Daniel Wagoner who tossed out the question.

I broke the silence. "I assumed that you would want to help your men."

"Of course we do," Sol Wagoner argued, "but like I said, we're shorthanded, and I can't afford to send off another bunch right now."

"How many could you send, Sol, if I was to ride up there with these two?" Ranger Bump asked. "I have permission to cross the Red River in cases like this."

Sol Wagoner stared outside for a while before he answered. "I'll give you two men, and no more, John. You know the chances aren't good that you'll find them alive if they've been ambushed."

"I know that," John Bump said, "but we have to give it a try."

"What do you suggest?" I said.

"We'll head out as soon as we can," he said. "We should be able to pick up his trail, but I'm guessing that the cattle got scattered in the woods. If the riders spread out to retrieve the cattle, we'll have to decide which way to go, but we'll want to stay together."

"Let's get going," I said.

"Miss Alexander must stay here," Sol Wagoner said.

"I think not," Jeanine said.

They all looked at me.

I shrugged.

CHAPTER SEVENTEEN

Red River County, Texas
July 17, 1867

The terrain was as bad as Sol Wagoner had described it—even worse in places. He had been kind enough to give each of us a pair of horse-hide chaps, which saved our legs, but the thornbushes chewed away the leather on our unprotected boots. Sting's coat was soaked with blood. I was getting angrier by the moment.

William Halsell had been a fool to take the herd this direction. He should have turned back and gone the other way once he discovered his mistake, but the evidence seemed to indicate that he'd pushed the herd onward through the thicket with devastating results.

As Sol Wagoner had predicted, the cattle had immediately begun to scatter once they were in the woods. As we grew closer to the Red River, the ground softened, and it was obvious that the cattle had encountered difficulty moving through the mud, further dissipating them.

Sol Wagoner's men weren't happy to be riding with us. Both were named Bob—one was Big Bob and the other was Little Bob.

We were told that they were good shooters. I found myself thinking about that.

Ranger Bump remained calm on the exterior. "I lost a good friend in woods just like this not long ago. Van Roberts was an outstanding Texas Ranger. He saved my life once."

"I owe my life to several fellow soldiers...I know how that feels," I said. "How long do you plan to stay with us? You'll be out of your jurisdiction once we cross the river."

"I'll stick with you until I think there's no more point to it," he said.

I wasn't extremely encouraged by that reply, but I admired the man for going with us in the first place. John Bump was rugged, but he had a soft side. He was easy to like. He could have easily sent us on our way alone, but he had chosen not to do so. The Texas Rangers had a great reputation for courage. They were some of the greatest fighters for the Confederacy, and the stories of their exploits reached all the way to Virginia. Colonel Mosby always wanted to meet one of them.

When we reached the river, we found the place where the largest part of the herd had crossed. "It looks like there were about seven riders here," Ranger Bump said. "I assume that one of them was Halsell."

I wasn't sure how he came up with that number, but I didn't want to ask. I was willing to concede that his tracking skills were much better than my own in this terrain.

The herd continued to scatter out after crossing the river, and by the time we stopped to make camp near dark, Little Bob estimated that less than six hundred cattle were left in the main group. We found a small cave that was nice and cool. There was water in a small stream nearby. We ate dried beef and beans.

"Most of these cattle are beeves," Little Bob said. He turned to Ranger Bump. "Beeves are at least four years of age...ready for market. Halsell took a lot of those...more than we expected."

"Texas cattle have long horns, large lungs, small intestines, and small bones," Big Bob said. "They'll take a lot of punishment before they show signs of wearing down, but they need to be watered and fed on a regular basis, so I expect that we'll catch up with them soon. Even on a good trail, they'll make only ten to fifteen miles a day... and this is hardly a good trail."

"We'd better find them soon," Little Bob said. "We're needed back at the ranch."

I didn't expect Ranger Bump and the Bobs to be with us much longer. I hoped to find William Halsell and the cattle before they turned back. I looked over at Jeanine. I think she was reading my mind.

Ranger Bump set the order for the night watch. Jeanine insisted on taking the first watch, much to the surprise of the others. By now, I wasn't surprised.

Sleep came quickly for most when the opportunity was there. I found myself thinking about the war. I'd spent many nights like this, but I couldn't remember being this worried. It's one thing when you worry about yourself, but it's something quite different when you're worrying about someone else. I had to make sure that John T. Alexander's daughter returned home *on* the saddle instead of *over* it.

CHAPTER EIGHTEEN

In the Woods North of the Red River
July 18, 1867

It was about noon the next day when I heard the riders approaching from the east. The dense woods had begun to thin out, making things a bit more comfortable for us. I raised my hand to halt everyone, as if I was in the cavalry again. I turned Sting to the right to face the threat. John Bump also heard them and turned his mount; he was the first to pull a long gun from its saddle sheath, a breech-loading Sharps Model 1859. Jeanine and the Bobs were confused, but they turned their horses to the east as we had and raised their weapons.

The riders raced through the woods with reckless abandon, hoping to overwhelm us with their charge. Instead, they were greeted with a hail of bullets that knocked the lead attackers from their horses. The others quickly pulled back to dismount and attack on foot. I sensed that few of them had been trained in the military.

Big Bob took a bullet through the top of his hat, but he wasn't harmed. I was sure that we took down at least four riders in the initial altercation, but I knew that more than four remained in the woods. I was relieved to see that Jeanine was all right. I saw that she could handle a gun.

Jeanine's rifle was the brand-new replacement for the Henry that I borrowed from her brother. It had a comforting wooden forearm to protect the fingers on the left hand—mine were already burning from the ongoing action, but she was still firing away with ease.

"If we make it through this," she said, "I'll buy you one of these."

"I'll buy my own...but thanks anyway," I said, hoping that we would make it through this. I shouted the order to dismount.

We dismounted. My cavalry officer training kicked in with full force. I ordered Little Bob to gather the horses so that the rest of us were free to carry on the fight. I kept us close together and concentrated our firing on the most threatening target.

The attackers quickly recognized their disadvantage and began to back off. They had abandoned their horses, so they were permanently on foot. A loud voice attracted my attention, and I slowly moved our position toward it. Just then, a long gun grew out of a tree.

Four of us fired in unison, and the gun flew away with part of an arm attached. The loud voice returned from behind the tree, but this time it was a wailing scream.

When we passed the tree minutes later, we saw a large man with bulging eyes crawling in a pool of blood looking for the rest of his arm. His scream had drained to a whimper. Soon, we stopped and listened. It was quiet now...except for the cries of the wounded. The others had long departed.

We scattered and checked the immediate area. We found one man that we could save, and as Jeanine tended to him, the others reported in one by one.

"Stumpy's dead." We looked at each other. Little Bob had a way with words.

We found a horse for our captive and rode out of the woods. We made sure that we weren't being followed as we rode well into Indian Territory before we camped for the night.

CHAPTER NINETEEN

———— ✦ ————

Indian Territory
July 19, 1867

Our captive revealed that he and his fellow bandits had also attacked Halsell and Wagoner's cowboys several days earlier. They used the woods as a hideout, and they were surprised to find a gift of a cattle drive fall right into their hands.

Ranger Bump took the lead in questioning his prisoner. "What's your name?"

"Smith."

"What happened to the men who drove the cattle into the woods?"

"They all ran off," he said. His shifty eyes gave himself away.

John Bump saw it, too. "I don't have a lot of time, Smith, so we can do this your way or my way...you decide." He drew his pistol. Jeanine walked away.

"Well, go ahead and shoot me if ya want," Smith said, "cuz ya ain't gonna get those cows back...they're long gone. We split 'em up and sold 'em off to the Injuns."

"There're five tribes in this area," Big Bob said. "The Choctaw and Chickasaw fought with the Confederates, but some of the Creek, Seminole, and Cherokee fought on both sides. None of them are happy about how they're being treated at the moment. If they bought the cattle as this fellow says, we'll never get them back."

"What if he's lying?" I said.

"Selling the cattle to the Indians is the best way to get rid of them quickly," Big Bob said. "He's probably telling the truth."

"So what happened to the men?" Ranger Bump asked.

This time Smith looked him straight in the eyes, "They wuz busy tendin' to the cows...we ran up on 'em fast...we dropped all of 'em." It took a moment for his words to settle in.

Little Bob was the first to speak. His words came as he drew his pistol. "Enough said."

Ranger Bump's pistol was suddenly aimed at Little Bob. "I'm taking this man back to Texas to stand trial. Justice will be served in the court, not here."

"Justice will be done *here*." Big Bob's pistol came up quickly. It was pointed at Ranger Bump. "We're not in Texas."

Jeanine and I drew our pistols in unison and covered the Bobs. Awkward silence filled the air. Smith chuckled. A soft breeze washed warm air across my face. Jeanine's gun hand was shaking. She was very close to killing someone who was a friend moments ago.

Smith was enjoying the scene. "Why don't you folks kill each other so I can git on 'bout my business?" The thought occurred to me that we should all turn and shoot *him* instead...just as the Bobs had suggested.

Little Bob tilted his pistol upward and eased the hammer back to its resting point. He holstered the gun and said, "That's fine, Ranger, you take him back, but Bob and me will have no part of that. We're going back to let Mr. Wagoner know what's happened. I'm sure you'll be hearing from him real soon."

Big Bob responded immediately with a grunt and put his weapon away. He walked off to get their horses.

I looked at Little Bob and said, "I'll need your word that you're not going to cause any further trouble for Ranger Bump and his prisoner."

"You have that," he said. "We'll leave the two of them alone."

John Bump joined in. He kicked some dirt at Smith. "This man will hang, and I'll return to the woods with some additional rangers to find the others. They'll hang, too." He turned to look at me. "You and Miss Alexander need to forget about getting her father's cattle back...and start working on getting back to his farm in one piece."

I wasn't one to give up so easily, but I knew that he was giving me good advice. I wasn't sure how Jeanine Alexander felt about it. I looked at her.

Jeanine's stiff upper lip softened. "I suppose he's right. I'm in enough trouble already."

CHAPTER TWENTY

—◄►—

John T. Alexander Farm
August 1, 1867

Activities blurred in a rapid pace after Jeanine and I returned to the farm. I was greatly relieved, but not surprised, to find that Mr. Alexander's concern for the well-being of his daughter overshadowed his misfortune in the loss of his cattle. This was the first of many revelations that I would witness regarding the stalwart character of this man. He was much more than "the Cattle King" that many called him.

I learned that John T. Alexander had sent additional funds to Joseph McCoy in Abilene to help him with his venture. He also stepped up the timetable for the completion of the new stockyards at the two railroad stations in Tolono. John T. Alexander would bear the entire burden of the cost of the new stockyards because the railroads had refused to contribute. Jason and Jerome Alexander were caught up in the details of the Tolono activity, and I saw very little of them after I returned to the farm near the town of Alexander.

Jeanine avoided me entirely. My experience with women was somewhat limited, so I decided that I wouldn't try to figure out what was wrong. I thought that I'd treated her well during our trip to Texas, but apparently, she didn't agree.

I met the Chief. He worked for John T. Alexander and helped Jeanine with the horses. No one seemed to know what tribe he was from. He'd picked up some words of English from the other farm hands...some good, some not so good. The Chief and his large family stayed in a small house just to the west of the Alexanders.

I tried to convince Mr. Alexander that I should return to the Indian Territory to find the missing cattle. He was adamant about not doing so. "I only paid four dollars a head for those longhorns, and I could easily spend a lot more than that in trying to get them back. They're water under the bridge—part of doing business. Besides, I need you here...if you're willing to stay on, that is."

"What do you have in mind?" I asked.

I didn't have to wait long to find out. "I need a fresh set of eyes and ears to go to the state's capital, Springfield, and examine what's happening there. I want you to sit with the people in the saloons around the state buildings and find out what's on their minds. They don't know you—and you make friends easily. They'll talk to you in ways that they wouldn't talk to me."

We were sitting in his library when he spoke to me about this. The room reminded me of Doc Durant's library back in his home in New York. It was very orderly, each book seeming to have its assigned place. A large map of Champaign County rested on John T. Alexander's hardwood desk. His looking glass held back a curled corner of the yellowed paper.

"I can't really trust the newspapers. They're such political things, providing only one point of view. I need to understand both sides of the issues. Good decisions cannot be based on one-sided judgments. That kind of thinking carried us right into the worst war of our history. I didn't favor slavery, mind you, but the North failed to recognize that, right or wrong, the slaves represented a form of property to the plantation owners, and if their workers were to be taken away, there had to be some compensation of sorts to make amends. Absent that, a fight was a sure thing."

He rose from his chair to stretch. "I wouldn't let people take any of my property without a fight, would you?" He sighed. His eyebrows seemed to dance above his eyes. "But I guess I just let those outlaws take some of my property, didn't I?" He sat back down and thought about what he'd just said. "We all make mistakes, and no matter what, we live with the consequences. It was right to stop the slavery. It's right to bring up the longhorns from Texas."

I enjoyed listening to him. He was a smart man, more than just a good businessman. I had met a lot of businessmen, and some of them weren't very smart. I agreed to take on this assignment for him. Another short delay wouldn't matter that much; I would head west afterward.

"I'm planning to bring a lot of Texas longhorns into this state very soon. I need to know if the government intends to enforce that foolish law that it put in place back in February, or will cooler heads prevail?"

"The law, as I understand it, won't allow Texas cattle to be brought into the state," I said. Jeanine had explained this to me as we rode along the Shawnee Trail in our journey back to Illinois. She was concerned about the situation, just like her father. I think she knew more about the cattle business than her father and brothers gave her credit for.

"The law applies to Texas cattle and Cherokee cattle," he said, "essentially longhorns. It's a bad law. It was slipped in when nobody was looking, and I don't think many people expect it to be carried out...but I need to know for certain."

"I'll find out," I said.

CHAPTER TWENTY-ONE

The Gavel Inn
Springfield, Illinois
August 16, 1867

After spending some time in Springfield, I discovered that Thursday evening was the best time to mingle with the legions of men, and the few women, who called the city their home when the legislature was in session. They spilled out of the buildings in large numbers in the late part of the afternoon. They came from all walks of life. They came from all parts of the state, the country, and the world. I didn't particularly like being around most of them, but it didn't take long for me to understand their power.

"These people control the *higher-ups*," the gangling Buck Lathrop said, waving his hand out across the shoulder-to-shoulder sea of bodies that packed the stylish inn. "They're the ones who determine how much money will be spent on waste management, and my business will stink if it's not enough."

We laughed. Four of us stood together at our chest-high table, drinking the Gavel Inn's own brew. "Buck, you never cease to amaze me." This time it was Brock McMunn who spoke up. "You convince legislators to spend thousands hauling human and animal waste to big holes in the ground, when all we have to do is run it off into the waterways that'll carry it off for nothing." Sometimes, I had trouble telling if McMunn was serious, or not.

"I agree," Samuel Walters said. "Let the folks in New Orleans take care of it...they decided to live there." Sam was a heavy drinker who smoked expensive cigars.

"Brock, you and Sam both know that we must address social issues if we're to move forward and grow the economy," Buck Lathrop said. "A strong economy will help you send money to Chicago, Brock, and it will also help you bring in more money from the other states and countries, Sam."

"I'll drink to that," Brock said. We raised our glasses. McMunn Enterprises was fast becoming a funnel for large sums of tax dollars making their way to Chicago, the fastest-growing city in the state. For some reason, I had struck up a nice relationship with McMunn about a week ago, and he had introduced me to the others. It didn't take me long to discover that all three of these men were at the center of the new power structure that was building in Springfield.

"John, you said you were interested in beef," Brock said. "I'm sure you must know about the meat packers."

"Yes, I've heard about their planned start-ups in Chicago and Kansas City," I said. "But how will they manage to make it work if the Texas longhorns are kept out?"

"Damn good question, Demsond," Buck Lathrop said. "You might want to ask the legislators who slipped that law in, right under our noses."

"What happened?" I asked.

Samuel Walters jumped in. "Word is that our esteemed legislators were *persuaded* by enticing promises from highly influential people from the East...big money people who add six zeroes to the end of the dollars that find their way into the hands of our politicians."

"Don't kid yourself," McMunn said. "Some of that money came from Chicago and St. Louis, too."

"All of them motivated by their self-interests, no doubt," I said.

"Of course," Walters said, "and also by a desire to further punish the South...and Texas is part of the South. They want to see the Texas cattle die there, causing the ranchers to lose their businesses... and then the money people will dive in and buy them on the cheap."

"And then they'll change the law to make it legal to bring in the Texas cattle," I said.

"Precisely," Walters said. "You're learning fast, Demsond."

"Do you think the law will be enforced?" I asked.

"That's hard to say," Lathrop said, suddenly getting serious. "There are some who believe the trumped-up story that the Texas and Cherokee cattle are sick." He smirked. "I've seen them, and they don't look sick to me. You've seen them, John. What do you think?"

"They don't look like they're sick," I said. "I've seen a good number of them up close."

"Of course they're not sick," Walters said. "There're millions of them in Texas!"

"So back to my question about the law," I said. "Will it be enforced?"

Brock McMunn grunted. "It'll probably come down to each local jurisdiction to decide on its own whether or not it'll carry it out. If a lot of the local economy is dependent upon the cattle business, I suspect that they will turn their heads the other way."

That was the opinion that seemed to carry the day during this conversation, as well as most of our talks that followed in the days afterward. It wasn't hard to make friends when you were willing to buy them drinks. The Springfield crowd wasn't as concerned about the Texas cattle matter as I thought they might be. They seemed to have many more items on their plates of much greater importance to them. In fact, I found that a good number of the people whom

I talked to didn't even know about the law, and a few of them even told me that I couldn't possibly be right about it.

As the days went on, I began to prepare my report to Mr. Alexander. I wanted to discuss the matter with him face-to-face and leave him with a written statement of my findings. I would include the names of the people with whom I had discussed the issue, but I would ask him to keep these in confidence, which I was sure he would do.

CHAPTER TWENTY-TWO

John T. Alexander Farm
September 1, 1867

I completed my business in Springfield in late August and waited for John T. Alexander to return from a trip to Canada. I felt that I might have overstayed my visit as a guest of the Alexander family, so I took up a room in the Grande Jeanne Hotel in town.

The Grande Jeanne was located on the corner of Front Street and Hardin Avenue. Almost all of the rooms were occupied. The rooms were large, clean, and comfortable. However, everything, including my teeth, rattled when the express trains rolled right through town at night without slowing. The dining room was very pleasant, and the people were friendly. The one exception was the neighbor across the hall from my room; Henry Fitch didn't seem to like me for some reason.

It was a Sunday afternoon when I was able to sit down with John T. Alexander in his library. I placed my report in front of me on his desk. "I have a written report of my findings, Mr. Alexander, but I wanted to discuss things with you before I hand it over."

John T. Alexander smiled and nodded his approval.

"I was able to meet with a lot of people in Springfield. You'll find the names of thirty people in my report. I frequented many different locations, and I didn't spend the night in one spot for more than a week at a time. All of my expenses are detailed for your review and consideration."

Again, he nodded. He seemed to be more serious than I had noted in the past. I guessed that something was bothering him, and I hoped that it didn't have anything to do with me.

"It would be wrong of me to say that I have a unanimous opinion regarding the matter of the enforcement of the law of February twenty-seven," I said. "However, I can say that I am quite confident in my findings. My conversations in Springfield included two judges and four peace officers as well as four members of the legislature. I had to pay only one of the legislators for his information. The others offered their opinions freely."

I paused to wait for any questions, but hearing none, I went on. "The law seems to have been some kind of a contrived operation, to borrow a term that we used in the Confederacy. Swaps and behind-the-scene deals seem to have given birth to this legislation. Not one of the four legislators whom I spoke to remembered it, if you can believe that. None of them claim to have voted for it, but when I checked on that, I found that three of them had."

This time, my pause produced results. "I didn't know anything about it until I heard that the law was passed," John T. Alexander said. "It surprised the heck out of me. Is there any chance that it will be repealed or superseded in some way?"

"I don't think so. There are too many other issues to address for the next couple of years at least."

"So we're stuck with a piece of garbage?"

"Yes," I said, "that's about it, but the good news is that it isn't likely to be enforced—unless the cattle get sick or cause other cattle to get sick. One person I talked to said that this is what happens… they carry disease to the local livestock."

"I've heard this claim," Alexander said, "but I haven't seen it. All of the cattle that I've brought up from Sol Wagoner have been clean. I told Halsell to look them over before he bought them for me, so he wouldn't have brought any of them back here if they were sick."

"So this sickness story seems to have been made up by someone for some reason," I said.

"It would seem so," he said. "So you're telling me that I should proceed at my own risk?"

I pushed my document forward to him. "Yes, that's the recommendation that I've included in my report."

"Thanks, John, you've done a fine job. I'd like for you to stay on and do some more work for me. Can you put off that trip to California a bit longer?"

He didn't wait for an answer. He knew that I would stay.

"I'd like for you to go with me to Abilene for the McCoys' grand opening out there on Thursday. We'll leave tomorrow morning."

CHAPTER TWENTY-THREE

*New York City
September 1, 1867*

Raven reluctantly agreed to meet with Badger. The two men didn't like each other, and they didn't try to hide it. "Your resources haven't done a thing to eliminate our problem," Badger said. "In fact, your bungling has probably made matters worse, if the truth be known."

Raven seethed. "You know nothing of the truth. While you sit back in Albany and criticize, I've been working the issue. If things were going well, you'd probably be taking credit for it, wouldn't you?"

Badger didn't respond. He brushed dust from his expensive suit, trying to maintain his composure. Raven's arrogance had reached an insufferable level since the ending of the war. His close ties with Grant were well-known. Some claimed that he manipulated Grant like a puppet. Badger knew better than to push the powerful man too far.

Only a few other patrons were in the Black Duck restaurant this evening. This was one of the many New York restaurants that served the very expensive fine cuts of beef savored by its wealthy customers.

The population of the city rapidly expanded after the war ended, but the supply of beef diminished. It was a delicacy and a rare treat for most.

Raven and Badger didn't let their bad feelings for each other go beyond their table. Their sharp discourse wasn't revealed by facial expressions or tone of voice. The men had iron in their veins and hearts as cold as ice. There was disagreement, but if their common enemy was to show its face, they would strike out as one against that foe.

Raven leaned forward in his seat, restraining his booming voice. "You underestimate my resources," he said. "You always do."

Badger snapped back. "This problem is much worse than you think it is. Our lock here on the New York market isn't as strong as you think it is. You're overconfident."

"You failed to understand the significance of our victory over the South, *my friend*. We are now a society that is controlled by law. Only law matters now. The law need not be sensible or fair. The law is our deity. We worship the law. Those who control the law are the masters over the citizen slaves."

"I wish that it was that simple," Badger said.

"It is absolutely that simple," Raven said. "Once the laws are in place, the judges and law enforcement people become our pawns. They are bound to carry out our agenda. It's actually quite remarkable when you think about it."

Badger ignored his claim. "Our ability to manipulate the law is limited," Badger said.

"You're wrong. Let me give you an example as to how it might work...a hypothetical, if you will. Let's say we decide that we don't like something the president of the United States is doing. We can use the law of impeachment to remove him from office, and even if we fail at the attempt to remove him, we tarnish his reputation by putting the cloud of doubt over his head, thus diminishing his ability to carry out the duties of his office...either way, we accomplish our objective."

Badger was well aware that Raven was involved in the attempts to remove President Johnson from office. "All right," Badger said. He stabbed a piece of steak and held it up at the end of his fork, waving it in the air. "I'll remain patient a bit longer."

"I will create a cloud of doubt that will cause a *storm*," Raven said.

Suddenly, he grabbed Badger's hand and pulled it forward, just long enough to devour the meat at the end of the fork with one swift bite.

"Don't mess with me," Raven said and laughed.

CHAPTER TWENTY-FOUR

—•—✠•✠—•—

Abilene, Kansas
September 5, 1867

I enjoyed the good fortune of riding the railroad cars to Abilene with John T. Alexander and many of the other cattlemen who were contemplating an investment in Texas longhorns. In Mr. Alexander's case, the decision had already been made, and he intended to make a statement to the industry by purchasing some cattle immediately upon his arrival—enough cattle to fill the first twenty railroad cars departing Abilene on Thursday morning. "My men will be here in the morning," he said. "They'll help load the cars and accompany the cattle all the way to market."

He planned to ship these cattle directly to Chicago without stopping to fatten them up in Alexander or Tolono because he wanted it to be known that they had come directly from the new railhead in Abilene, Kansas. Many of them would immediately be carved up and served at Chicago's multitude of restaurants at special introductory prices. "This approach works out well for me," Mr. Alexander said, "because we had a poor crop of corn this year."

The second shipment from Abilene was destined for the New York market. John T. Alexander did not intend to invest in this second shipment. "I send a lot of my native cattle to the New York market. It's large but tightly controlled. The metropolitan district of New York alone requires about one thousand five hundred head of cattle *each day* to meet its needs. I don't intend to send any Texas cattle to New York for a while. I think it's foolish to rush the Texas cattle to that market."

I sat with Mr. Alexander in one of the many tents that had been erected for the big event in Abilene. All sorts of food adorned the tables—especially Texas beef—and plenty of beer and wine. Musicians wandered from tent to tent. Longhorns filled the stockyards as well as the multitude of holding pens that surrounded the town. Rumors were that there were ten thousand head of Texas longhorns ready for the railroad cars and another ten thousand head less than two days away on the trail. Millions more were waiting in Texas.

I was astonished at how the town had changed in just the short time that I'd been away. J. G. McCoy and Company had finished the three-story Drovers' Cottage, which sat on Texas Street, paralleling the railroad. All one hundred rooms were occupied for this event.

The stockyards had also been expanded. McCoy coaxed the railroad construction people into expanding the sidetrack to an impressive one-hundred-car length. A lot of cattle could be loaded in a very short time.

Cedar Street ran south from Texas Street. Two additional hotels were under construction there, including a Merchants' Hotel. Two large saloons were ready for business, and ten more were under construction. These enterprises were bound to be attractive havens for the cowboys coming in off a long trail drive payday. In the distance, several new houses had been thrown together, and I guessed that one of them might belong to Joseph McCoy.

I was glad to see that he was carrying a gun now. "We still don't have a lawman here," he said. "Are you interested in the job, Demsond?"

I guess I still looked like a lawman.

"He works for me now, Joe," Mr. Alexander said. "But I'll try to find someone for you."

I met James McCoy. He was full of energy, just like his brother, Joseph. James was busy taking an inventory of those in attendance and making sure that all of their needs were met.

In addition to the buyers and sellers, a number of dignitaries had taken advantage of the all-expenses-paid opportunity for a trip westward. A number of them were taking turns bashing our ears with pompous speeches in between the sounds of music. Even the representatives from the railroad who had refused to fund the initial venture were speaking about Abilene's potential. "If it works out very well," John T. Alexander said, "you can be sure that it will be described as having been their idea from the beginning."

"If they invest money into the venture," Joseph McCoy said, "I'll be more than happy to let them take credit for it."

I had dealt with enough railroad people to know that this is exactly what they would do, but I also knew that the railroads had a lot of very good people, and they were the ones who made it all work... not the same people who were here for the extravagant celebration.

And, to be sure, there were a lot of people here. Most of them knew John T. Alexander, or at least knew who he was. Mr. Alexander introduced me as his friend rather than his employee, and I was grateful for that important distinction.

After a while, we parted company, as Mr. Alexander wanted to have a private conversation with several individuals. This gave me an opportunity to explore on my own.

I was having a nice time until I heard a voice that I was hoping to forget. "Demsond, I'm finding you in places where you shouldn't be."

I turned to face Tanner Biggs. I didn't speak right away. I wanted to be careful about my choice of words. "Why is that, Tanner?" I asked.

"You're sharing company with the wrong folks," he said. "These people are hell-bent on sending sick cattle to the East...and the people in the East don't want sick cattle."

"What do you mean? I don't see any sick cattle here."

"They're sick all right...and they rub their sickness on anything that they come in contact with. They need to stay down in Texas where they belong."

"The East needs beef, Tanner," I said, "and there're millions of longhorns in Texas. I've eaten the meat, and it tastes just fine."

"You're not listening, Demsond," he said. "These cattle aren't welcome in the East. Anyone who tries to take them there and sell them is going to get hurt."

"Is that a threat, Tanner?" I said.

"No...that's a promise, Demsond," he said.

⌘ ⌘ ⌘

I sat down for supper just after sunset. John T. Alexander invited two of his good friends from Texas to eat with us at the Drovers' Cottage. Major Seth Mabry from Austin and J. D. Reed of Goliad had large herds of longhorns that they wished to bring northward out of the depths of Texas. Most of the early cattle drives out of the state had originated from northern Texas, but much larger herds were present in the heart of the state in an area known as the Cross-Timbers Region. Massive herds were also located in the deep southern part of the state known as the Diamond Region.

Like me, both men had fought for the Confederacy. Major Mabry led the Seventeenth Texas Infantry, and Captain Reed led a company at the Arkansas Post. Captain Reed was wounded, captured, and taken to a prisoner of war camp in Alton, Illinois. His right arm was amputated there.

Very soon, both men intended to divide their herds, sending some of the cattle directly northward to Abilene and others northeastward to Cairo, St. Louis, or Hannibal. John T. Alexander was interested in receiving cattle from all these locations.

"I'm rapidly expanding my operations to the point where I can take on large numbers of longhorn cattle from multiple points simultaneously," Alexander said. "I'm interested in making an arrangement with the two of you to guarantee that I get what I call the first right of refusal to purchase your cattle."

"Go on, John," Major Mabry said, "but please make it clear what's in it for me." Smiling, the large man shoveled a spoonful of fried potatoes past his thick moustache and beard.

"If I have a purchasing agent present when your herd arrives, that agent is the first person that you talk to regarding the purchase of all or part of the herd. My agent could also decide not to make a purchase—but that's unlikely. If you notify me in advance of your arrival, I will promise to have someone there, and they'll have cash."

'I like where you're going with this," J. D. Reed said. "It's comforting to know that I'll have a potential buyer standing there waiting for me. It should reduce the amount of time that I have to hang around waiting for a buyer...and spending a lot of money feeding my cattle while I wait. I'm inclined to go along with your proposal."

"Not so fast," Major Mabry said. "I'd like to understand why you would *not* make the purchase."

"Well, I know you've heard the stories about the sick cattle that are supposedly coming up from Texas," Alexander said. "I have yet to see one, but the stories are there. As a protection for me, I don't want to be forced to buy sick cattle."

"That seems fair to me," J. D. Reed said. "I'm not worried because I don't have any sick cattle...and I'm sure that you don't have any, Major."

Major Mabry rearranged the food on his plate. "I suppose you're right. I probably don't need to worry about that."

"While we're on the topic," I said, "do you gentlemen have any idea what this sick cattle scare is all about?"

"It's a continuation of the Yankee punishment of the former Confederacy," Major Mabry said. "Look at what's going on in Washington. They're doing whatever they can to push President Johnson out of town. That kind of behavior will seal the fate of the nation for years to come...perhaps forever. In the future, I'd hate to think that the federal government would be as large as it is today."

"Let's hope not," I said, "but getting back to the sick cattle, do you know anyone in Texas who has seen any?"

They answered in unison. "No."

CHAPTER TWENTY-FIVE

Cameron, Missouri
September 6, 1867

John T. Alexander's men arrived in Abilene on Friday morning as planned, and the twenty carloads of cattle departed on schedule when Engine Number Seventeen pulled out of the station with a lot of bells and whistles. The engine was emblazoned with the new Kansas Pacific Railroad moniker, which wouldn't become official until next spring. They just couldn't miss the opportunity to show off their new name.

Instead of staying on in Abilene to enjoy more of the festivities, John T. Alexander and I were riding along with the others on the outgoing train. This was a change in our original plan. Just after Major Mabry and J. D. Reed left our table at the Drovers' Cottage on Thursday night, I told Mr. Alexander about my conversation with Tanner Biggs. He responded immediately.

John T. Alexander wasn't going to take any chances that the cattle might not make it to Chicago. "It's imperative that the Chicago newspapers announce the arrival of Abilene cattle. It's headline news, and the story puts my whole plan in motion. I won't let a fool like this fellow, Tanner Biggs, put a stop to it." John T. Alexander decided that we would accompany his men on the train today.

Mr. Alexander purchased more guns and ammunition at the stops along the way, and we didn't hide the fact that we were heavily armed. We never left the cattle alone. We held the cattle longer than necessary at some of the feeding and watering points, making it more difficult for someone to anticipate our exact arrival at future points along the way.

I thought I might have caught a glimpse of the troublemaker when we transferred the cattle to the Kansas City and Cameron Railroad, but I couldn't be sure. If Tanner Biggs was going to mess with us, it was going to be a costly decision on his part; however, in my mind, he wasn't one who would press the matter unless the odds were stacked in his favor. I'd fought a number of battles alongside this man, and he wasn't to be taken lightly.

Tanner Biggs could handle a gun and a knife with great skill, and he had a mean streak that could cause considerable harm. When Colonel Mosby wasn't watching, he would scalp the wounded Union soldiers just to hear them yell. There were stories that he had hung a man upside down, tying his feet to the tree and his head to the saddle horn.

⌘ ⌘ ⌘

We stayed overnight in Cameron at a hotel near the stockyards. We took turns watching the cattle. I was with John T. Alexander just before midnight. A coal oil lantern provided a soft light that danced across the backs of the cattle nearby. The long, gangly horns stabbed the air like menacing spears.

The cattle seemed to be healthy. I couldn't find telltale signs of any sickness, and I'd noticed that John T. Alexander had looked them over pretty well. I was sure he was confident that there wasn't any truth to the rumors of bad meat.

After we stood together for a while, John T. Alexander placed his hand on my shoulder. "What are you going to do when you get to California, John?"

His question took me by surprise. "I'm not sure," I said. "I suppose that I'll wait for God to tell me what to do. He's watched out for me so far."

"Good answer," he said. I was aware that the Alexanders were very involved in the First Presbyterian Church in Jacksonville. My family had been Baptists, but I was now attending the Catholic Church in New Berlin with the Kumle family.

Just then, a shot rang out and the lantern erupted in a ball of fire. Part of the wooden fence and some of the hay that was scattered at the foot of the fence caught fire. The cattle bellowed and bunched up as far away from the fire as they could get. I could hear boards snapping in the fence.

John T. Alexander and I were fortunate to have avoided the flames. Several of his men came running to our aid as we tried to stomp out the fire. Charlie Drury ran to the back end of the holding pen and opened a gate that allowed the cattle to move into another fenced area that was farther away. They tore the gate from its hinges as they rushed madly away from what they feared.

Some of the other hotel guests and a few of the townspeople joined in to help us, and we got the situation under control very quickly. Charlie came back with a bleeding shoulder. "Those horns are sharp," he said. "There's no point trying to find the shooter…it's too dark."

We doubled the size of the watch for the remainder of the night.

After we finished our turn, John T. Alexander and I stood on the front porch of the hotel. "I'll stay with the cattle all the way to Chicago," he said. "Gustavus Swift has plans to get the steaks into

Chicago's restaurants. I'll try to arrange to be interviewed by the *Daily Tribune* while eating in one of those places. Maybe I can get my picture on the front page."

He was interrupted by a pain in his stomach that caused him to pause and bend over for a moment.

"Are you all right?" I asked. He didn't look well.

"It's nothing serious—I just need some good home cooking," he said. "I have a sensitive stomach that doesn't like anything it's not used to. I'm all right now...I want you to head back to the farm. Pass on what we've learned to Jason and Jerome. The two of them may still be in Tolono. If that turns out to be the case, go see them there."

"And Jeanine?" I said.

"She's in Chicago...visiting the Swift family."

"I see," I said.

CHAPTER TWENTY-SIX

—·—◄│►—·—

Tolono, Illinois
September 18, 1867

The Alexander family was making good progress in Tolono, largely due to the efforts of John T. Alexander's two sons. I met Jerome as soon as I arrived. He was only two years younger than his older brother, but he wasn't at all like him. "He has a lot of growing up to do," Jason said to me in confidence, "but I envy that thick curly hair."

The new stockyards at the Toledo, Wabash, and Western and Illinois Central stations were coming along nicely, and a near duplicate to the set of buildings at the farm in Alexander was being constructed here on the outskirts of Tolono in Champaign County on the family's new piece of property.

John T. Alexander had purchased just over twenty thousand acres of land from Michael Sullivant, a prominent landowner in the area. Sullivant had accumulated his substantial holdings of nearly seventy thousand acres in four eastern Illinois counties over about fifteen years. In 1865, the state of Illinois passed a law that greatly increased the taxes on landowners like Michael Sullivant without any regard to the implications that it created for such people. Some legislators had successfully argued that increasing taxes on the wealthy did not impact their businesses in a negative way.

Politicians who supported economic growth complained vehemently about such laws, but the proponents of big government praised it. The result was a tax bill that Michael Sullivant could not pay without selling off part of his land and reducing the size of his business.

John T. Alexander was the grateful beneficiary of this plight, as he was able to procure a large holding that Sullivant called the Broadlands Farm. Alexander had mixed feelings about the purchase, believing that it was morally wrong to benefit from another's misfortune, but his conversations with Michael Sullivant revealed that Sullivant preferred that the land go to someone like Alexander, who was involved in a business much like his own.

John T. Alexander agreed to take on Sullivant's loan with Goodell and Warren Loan Company located in Loda, Illinois. George McConnell, son of General Murray McConnell and a graduate of Harvard Law School, served as John T. Alexander's legal counsel for the transaction. There was some delay before the deal was closed because a number of Goodell and Warren's large investors in New York objected; however, John T. Alexander contacted Richard Oglesby, the governor of Illinois, and the matter was resolved.

Alexander's honorable behavior created a longstanding friendship between the Alexander and Sullivant families. Shortly after the forced sale of Broadlands, Michael Sullivant lost faith in the government and interest in his enterprise. He began to turn over the business to his son, Joseph. Like the Alexanders, the Sullivants also planned to bring Texas longhorns to their farm, a strategy that further bonded them.

Broadlands was perfectly located near the railhead at Tolono. Ample water was available on the property for the cattle, and the soil was able to support the large corn crops that Alexander needed to feed his cattle.

"This is a great setup for us," Jason Alexander said, "but some of the people around here aren't very friendly. There was a big battle between Jacksonville and Champaign for the federal land grant college, and the people of Jacksonville accused the people of Champaign of bribing the decision makers.

"It was a great disappointment for Jacksonville and Morgan County because Illinois College's Professor Jonathan Baldwin Turner and our neighbor in Sangamon County, Captain James Brown, were involved in helping push the Morrill Land Grant Act through Washington in 1862. Once the people in this area heard that we were from Morgan County, they turned a cold shoulder to us."

"I'm sorry to hear that," I said. Without further delay, I quickly changed the subject and filled them in on the latest developments in Abilene. "Getting the acceptance of Texas cattle is going to be difficult. I'm beginning to get the feeling that we are up against an organized form of resistance that goes far beyond a few people worrying about some sick cows."

"I think you and Jason are still recovering from the war, John," Jerome Alexander said with a laugh. "Once we get this place ready to receive the cattle, we'll be on our way, and there'll be no stopping us. You two are making too much out of nothing." Jerome had been sheltered from a lot of the experiences that had shaped his older brother and me. He didn't seem to recognize his good fortune in this regard.

"Take it from me, Jerome," I said. "I know trouble when I see it, and I can see it very clearly...I just don't know where it's coming from."

"That's what worries me," Jason said. "I like to have my enemy out in the open."

"I agree," I said.

Jerome shrugged.

CHAPTER TWENTY-SEVEN

The People's Bank of Chicago
September 20, 1867

The small fishing boats on Lake Michigan attracted the attention of John T. Alexander as he sat across from the desk of Spencer Dugan, the president of the People's Bank of Chicago. The view of the lake from the top floor of the brick and stone building was spectacular, and John T. Alexander never failed to comment about it. But today he noticed a demeanor in the bank's president that he hadn't observed before.

"Is something wrong, Spencer?"

The man was forty-seven years of age, just like John T. Alexander, but today he looked to be a good bit older. "I'm sorry that I missed your birthday party at the steak house on Sunday night, John. I had a family emergency, and I knew that you'd understand."

John T. Alexander nodded. "Of course I understand. I don't make a big commotion out of birthdays anyhow."

A short time passed as Spencer Dugan examined a cigar that he held in his hand. "I don't know any other way to say this," he said, "so I'll just say it outright. John, I don't have the authority to approve your fall loan."

John T. Alexander had to give the words time to sink in. He lost his interest in the fishing boats on the lake. He turned to face his banker. "What are you talking about?"

"The bank's board didn't approve your fall loan. I wasn't given much of an explanation." Spencer Dugan was visibly disturbed.

He squirmed to find a comfortable position in his chair.

He couldn't find it.

"You know how it works, John," he said. "The farmers borrow in the spring and the fall to cover planting and harvesting. In order to cover the loans, we pull money from the big banks in New York, making it tougher for them to make loans to their customers in the East during that same time. I was simply told that they couldn't part with the money right now."

"I find that hard to believe," John T. Alexander said. "So what is the heavy borrowing that's going on in the East this fall that's so important?"

Spencer Dugan looked John T. Alexander in the eyes. "I honestly don't know, John."

One of the bank's largest customers brushed away a speck of dust from the top of the bank president's desk. "Who's behind this, Spencer?"

Spencer Dugan sat there in silence. He looked at his longtime friend and said, "John, if you mention this to anyone, I'll have to deny that it came from me."

"I understand."

Spencer Dugan rose from his chair and walked to a window. He was obviously choosing his words carefully. John T. Alexander hadn't seen him this way before.

"Henrietta Green is the person who convinced the rest of the board to go along with this decision. She's one of the wealthiest people in the country. The others wouldn't dare to stand up against her."

"What can you tell me about her?"

"Not much. Her maiden name is Robinson. She is said to have learned about stocks and bonds when her father read to her from the *New York Tribune* and the *Boston Herald* on a daily basis. She refused to see her husband for years after he made a bad investment."

"I suppose I could appeal to the board," Alexander said.

"The decision is final, John. There can be no appeal."

John T. Alexander rose from his chair. "You know that I'll not return here...ever."

"I know," he said. "I'm sorry, John."

CHAPTER TWENTY-EIGHT

——— ⚜ ———

John T. Alexander Farm
December 14, 1867

Central Illinois quickly exploded with color, and then, just as quickly, the countryside stood bare and naked, braced for the onslaught of winter. The fall months represented a race against time. Corn and hay were harvested and stored for the winter. The corn was shucked and cribbed on the cob. The barns were filled with hay, and the rest was scattered about in huge stacks that the cattle would reduce to nothing before the barns were emptied.

After John T. Alexander returned from his trip to Chicago in late September, I began to spend a lot more time with him. "I need to take advantage of your experience working with large operations like the railroads," he said. "I've come to realize that there is a lot more to expanding my business than what I first thought. I didn't understand that as well as I should have. I suppose the additional risk that I'm taking on is the reason the big banks are pulling the rug out from under me."

I wasn't so sure about that. I accompanied him on the meetings of October and November that took place with his many bankers.

Mr. Alexander relied quite heavily on Christian Hays of St. Louis, Thomas Condell of Springfield, George Wilson of Geneseo, and William Orear of Jacksonville, but his dealings also included many other smaller banks, particularly after he was pushed out of the very large cities by "the New York club," as he called them.

Jason's attempt to investigate Henrietta Green hadn't turned up anything. She was an eccentric loner. She lived on oatmeal and wore one black dress. She had no friends.

We were pleased to find that the reach of the New Yorkers didn't extend to the Bank of Ontario, where Mr. Alexander's loans were still good. His good friend Danford Christie, Canada's cattle commissioner, was still on the board of directors of that bank.

When Jason and Jerome were home, they joined us in our meetings with the bankers, but they were often away on other business. Jeanine's interest in her father's cattle business began to wane as she took an increased interest in horses...and Gustavus Swift.

"I've got purchasing agents permanently posted in St. Louis, Cairo, and Abilene," John T. Alexander said. "They've all been buying Texas longhorns for the winter. Even so, they still represent a small portion of my entire stock. My primary investment remains in the native cattle." I estimated that he had at least fifteen thousand head of native shorthorn cattle on hand at the moment.

He leaned back in his favorite chair and locked his fingers behind his head. "The extra room in my feeding pens is almost filled up. I'm trying to buy enough additional hay and corn to feed them until they can graze on their own in the spring, but I don't want to buy any more than I need—or more than I can store. If we have a rough winter, I could be in trouble. If I think about all of this too much, I can't sleep."

"The larger upside opportunity carries with it a larger downside risk," I said. "The railroad business was certainly that way. Doc Durant often explained it to me. He said that he reluctantly shared his reward but happily shared his risk, by selling shares in the business." My long conversations with Doc Durant were extremely informative, and I always took notes. He also wasn't shy about telling me when I should not write something down.

"I read that his company called Credit Mobilier declared its first dividend on Thursday."

"Yes, I saw that in the newspaper. And I'm happy to say that I have a few shares of my own," I said. "Doc owns about a fourth of the twenty-five thousand shares that are outstanding. He paid me for some of the work that I did for him in Credit Mobilier shares, and I was happy to take them. The shares weren't worth much at the time—but I was sure that they would soon be quite valuable, and I held on to all of them."

"Actually, that's a dream of mine," Alexander said. "If things go right, I'd like to issue some stock in J. T. Alexander and Company someday. I want to pound that gavel at the stock exchange opening."

"I'd like to add that to my portfolio," I said. "Can I put in my order now?"

"Are you proposing a stock swap?"

We laughed. I sincerely enjoyed being around this man. I could have been making more money with the railroad, but I liked it here. In some ways, John T. Alexander was a lot like Doc Durant—his mind was sharp like Doc's—but John T. Alexander had a soft heart.

⌘ ⌘ ⌘

I stayed for supper at the Alexander residence on this Saturday night. Afterward, I sat with Jeanine near the fireplace in the great room while John and Mary visited with their other guests, who remained at the table, taking an additional cup of coffee with brandy.

We jumped from topic to topic, but then we settled on horses. "I'm beginning to build a nice stable of trotters," she said. "The

Morgan horse is finally being recognized as a trotter. There is a new
registry, or studbook, which is being created this year."

Jeanine's eyes lit up with excitement as she described her dream.
"I've purchased some horses from my father's cousin in Spring
Station, Kentucky. A. J. Alexander is a member of the committee at
the National Trotting Association that is putting together the registry. He knows all of the stock raisers.

"A few years ago, he helped me buy a Morgan stallion from a
gentleman in Vermont. The stallion was grandsired by Sherman
Black Hawk, a wonderful trotter who will be included in the registry. I call my horse The Black."

"I see you working with him quite often," I said. "He's a fine-
looking horse—a square-gaited, natural trotter—although a bit
buck-kneed."

Jeanine looked at me closely. "You know something about
horses?"

"I'm from Virginia," I said. "There are no finer horses that I'm
aware of."

"I beg to differ with you, John Demsond," she said. Her face was
getting red. "I've heard little about trotters from Virginia."

"All of the good Virginia horses were taken by the North by the
end of the war...and I emphasize the word *taken*...or should I say
stolen?"

"The new registry will clear up the lineage," she said.

"I wouldn't be so sure about that," I said. "It's easy to change a
piece of paper."

Jeanine rose from her chair. "So you're saying the registry is
worthless?"

"I didn't say that." I feared that I'd already said too much.

She sat back down. "So what is it that you are trying to say?"

"The registry will probably not list many, if any, of the Virginia horses," I said. "I suspect the document will show that the sire or dam was *unknown* rather than indicate it was a horse from the South."

Jeanine sat in silence. I couldn't tell if she was thinking about what I'd just said or whether she was formulating her response. It was obvious that she was disturbed.

It was an uncomfortable moment. I stared ahead, looking at the flames that reached out from the logs in the fireplace. Just as I started to get up to put another log on the fire, Jeanine abruptly rose from her chair and blocked my path.

She stood there looking down at me with her hands stiffly planted upon her hips. "That can't possibly be right," she said. Jeanine turned and stormed out of the room.

As I turned to watch Jeanine rush off, I saw that John T. Alexander was standing in the doorway. He made no attempt to impede his daughter's exit.

Instead, he walked over to the chair that Jeanine had vacated and sat down. "You hit a sore spot with her, John," he said.

"How's that?" I asked.

"The Black's sire was a stallion named Black Cloud," he said. "The Black's dam is *unknown*."

I shrugged.

CHAPTER TWENTY-NINE

─┄─ ≡✦≡ ┄─

M&W Railway Station
Alexander, Illinois
March 21, 1868

I stepped down from the passenger car on a chilly Saturday afternoon, reluctantly leaving the welcome heat from the car's stove behind for the remaining travelers to enjoy. I had been away since just before Christmas, when I was shocked to receive a telegram from my cousin Stephen Demsond.

I thought he was dead. Instead, he was recuperating in a soldiers' home in Chicago. He was one of the Confederate prisoners who survived the infamous, sixty-acre Douglas Camp. Stephen told me that the actual number of those who died there was far more than the four thousand deaths published in the Union papers. The camp was now being destroyed to cover any evidence that might later be found.

Stephen's parents had been killed in the same Union raid that took my parents' lives. He had returned home to check up on them when he was taken as a prisoner. He managed to escape, but he was beaten to near death when he was recaptured. His arms and legs were still a mangled mess because he received no medical help while in captivity.

I spent Christmas with Stephen, and I stayed in a boarding house nearby for several weeks thereafter. I noticed a gradual improvement in his spirit as we sat each day reminiscing about the past—the good times before the war. He had set his mind on returning to Virginia as soon as warmer weather arrived. We promised to keep in touch.

I still planned on going to California, but Stephen's presence in Virginia would put a root back in the ground there. I was actually happy about that in a way.

While I was in Chicago, John T. Alexander sent a bunch of his contracts with the railroad companies to me. In general, the contracts were poorly written. Mr. Alexander was a man of his word, and he preferred to close deals with a handshake rather than a detailed piece of paper. We had talked about this a few months ago, and he agreed that it was time to nail things down in a more proper fashion. He asked me to meet with each one of the railroad companies and negotiate new contracts. Mr. Alexander's attorney, George McConnell, provided me with some suggested wording for the contracts, but I was largely left on my own.

I started the lengthy process a few weeks after Christmas, and I ended up traveling to many cities in order to find the railroad officials who were able to legally sign the contracts. Edward Hinrichsen, John T. Alexander's good friend, was able to point me to the right people in the various companies. He informed me that many of the senior managers of the Big Four railroads of the East met at the Saint Nicholas Hotel in New York City during the holidays in order to avoid attention to their joint gathering. I decided against interrupting their clandestine meeting.

I arranged appointments in advance with every carrier of Mr. Alexander's freight. Some of my meetings with the railroad officials went well...some, not so well. On more than one occasion, I was offered a cash payment to sign off on a bad deal. Once I refused, the negotiations became very difficult. I intended to provide a listing of these bribes to Mr. Alexander. If he chose to pursue the matter, the railroad managers would, of course, deny that such offers had been made. It was a nasty business.

Because of the large shipments of cattle, we believed that J. T. Alexander and Company should always receive the lowest price that the railroad company offered from one point to another, and that was my position as we negotiated. I realized full well that it would be difficult for us to know that we had, in fact, received the lowest pricing when billed by the railroad; however, I intended to perform random audits as time allowed.

I was thinking about how I might go about doing this when I stepped from the train in Alexander and walked into the station building. Henry Fitch and Jeanine Alexander were waiting for me. Fitch dropped a bundle of mail and telegrams at my feet and walked away without a word. Jeanine gave me a half smile and said, "My father wants to see you right away." She turned around and called over her shoulder, "The horses are out back."

Such was the welcoming committee. I grabbed the bundle and followed her. She didn't look back.

I left my alligator skin traveling bag and the bundle of mail in the parlor of the Alexander home and entered John T. Alexander's study. Jeanine didn't follow. Mr. Alexander and Jason greeted me warmly before we sat down to talk.

Jason saw me looking at the bandages on his leg. "I have some complications...a bit of infection," he said. "Dr. Baker has things under control."

"Good," I said, but it didn't look so good. I began to feel uneasy.

John T. Alexander didn't waste any time getting our meeting started. "John, we have a bit of a problem. The ice is breaking up on the Mississippi River, and the cattle boats from the Red River have begun to push upriver to Cairo. I'm getting reports from my purchasing agent in Cairo that the condition of the arriving cattle is very bad. He doesn't think we should buy any of them right now."

Mr. Alexander rose from his chair and walked over to the large fireplace. He picked up a small log from the woodpile and used it to stir the fire. "The heavy snows in Kansas will keep Abilene out of operation for several more weeks," he said. "Likewise, the trails through the eastern counties of Kansas and the western counties of Missouri are still too risky. I desperately need to get some Texas cattle up here to replace some of the native cattle that I've moved out over the winter. John, I want you to go to Cairo and take a look for me."

"When do you want me to leave?" I asked.

"Monday," he said.

CHAPTER THIRTY

Cairo, Illinois
March 25, 1868

Cairo was a busy town where the waters of the Mississippi and Ohio come together. It was a place of great unrest during the War Between the States. It was farther south than Richmond, deeply planted among Confederate sympathizers.

William Clark wasn't happy to see me. Mr. Alexander's purchasing agent was concerned that I might be here to fire him. "I thought I was doin' a good job here," he said. Clark's beet-red face and bulbous nose told me that he was a drinker.

"As far as I know, you are," I said. "Mr. Alexander wants me to look into the condition of the arriving cattle. Your telegram worried him because he was counting on getting these longhorns up to his ranch before the end of this month."

Spring had come early, and as soon as the Mississippi River was able to handle the steamboat and barge traffic, the longhorns were moved eastward along the Red River to be loaded up and headed northward. It was a rough trip just to get to the Mississippi River, but the difficulty didn't end there.

"There's a barge head'n in now," he said, pointing to the south. "I'll show you how bad things are." Just as he said, a large barge was heading our way. The steamship that was pushing it along had begun to slow.

We walked to the stockyard pier. Even before the barge tied up, I could see that the cattle were jammed together in a way that allowed no movement whatsoever. "They've been standin' that way for eight days," Clark said. "The only food they get is what they eat off another's back when a small bit of hay is tossed in for 'em. Their water comes from an occasional hose'n down. If they're lucky enough to be face'n in the right direction, they catch a small drink."

I was appalled. "They look terrible." There were at least six hundred head on the barge.

"I believe that's what I reported to our boss, if I'm not mistaken," he said. "Watch'm stumble when they try to walk down the ramp."

And stumble they did. One by one, the wide-eyed creatures ambled to the holding pen. A few of them fell off the ramp and into the river. The pace of those who made it quickened as they discovered the food and water that awaited them. Several of the animals remained on the barge, hobbling about with broken legs.

"They don't appear to be sick," I said. "They're just worn out... and nearly starved to death."

"What's'a matter wit'chu, are ya blind?" Clark asked. "Look at 'em...they're sick...pret'n'near dead."

"I don't agree," I said. "I want you to buy them and put them on the next barge to Hannibal tomorrow, so we can ship them to Alexander on the TW&W."

Clark tilted his hat back on his head, and laughed. "Well, Demsond, I'm sorry to tell you that the barges're turnin' around right here and head'n back to the Red River. Seems there're some folks up ahead in St. Louis and Hannibal who aren't allow'n the barges full of

Texas cattle to be offloaded at the moment." He stared at me with a smirk on his face. "And I hear that they're a rough bunch, too."

I'd heard a rumor about this on the train. I had to think quickly. "Put them on the Illinois Central train to Tolono after they've been fed and rested here for three days," I said. "When the train reaches Farina, about halfway between here and Tolono, I want all of the cattle taken off the train to be fed and rested at Edward Richardson's place for two days before they're sent on to Tolono. Is that clear?"

William Clark seemed to be taken aback by my suggestion. Sweat beaded on his forehead. "I'm hav'n trouble believe'n this."

"Believe it!" I said. "Keep purchasing and shipping the cattle to Tolono in this manner until you receive instructions to stop doing so."

He nodded reluctantly.

I had him repeat my instructions. I left the area, and then I circled back to watch Clark. I didn't trust him.

At first, I couldn't find him, but then I saw him come out of the Western Union office. I was pretty sure that his telegram hadn't been sent to Mr. Alexander to complain about me.

I was right…it went to someone else.

CHAPTER THIRTY-ONE

Champaign County, Illinois
April 30, 1868

The summer heat had come early. Isaac Larmon stood on the front steps of his porch listening to the reports from his hired hands. More of his animals had been found dead. First, it was the cattle, but now the horses and sheep were dropping, too.

"It's those damn Texas cattle that John Alexander's men are driving to the Broadlands from the stockyards in Tolono, Isaac," his foreman said. "All they have to do is rub up close to our fences when they pass down the open road. If there's a section of fence down, they wander in amongst our stock. All they have to do is breath on our stock to kill them. They're poison."

The others agreed. Isaac noticed that most of his men were now wearing guns. He knew that a good part of what they were telling him seemed to be true. The problems started to occur shortly after Alexander's Texas cattle arrived in the area late last month.

"Abe Gaston is shooting them if they get into his pens," another man said, placing his hand on his holstered pistol. "He drags the carcass out on the road and leaves it there for Alexander's men to find.

Abe's talking about blocking off the roads with armed men to keep
the Texas cattle away from his fences."

"I've known Alexander's foreman, Rand Eaton, for a long time,"
Isaac Larmon said. "He tells me that the Texas cattle aren't sick."

"They're sick on the inside, Isaac. I wouldn't eat that meat for
anything."

"I'll ride over to the Broadlands Farm and talk to Rand," Isaac
Larmon said.

⌘   ⌘   ⌘

Randolph Eaton wasn't surprised to see his old friend, Isaac Larmon,
riding up to the house. The tension in the area where both of them
had been raised had continued to build since the first downers were
spotted a week or so ago.

They sat on the porch, enjoying the calm breeze of the late afternoon. Rand's wife, Betty, brought out a pitcher of lemonade and a
couple of glasses on a silver tray. She spoke with Isaac briefly and then
returned inside. The two men sipped their drinks in silence.

"We've got a problem, Rand."

"I know, Isaac. But I just can't believe these longhorns are the
cause of it."

"What other explanation can there be? Everything was fine until
you started bringing those Texas cattle in here for John Alexander."

"The Sullivants are starting to bring longhorns in here, too...
and so is John Sidell," Rand Eaton said. "Honestly, Isaac, not one of
those longhorns has died since we started shipping them here from
Cairo last month. We've butchered a few of them for food. All of us
have been eating the meat—none of us have been sick." Rand Eaton
poured another glass of lemonade for the two of them. "How have
your animals died?"

Isaac Larmon told him what he had seen and repeated the stories that he had heard from his men. "It's similar to a horse with the botts or colic. They seem to suffer with inward fever. When we cut them open, they appear to be dry and scorched inside. We've tried a bunch of different remedies. Most haven't worked."

"Which ones seemed to work?"

"We drenched a few with lard, and they recovered," he said.

Rand Eaton had to ponder that for a bit before he responded. "That tells me the problem's *outside*, not *inside*."

"We have to get this taken care of, Rand," Isaac said. "We'll all be destroyed if people are afraid to eat our beef."

"I know," Rand said. Isaac Larmon was absolutely right about that.

"Would you be willing to let the doc come over here and inspect some of your cattle?"

"I'm sure Mr. Alexander would approve of that."

"I'm sure he would, Rand," Isaac said. "I think you know that I'm not one of the people who believes he doesn't have a right to be here in Champaign County."

"I know," Rand said.

The two men parted with a handshake. As Rand Eaton watched Isaac Larmon ride away, he was fearful that his new job running John T. Alexander's operation at the Broadlands Farm might cost him one of his best friends.

CHAPTER THIRTY-TWO

John T. Alexander Farm
May 4, 1868

I sat in John T. Alexander's office on a Monday afternoon. Jason Alexander and Randolph Eaton were also in the room. The windows were wide open, and a warm breeze from the west moved the curtains gently in a soft motion that reminded me of my mother's clothesline.

My eyes went to the looking glass that rested on the corner of his desk. This was his usual companion when he sat upstairs in the cupola, looking out over the vast expanse of his farm. I once made the mistake of calling it a spyglass, and I was quickly corrected.

His presence in the cupola was often revealed when the sun occasionally reflected from the outer lens of the looking glass with an explosion of dazzling light. Whenever I saw this, I was always taken back to my days in the cavalry when the mistake of not shielding the reflection could have brought dire consequences. I longed for these recollections to go away, but I feared that I would carry them with me forever.

"What did Dr. Lawrence have to say, Rand?" It was unusual to see John T. Alexander in so tense a mood. It was impossible for the rest of us not to notice.

"He didn't find any problems with our cattle. He found some bugs, some sore feet, some cuts from the horns...the usual things." Rand Eaton seemed to be confident that Mr. Alexander's property was in good condition. It was his job to make sure of that.

"Do you think that will satisfy Isaac Larmon and the others?" Jason said.

"No, I don't." Rand Eaton moved around in his chair to face Jason. "They're an angry bunch, Jason. They believe that our cattle are the cause of their problems, and they won't be happy until our longhorns go away."

"And that's not going to happen," John T. Alexander said. "I paid a lot of money for Broadlands, and I have to make it return a profit." He stood up and walked to the window, taking a deep breath of fresh air. "What can we do to change their minds?"

His question didn't seem to be addressed to anyone in particular, so the three of us sat there in silence, watching the drapes flap across Mr. Alexander's shoulders. For a moment, he looked like an angel.

"Perhaps it will help if we show them that we're not afraid to mix the longhorns with *our* native stock," Jason said. "So far, we've shipped all of our Texas cattle to Tolono this spring, but now that the Kansas winter is over, we'll soon be bringing some of them from Abilene to this location right here. And if enough drovers try to push the cattle through eastern Kansas and western Missouri, some of those will get through to us as well. We can mix the longhorns with the shorthorn stock that we have here and send the rest of our native stock to Tolono to mix in with the longhorns there. That should be enough to convince them that it isn't our longhorns that are causing the problem."

"But Jason, we don't know for sure that we can mix the cattle, do we?" I said. All eyes were on me instantly, implying that I was taking the side of our opponents.

I held my ground. "All I'm saying is that you should stick your toe in the water before you plunge in. Why not take the longhorn cattle that you get from Abilene and mix them in with your native stock here, and if all goes well, *then* you move the native stock to Tolono to mix with the longhorns there?"

John T. Alexander returned to his chair behind the desk. He sat there for a moment, appearing to be deep in thought. He leaned forward in his chair. "We're expecting a shipment from Abilene this week, are we not?" He was looking at Jason.

"On Thursday," Jason said, "we should be getting five hundred head. And then, we should be getting five hundred head on both Tuesday and Thursday, well into August."

"That's what I thought." John T. Alexander appeared to be doing some quick calculations in his head as he rolled his eyes up to the ceiling. "I should be getting some more Devons and Herefords from the Browns over in Grove Park very soon, so we'll have plenty of native stock to send to Tolono." He rose from his chair and went to the window once more.

"It's all set then," he said. "We'll do as John suggests, mix the cattle here, and if that works, we'll mix them in Champaign County afterward."

Jason and I left his father and Rand Eaton alone in the room to discuss a few more matters before Rand was to catch the train back to Tolono. Jason had an appointment with his doctor, so he promptly headed into town. I decided to walk over to the horse barn to see if Jeanine was around.

I said hello to the Chief as I entered the barn. He smiled and nodded. Without asking, he pointed to a stall farther in.

Jeanine was busy brushing down a Morgan mare. I stood there watching her for a moment before speaking up. Even though Jeanine didn't treat me very well, I still liked her.

"Hi, Jeanine."

She stopped her work and turned to look at me. "Hello, John."

"You sure have some fine horses," I said. "Are you planning on racing any of them this season?" Jason had already told me that she was planning on entering some of the local races.

"I'm not quite sure yet," she said. "What do you think?"

I was surprised that she asked for my opinion.

"I think they'd do fine." I wasn't just saying so to make her happy; I believed that her horses were some of the best stock that I'd seen in a long time. She had a special way with horses that couldn't be denied. She still let me ride Sting, and Sting was the finest horse that I'd had the pleasure to ride. He had a rocking horse canter that was as smooth as silk.

"Thanks for the vote of confidence," she said. Then she abruptly changed the subject. "My father's still worried about all of this longhorn talk. What's going on, John?"

I told her about my conversation with her father, her brother, and Rand Eaton. Her face registered grave concern. "Jeanine, I want you to be sure to keep your horses away from the longhorns," I said.

She looked at me with great surprise. "What are you talking about?"

"I'm talking about being very careful, Jeanine. There are just too many unanswered questions right now. Some horses have died in Champaign County—that's all I'm saying. I don't know any more than that."

She turned and went back to brushing the mare that was anxiously awaiting further attention. "John Demsond, there are times when I just don't understand you at all."

I turned and walked toward the barn door. "I know," I said. "How well I know."

"What did you say?" she called.

"Never mind," I called back.

The Chief chuckled as I walked by him.

CHAPTER THIRTY-THREE

— ⚎ —

River Rat Saloon
Hannibal, Missouri
May 4, 1868

"Honest to God, boss, as much as I'd like to take credit for what's gone on there in Champaign County, I honestly didn't do a damn thing to stir up the trouble."

"You surprise me, Tanner. That's a word that I didn't expect to be part of your vocabulary."

"What word's that?" Tanner Biggs wasn't smiling.

"Honest," Red Beard said.

Tanner Biggs still wasn't smiling. "Don't make fun of me." Red Beard was a Yankee, and Tanner Biggs didn't like Yankees.

"Oh, lighten up, Tanner. You're doing a good job for me. I have no complaints."

Tanner Biggs relaxed somewhat and gulped down what remained of his beer. Red Beard bought another round. They stood alone at the end of the long oak bar at the busy River Rat Saloon. Hannibal, a town with ten thousand residents, was known for having well over twenty saloons. Red Beard motioned for another round for the men sitting at a nearby table.

"Me and the boys have been raising holy hell here, making sure that none of the cattle barges and boats get unloaded." Tanner Biggs was raising his voice as he consumed more beer.

"Keep it up as long as you can. I know the local authorities will step in at some point and shut you down, but the news about the animal deaths in the Tolono area has spread fast...so that should help our cause."

"Getting back to what I said before," Tanner Biggs said, "I didn't do a thing about that."

"And here I was thinking that you'd killed those animals and set the blame on John Alexander," Red Beard said.

"Nope, I'm innocent, boss."

Red Beard wasn't convinced. "Do you think it was someone else?"

"Could be, I suppose." Tanner Biggs was losing interest in the conversation. He didn't think the Yankee was very smart, but he was happy to take the man's money.

"Well, whoever did it sure did us a big favor," Red Beard said.

"You want me to go take a look for myself?"

"Yes, do that," Red Beard said, "but don't raise too much attention."

"Maybe I'll get lucky and run into my old friend, John Demsond."

Red Beard put his mug down on the bar and turned to face Tanner Biggs. "No killing."

"Of course not," Tanner Biggs said, "that word's not in my *vocabulary*."

CHAPTER THIRTY-FOUR

——— ≡✦≡ ———

Alexander, Illinois
May 31, 1868

After the churches in the area concluded their services on Sunday morning, the townspeople gathered for a picnic in the central park. It was a perfect day...bright and sunny with a cool breeze from the north. The Alexanders and all of their employees and families sat together on several tables that were clustered under a large tulip tree at the north end of the park.

"This is a great spot," I said. The yellow tulips were in full bloom above us, and the food was magnificent. I was grateful for days like this. They helped to heal the wound of losing my family...but I still had my cousin Stephen.

Gustavus Swift was quick to agree. "Yes indeed, a perfect day with perfect company." He had managed to squeeze into a place that Jeanine created for him between the two of us. I was disappointed but not surprised. I didn't look at the Chief, but I knew that he was laughing again.

Gustavus arrived last night and stayed at the Alexander home as he always did. His meatpacking business in Chicago was thriving, as the people who had been deprived of beef during the war now found it to be readily available. But it was still expensive. The Texas cattle were gradually being moved northward, slowly forcing the slaughter-houses to reduce the prices.

I actually liked Gustavus Swift, and that made things more difficult for me when I watched how Jeanine seemed to adore him. He was good-looking and wealthy and about to become one of the most successful people in the whole state...how could she not like him? I was still trying to find my calling, and I seemed to be wasting a lot of time in the process.

"Jeanine, I hear that you're racing some of your Morgan horses," Gustavus said.

Jeanine smiled. "I've entered a few local races, that's all."

"You should put some of them up at the Broadlands Farm," he said, "and then you could run them up to Chicago on the Illinois Central and enter some bigger races there." His thick eyebrows danced over deep-set brown eyes that sparkled when he smiled.

"I don't think that's such a good idea," I said.

Jeanine was quick to respond. "Why not, *John?*"

Her tone of voice warned me not to continue, but I ignored the alarm. "Animals are still dying over there...even horses."

I immediately collected some glares from those at the table who heard my comment. "It's true," I said in response to their looks. "All I'm saying is that it might be a good idea to hold off until we find out more about what's going on there." The stares remained.

"John's right," Jason Alexander said. Most of the glaring faces subsequently relaxed. "It's wise to be cautious."

"They're my horses, Jason," Jeanine said, "and I'll do what I please with them."

"Suit yourself," Jason said. He rose from the table and walked away. I joined him.

We walked to the northwest end of the park and looked across the street to the new post office that had just been constructed. "Jeanine's a bit high-strung, but she means well," Jason said.

"I know that," I said. "She wants to prove that she is as capable as the male side of the Alexander family—and she is. I just don't want to see her make a big mistake to prove the point."

"She's going to marry Gustavus Swift, so you'd better get used to it, John," Jason said.

I didn't reply. I knew that he was probably right, but I didn't like to hear him say it.

"By the way, John, before I forget it, Rand Eaton said he saw a guy who fits the description of Tanner Biggs. He's probably mixed up in this thing somehow."

"Most likely," I said. "I'll head over there tomorrow and see if I can find him. I've got some questions for Tanner."

"You can ride on the train with some of our shorthorn stock that we're moving over there. It's been about three weeks now, and we haven't had any problems here with mixing the longhorns from Abilene in with the shorthorns, so father wants to move some of the stock to the Broadlands Farm."

I shrugged. "I don't think that's a good idea, but I'm not the boss." No one was listening to me now.

Jason nodded. "We have to show our neighbors over there that we're not afraid." Jason wasn't convincing. I'd known him long enough to read between the lines, and I knew that he was scared.

Just then, a Western Union courier walked up to Jason and delivered an urgent telegram. Jason promptly tipped the courier and sat down on a nearby bench to read the message. I stood by, waiting to see if I was needed in any way.

Jason closed the message and sat there for a moment. "John, I need to travel to Washington to help my old friend Anna Carroll. She's involved in a congressional hearing, hoping to gain payment for a lot of the writings and other work that she completed for President Lincoln and the War Department during the war. She has asked me to be a material witness on her behalf."

"I thought she worked closely with General Grant," I said. "Can't he help her out?"

Jason shrugged. "General Grant is now a *politician*. My sense is that he is being manipulated by a group of powerful Republicans led by Senator Roscoe Conkling from New York, among others."

"It looks like Grant will be our next president now that he got the nod at the Republican National Convention in Chicago a few days ago," I said.

"Yes, but that won't help Miss Carroll, because she was pushing for Senator Benjamin Wade from Ohio, her good friend."

Jason rubbed his leg and rose from the bench. "It looks like I'll be riding along with you on the train tomorrow, but when you get off in Tolono, I'll have to continue on. I'm not anxious to return to Washington, but I will do anything that I can to help Miss Carroll. She is one of the most impressive people that I have ever met."

The eastbound train was filling up fast.

CHAPTER THIRTY-FIVE

M&W Railway Station
Tolono, Illinois
June 1, 1868

Even before we reached the station, Jason and I could see the large crowd that had gathered on the platform. We knew that they were waiting for us to arrive with the cattle, but we couldn't understand why they would have a problem with us bringing in the native stock.

Shouts filled the air as the train screeched to a stop. The engineer moved the crowd back a bit when he released a double blast of steam from the bottom valves. He laughed as they backed away and bunched up in a heap.

Just before Jason and I began our descent, I could see that Rand Eaton had worked his way to the front of the group. He quickly climbed up onto the steps of the passenger car in front of us and turned to face the crowd of people. He raised his hand, hoping for silence.

Reluctantly, the people quieted. Rand Eaton put his hand down. "I've known you folks for a long time. I was born and raised here, just like most of you. You've heard that the cattle in these cars to my left are full of Texas longhorns, but that isn't true. They're native shorthorn stock, just like your cattle. The man I work for, John T. Alexander, your new neighbor, has brought some of his best cattle here so you can see that he isn't afraid to mix these cattle in with the longhorns he brought in here from Cairo on the Illinois Central."

"He isn't our neighbor," someone shouted. Several others murmured in agreement.

"We've always welcomed newcomers to this area," Eaton said, "and we've called them neighbors. My boss is no different. He is a good man, and he brings these cattle here to show you that it isn't his cattle that are killing your animals."

"Maybe these cattle are poison, too," another shouted. "That's right," others called.

I noticed that many of the people in the crowd carried firearms. I was glad that I had mine, and Jason was armed with his Pocket Colt. I saw him fold back the front of his coat so he could reach it quickly if needed. I lifted my pistol from its holster ever so slightly and gently let it settle back into place, very loosely. I was hoping that I wouldn't have to use it, but if someone pointed a gun at me, I wasn't going to let him get off the first shot. If I learned anything in the war, I learned that.

I was sure that Tanner Biggs was in their midst, but I couldn't see him. Rand Eaton was beginning to gain control of the crowd. "Let me and my men unload these cattle and drive them on out to Broadlands. They'll walk along the same roads that your animals walked and rub up against the same fences."

Just then, a rider appeared, shouting out to Rand Eaton as he pulled up his lathered horse within inches of the end of the station platform. "Somebody killed Joe Hall, and they killed a bunch of our cattle, too…shot Joe down in cold blood."

The crowd buzzed and swarmed near the rider. Jason reacted quickly. "Rand, stay here and get these cattle unloaded. Move them out to Broadlands slowly. John and I will find a couple of horses and ride out with your man to take a look."

"I'm going, too." It was James Pierce. The local blacksmith and sheriff had suddenly appeared from within the crowd.

Others joined in, and before long Jason and I raced to the scene with a dozen other riders. I glanced down at Jason's peg leg to remind myself that this man was riding just like the rest of us. His saddle back at the farm had been fitted with a special stirrup for his wooden peg, but now he was forced to ride without it. I was never sure whom I admired most, him or his father.

We rode about five miles before we came upon a small group of men who clustered around Joe Hall's body, which they had dragged from the road to the bottom of a maple tree. He had taken a bullet in the chest at close range. "It looks like he rode right up to the shooter before he was discovered," Sheriff Pierce said. "I suppose the shooter was too busy killing longhorns and didn't see Joe right away." There were about a dozen carcasses scattered around in the large holding pen, and the other animals were moving around nervously in bunches. "He turned on Joe as soon as he saw him. He never had a chance."

"As soon as Rand gets here with the other cattle, I'll ride with him over to the Hall's place to tell his wife," Jason Alexander said. "I think he's got a couple of young ones, too." Several of the men nodded. "Let's get Joe on into town, and get those carcasses out of there. The men can take home as much meat as they want, and we'll put the rest in the smokehouse." The men followed Jason's instructions and went about their business without a word.

"I'll try to put a stop to this thing before it gets out of hand," the sheriff said. "I don't suppose you have any idea who did this?"

"No," we said. However, I immediately thought of Tanner Biggs. I'd been informed that he might be in the area, so it seemed to make sense. I would try to find him, but I had to remind myself of the need to move cautiously. The war had taught me the lesson that the bullets come much more easily after the first shot is fired...and the first shot was fired here today.

CHAPTER THIRTY-SIX

✦

Alexander Station
June 3, 1868

When Jerome Alexander stepped off the westbound train that arrived on the main track, he found his father and his sister standing on the station platform. They were watching the cattle being loaded onto the cars of the eastbound train that filled the sidetrack located just south of the main track. Jerome received a warm greeting.

After a short time, the westbound train moved on. "This entire load will go to the New York market," John T. Alexander said, waving his arm in the direction of the stock cars.

Jerome shook his head. "You're sending out only the shorthorn stock. Isn't it about time to send some longhorns out there?"

"Not yet," Jeanine said. "Father wants to go slowly out there. It's a tough market."

Jerome was annoyed, but he didn't press the issue. He'd telegraphed some information about what happened in Tolono on Monday, and he wanted to fill them in on the latest developments. "They'll bury Joe Hall tomorrow afternoon. We can all travel back there together on the morning train." They both nodded.

"Did John Demsond find Tanner Biggs yet?" Jeanine asked.

"No, he's still looking for him," Jerome said. "I'm not so sure that it was him. I expect one of the local people. They don't like us."

John T. Alexander shook his head. "Have there been any more sick animals in the area?"

"Not as many as before," Jerome said, "but some animals are still dying. I think someone is killing them and blaming it on our Texas cattle."

"John Demsond thinks we should keep the Texas cattle away from the other animals," Jeanine said.

Jerome grunted. "We don't work for *John Demsond*...he works for us."

"I'm aware of that," Jeanine said. Jerome was only four years older than Jeanine, and she didn't like it when he seemed to present himself as being much older and much smarter.

John T. Alexander had heard enough of his children's banter. "Let's get over to the house so we don't miss dinner. As far as mixing the cattle goes, there's no need to put them together in the same pens. We don't want mixed breeding; however, we'll continue to move the herds from one holding area to another, just as we've always done. They eat grasses for a while—then we bring them in closer to our corncribs to fatten them up. Then we start all over again. It works just fine."

"John says we shouldn't put the longhorns in pens right next to the native stock," Jeanine said.

"I told you," Jerome said. "John works for us."

They were about to walk away when Henry Fitch appeared from the station building. "Some of the folks around here are getting nervous about the stories coming out of Tolono," he said. "Is there any truth to the claims that your Texas cattle are the cause of those deaths?"

"None whatsoever," John T. Alexander said. "You've seen the longhorns that started to come in here from Abilene last week. Did they look sick to you?" John T. Alexander still missed his old friend Edward Hinrichsen, who used to occupy Fitch's office.

"No," he said, "they looked all right." Fitch had refused to use the telegraph line out to Alexander's farm to communicate with him as Hinrichsen had done. He wanted to remove it.

"We'd appreciate it if you didn't spread the stories, Fitch," Jerome said.

"People talk...I can't stop that."

It was obvious that Jerome didn't like the man. "No, you wouldn't want to do that, would you?"

"What does that mean?" Henry Fitch wasn't one to back down.

"You're a smart man," Jerome said, "figure it out for yourself."

"Good day, Mr. Fitch," John T. Alexander said, "I think I hear the dinner bell ringing."

Just as they reached the steps leading down from the platform, Jeanine turned and called to Henry Fitch, "By the way, I'm going to send some of my horses to Tolono next week. Can you arrange for a special car for them?"

Fitch waved his response. He turned and entered the building, mumbling to himself, "Special cars for special people."

CHAPTER THIRTY-SEVEN

Marion House Inn
Tolono, Illinois
June 5, 1868

On Thursday I attended Joe Hall's funeral services with the Alexander family and Rand Eaton. All of his fellow workers at the Broadlands Farm were also there along with many other people from the area.

After saying good-bye to Jeanine and John T. Alexander at the TW&W Railway Station on Friday afternoon, I joined Jerome Alexander and Rand Eaton at the Marion House Inn for a beer. The place was rebuilt after it burned down a few years ago, and the wood still smelled as if it had just been cut. The promise of the weekend brought in a large, noisy crowd. A drunkard pounded away on the keys to the out-of-tune piano in the far back.

The menacing glares at Joe Hall's burial from a day earlier were back again today. "Sometimes, I wish we hadn't expanded to this area," Jerome said. "These people don't want us here, and they're looking for any reason they can find to push us out."

"They're losing valuable animals, Jerome," Rand Eaton said. "You would've seen the same kind of response no matter where you'd gone if the same thing had happened there."

I was listening to the exchange, but I was watching Tanner Biggs. I knew that he would show up here sooner or later. The timing was bad, but I needed to talk to him.

I told the others what I was going to do before I walked over to the table where Tanner Biggs was playing poker. He saw me coming. He dropped his right hand close to his pistol, a Starr Arms Company, single-action, Model 1863 Army revolver.

"Tanner, I need to talk to you," I said. My right hand was also near my pistol, but I didn't think he'd pull a gun on me in here. The knife in his boot was another issue.

"Demsond, can't you see that I'm busy right now?" He spat his words along with bits of tobacco through the few teeth that remained in his mouth.

One of the other men at the table looked up at me. "The man's playing cards...get lost, cowman." He was the same big man whom I had wrestled with in Abilene last year. The playing cards were lost in his huge hands. I suspected that his two friends were close by, but I didn't notice them.

"I need to know where you were when Joe Hall was killed," I said.

Tanner Biggs threw his cards down on the table. "Did I miss something, or is Pierce still the sheriff around here?"

"I asked you a question," I said. The others put their cards down and pushed their chairs back from the table. The others in the inn quickly noted the confrontation. The room became silent.

"Let's take this outside, Tanner," I said.

"I like it right here, Demsond. I was having a nice game of poker until now, and you've disrupted things. You owe me and my friends an apology."

In one swift motion, the big man grabbed the table and threw it in my direction. I turned my head just in time to protect my eyes and nose, but the edge cut me on the forehead as the table slammed into me.

I fell to the floor with the table on top of me. I pushed the table in the big man's direction. While I was paying attention to him, Tanner Biggs hovered above me and landed a solid blow to my chin as I tried to get up. Others joined in the fray as Jerome Alexander and Rand Eaton came to my assistance. Before long, the whole place was getting involved.

Some were using beer mugs as clubs, and I caught one on the back of my head. I was seeing stars as I continued to defend myself from multiple attackers. I was trying to watch for guns and knives as I worked my way toward Tanner Biggs. He had moved back against the piano to enjoy the fracas.

He was waiting for me with his hand on his pistol. I didn't even know if my pistol was still in its holster. I was about to find out when I broke in the clear and faced Tanner Biggs. He smiled and raised his pistol.

Just then, a shot rang out, and everyone froze. Sheriff Pierce stood in the doorway, and he leveled his Tranter revolver at Tanner Biggs. "That's enough. There'll be no gunplay in here. If I see any man with a pistol in his hand, I'll shoot him." Tanner Biggs quickly complied, lowering his weapon.

I looked for Jerome and Rand. Jerome was out cold on the floor, and Rand was being held back by several of the local men. "Who started this?" Sheriff Pierce said.

"He did." Several fingers were pointed at me.

Jim Pierce walked over to me and took my gun just as I picked it up from the floor. "Come along," he said. "Somebody throw some water on these guys on the floor." He turned to Rand Eaton. "You and your young friend there on the floor might want to join us as we leave this place."

The sheriff waited for Jerome to be revived, and then the four of us walked down the street to the jailhouse. It was a small building with three cells. Sheriff Pierce didn't intend to put me in jail, but he was ready to dish out a stern warning. "Demsond, I take it that you and this fellow, Tanner Biggs, have a history. I really don't care about that unless you start causing trouble around here. If you have some proof that he was involved in Joe Hall's killing, then bring that to me; otherwise, I don't expect any further disturbances. Do I make myself clear?"

"Yes, Sheriff," I said. "I handled it poorly." But in fact, I had accomplished exactly what I'd set out to do. I didn't expect to get any kind of a confession from Tanner Biggs—all I wanted to do was to let him know that I knew what he was up to.

"Jim, I think you should keep a close eye on Tanner Biggs and his friends," Rand Eaton said. "We're pretty sure that they have something to do with the deaths of these animals around here...and now, Joe Hall is dead."

Sheriff Pierce shrugged. "Like I said, bring me the proof."

CHAPTER THIRTY-EIGHT

Alexander, Illinois
June 24, 1868

John T. Alexander and I sat with Edward Hinrichsen on his back porch drinking some German beer that he had brought home from New York. It was a refreshing relief from the summer heat that had arrived in full force. "There are actually some fine breweries in New York," he said in his gruff way. "Of course, I didn't believe it until I tasted it for myself...one of the benefits of being the railroad's general stock agent...not to mention the pay."

This was the first opportunity for me to spend some time with Mr. H., as everyone but John T. Alexander called him. I met him a few months ago, but he was always on the run. He was a strong man, full of energy, and a very shrewd businessman. I couldn't be sure about his age, but I thought that he was probably older than he looked. "Jason stopped by to see me on his way to Washington to help Miss Anna Carroll," he said. "He'll be out there a while. You know how slow things go in that place. They get the same pay no matter how long it takes to get the job done. If I ran a business, or for that matter, a railroad, like that, I'd be shown the door in short order."

"I'm afraid you're right, Edward," John T. Alexander said. "I could sure use his help right now. I'm fortunate that John here agreed to stay on for a spell." He put his beer down and reached out to put his hand on my shoulder. "You've done a great job, John."

"Jason said the same thing about you," Mr. H. said. "I'm sure glad you two didn't kill each other during the war." Jason had warned me about Mr. H.'s propensity for delivering the occasional shocking statement. He savored the responses that his quips would bring from his audience.

"Fortunately, we were both terrible shots," I said. He got a good laugh out of that.

Jason and I would occasionally talk about the war when we were alone. We had both seen enough to understand the futility in it, but we were intelligent enough to know that there would be more wars in our nation's future. "It is a natural result of the human condition," Jason claimed.

John T. Alexander's Wednesday cattle train left the yard about an hour earlier, and it was quiet in town until the next train arrived. Hinrichsen's home sat on an acre that was bordered by Cedar Avenue on its west side. The lot filled the entire block all the way from Main Street on its north to Front Street on its south. One of John T. Alexander's pastures was to the east, marking the end of town in that direction. It was the largest lot in town.

Hinrichsen's home was the largest building in town, and visitors always asked who lived there. "It's half-timbered, Bavarian Baroque architecture," he said when describing it. "Much of the materials came from my homeland."

We shared pleasantries while looking out upon his extensive beer garden, which stretched out across the backyard until it reached the horse barn at the rear of the property. A gardener was clearing out some weeds. The large barn provided a nice noise barrier to shield the house from some of the racket of the passing trains just to its south.

Edward Hinrichsen was a wealthy man, and a good bit of that wealth had been invested in this piece of property.

His grain business was thriving even though he was seldom around to closely manage it. He experimented with different ways of drying the grain for shipment on the rail cars. People came from all over the country to look at what he was doing.

Suddenly, his mood changed. "J.T., I hate to bring up business on a fine day like this, but I have to tell you about some of the developments in New York that are going to impact your business."

Edward Hinrichsen rose from his chair and paced a bit before he continued. "There are some incredibly powerful forces at work, and I regret that I cannot identify many of them. But I can tell you that they are well connected with Governor Reuben Fenton and his newly appointed lieutenant governor, Rafner B. Hale, who oversees all of the commissions and boards in the state. Hale just appointed the first president of the Metropolitan Board of Health of New York City... his close friend, George Lincoln.

"Lieutenant Governor Hale has a large budget as well as an open line of credit at the Mechanics' and Farmers' Bank of Albany. I've yet to meet the man, but I'm told that he has a take-charge attitude, so he'll likely be running the venture."

"Just what is *the venture* that you speak of?" John T. Alexander said.

"First and foremost, I expect that it's keeping out the Texas cattle," Hinrichsen said. "Millions of dollars are at stake there if the price of beef drops. You know how they jumped all over that first shipment from Abilene. A good number of the cattle were killed for examination purposes, and the rest were held so long that they couldn't be sold for a profit. Hale has set up examination centers at the major points of railroad entry into the state, including Buffalo, Campville, Elmira, Dunkirk, Jamestown, Salamanca, and Binghamton."

There was unmistaken seriousness in Edward Hinrichsen's voice. "There are no limits on how many of the cattle can be killed for examination, and there are no limits on how long they can be held in quarantine...and it all happens at the cattleman's expense."

John T. Alexander shrugged.

"Mr. Alexander just started shipping some longhorns from Tolono to New York last week," I said. "He waited as long as he could."

"J.T., I wouldn't dare try to tell you what to do or not to do," Hinrichsen said. "I'm just telling you what you're going to run into. And you can't ship your cattle to Canada—and into New York from there—because they have the Niagara Falls Suspension Bridge covered as well."

"We can push them through at night." I knew enough about the railroad stations to know that most of the night trains go right through as express runs.

"In my position, it's not ethical for me to condone such a thing, but now that Demsond has suggested it, I'll say that it's not a bad idea. Of course, you still have the option of droving them into the state from Pennsylvania."

"I read the inflammatory articles about the problems in Tolono that appeared in the *New York Times*," John T. Alexander said, "but the Texas cattle aren't sick, Edward. I have thousands of them here and in Tolono, and I must get them to market...I can only send so many of them to Chicago."

Hinrichsen winked. "My job as stock agent is to keep things moving on the railroads all the way to Buffalo, so I'll help out as much as I can."

John T. Alexander stood up and stretched his long frame. "These people in New York may be powerful, and they may have the governor and lieutenant governor in their pocket, but they cannot keep the Texas cattle out for very long."

"J.T., these people are more powerful than you or I could ever hope to be. When they come calling, *senators* clear their calendars in order to meet with them."

I watched John T. Alexander as Mr. H. spoke to him. He was getting the message. He studied the situation in silence.

Just then, a Western Union messenger arrived. The company no longer worked out of the train station because they had just completed a new office right next to it. Business was booming.

"I have an urgent message for you, Mr. Alexander," he said. It was Western Union's policy to hand deliver a message to the addressee, or in his or her absence, to an appointed agent, clerk, or family member.

John T. Alexander read the message and then responded to the messenger. "Please notify General McConnell that I'm on my way."

"Trouble, J.T.?" Edward Hinrichsen asked.

"It seems that one of my former purchasing agents who disappeared near Texas has arrived in Jacksonville, spending my money lavishly." John T. Alexander looked at me. "William Halsell is still alive."

Edward Hinrichsen grunted and motioned to a servant standing nearby. "I'll have my man prepare the carriage immediately."

CHAPTER THIRTY-NINE

Jacksonville, Illinois
June 24, 1868

When we arrived at General McConnell's place, his son greeted us and immediately directed the three of us to Judge Charles Constable's office at 336 West State Street. "My father is waiting for you there," George McConnell said. He was slowly taking the legal practice from the hands of his father, but in this matter, his father had retained control.

After a short walk in the heat, we entered the Heslep Tavern and climbed the stairs to the judge's office on the second floor. When we walked in, I was astonished to see Red Beard sitting in the waiting room to our left. He looked up at me and smiled, knowing that I probably remembered him from our encounter at the Missouri border almost a year ago.

I didn't have a chance to say anything because we were shown into Judge Constable's office right away. General McConnell rose to greet us, but the judge remained seated.

"Leave the door open. It's stuffy in here. Let's get on with business, gentlemen," Judge Constable said. "I don't have all day." Charles

Constable supported the Confederacy during the war by protecting local members of the Knights of the Golden Circle. He was held by Union troops on several occasions, but he always managed to obtain a pardon.

John T. Alexander obliged. "I assume that my attorney has informed you about what has happened, so I'm here to seek amends. I would like to have William Halsell arrested forthwith."

"Not so fast, Mr. Alexander...or may I call you John?" the judge asked.

"Certainly...if I may call you Charles."

The judge winced. "Mr. Alexander, I need to see the written agreement that you have with Mr. Halsell...I assume that you have one." Judge Constable already knew, as did everyone else, that John T. Alexander was a man of his spoken word rather than the written word when it came to dealing with individuals in his employ.

John T. Alexander turned to his attorney. General McConnell spoke up immediately. "This isn't Washington, or for that matter, Springfield. This is cattle country, Judge, and you know how things are done here."

We were all trying to maintain our composure while the judge played his little game with us. Judge Constable pushed back in his fine leather chair and made quite a show of lighting a large cigar. He didn't offer one to the rest of us in the room.

"You, of all people, should know that I cannot grant your request."

General McConnell and John T. Alexander looked at each other and shrugged.

"Your problem, gentlemen, is that you're still living in the past." The administrator of justice brushed away some ashes that had fallen on top of his desk. "Everything changed at the Appomattox Court House. Just ask Captain John Demsond here—he observed it firsthand."

"What do you mean?" I asked.

The judge ignored me and looked at John T. Alexander. He removed the cigar from his mouth and turned it in his hand, examining it as if it was something he'd just discovered. "When the colonies came together and formed the United States of America, they did so with the understanding that they were not giving up their freedom. No, they thought that the unification would guarantee their freedom...but they were sadly mistaken.

"The governing body's insatiable appetite for power steadily removed the states' independence...and in less than one hundred years, it was completely gone. The formation of the United States was based on trust, so as little as possible was placed in writing...much like the arrangement that you have with your agents, Mr. Alexander."

John T. Alexander could remain quiet no longer. "I'm having trouble making the connection here, Judge."

"That's unfortunate," Judge Constable said, "but let me assure you that the people in Washington, and Springfield, understand this issue quite well...so well, in fact, that they have redefined the meaning of freedom to include *only that* which is represented in writing.

"This devious twist has subjugated all of us...we are now nothing more than the minions of government, and since it is *impossible* for us to write everything down, we essentially have little freedom at all. And when several of our good states tried to pull out of this obfuscating arrangement, you know what happened to them...am I correct, Captain Demsond?"

I didn't respond. Jason Alexander had already informed me about Judge Constable's wartime escapades, and I wasn't going to give him any indication that I was still fighting the war, as he apparently was.

John T. Alexander rose from his chair and walked to a window that looked out across West State Street. "So you're telling me that because I don't have the arrangements with my purchasing agents in writing, I don't have arrangements with them at all?"

"Precisely," the judge exclaimed loudly.

The meeting was over.

Red Beard was gone when we walked out of the judge's office.

⌘ ⌘ ⌘

Edward Hinrichsen immediately returned home. John T. Alexander and I walked over to General McConnell's law office, where his son prepared a standard contract for the stock purchasing agents. John T. Alexander was upset. "I understand why I needed contracts with the railroad companies...but my own employees?"

I would spend the next few days getting signatures from J. T. Alexander and Company's agents. I also sent a message to Texas Ranger John Bump to let him know that William Halsell had shown up back in Illinois.

A strange feeling came over me as I was thinking about all of this at the end of the week. It had been a while since I'd felt this way.

I was sitting on my horse amidst a field of gray, facing a blue sea of riders twice our size, waiting for the senior cavalry officer to order the charge. I wondered why God had brought me to this point. What could I possibly accomplish here?

CHAPTER FORTY

—•— ⚎⬦⚎ —•—

Tolono, Illinois
June 26, 1868

I was back in Tolono on Friday. The situation had worsened. Armed bands of riders were trying to keep out the Texas cattle arriving from Cairo on the Illinois Central Railroad. Sheriff James Pierce had wired for assistance, and members of the state militia from nearby Springfield were in Tolono to help keep the peace.

Tanner Biggs was a prominent figure in the organized effort to disrupt the Texas cattle business. With the presence of the troops, he wasn't able to keep the cattle from being moved to the grazing areas during the day, but at night he was able to create a lot of problems. He and his renegade friends pulled down fences and scattered the cattle in many different directions. Last night, even some of Jeanine's Morgan horses got loose.

Following John T. Alexander's lead, some of the local farmers were also beginning to bring in Texas cattle, so the trouble began to spread beyond Broadlands in Champaign County all the way to the east beyond the Indiana state line.

I was riding with Rand Eaton and some of his men, rounding up stray animals from the night before. It was warm, and the air was still. We found native cattle, Texas cattle, horses, and oxen that belonged to J. T. Alexander and Company. Some of the Texas cattle had been shot. "You were right all along, John," Rand Eaton said. "That guy Biggs is nothing but trouble. It's a wonder that only Joe Hall has been killed."

He wouldn't believe me if I tried to tell him what Tanner Biggs was capable of.

Rand Eaton pulled back on his horse and stopped for a moment. "John, I do have some good news to pass on."

I waited.

"Most of our recent shipments to New York are getting through just fine…all the way to the big city. The organized effort to keep out the longhorns doesn't seem to be so well organized after all."

"That's great news," I said. "Once the people are able to sample the meat, they will find out that it's quite good, and the prices should begin to drop. People who have never been able to afford beef before now will be able to do so."

"They're tired of eating horse meat," Rand said, having read the stories about the substitution that was often made by the New York butchers.

⌘   ⌘   ⌘

Jerome Alexander and a few others were riding north of Broadlands, still looking for some of the animals that had escaped the night before. They had picked up a suspicious-looking trail of riders that was fresh from the early morning. Several of the men were getting nervous, suggesting that they turn back. Jerome would have none of that. "We're going to track these crooks down and turn them over to the sheriff."

Tanner Biggs had other ideas. He and his men saw them coming. It was like old times, riding with John Mosby and waiting for the Blueboys to wander into their trap like a bunch of turkeys. "Let'm have it," Biggs shouted. "Kill'm all!"

The quiet day erupted in a cacophony of gunfire.

Jerome took the first bullet in the shoulder. Another caught him in the leg. The man on his right had the top of his head taken off. The man on his left was hit so many times that there wasn't much left of him when he hit the ground.

Bullets and blood were flying everywhere. Some of the horses were falling with a loud scream. Jerome was sure that he was going to die.

It was all over in a matter of a few minutes. Only one of the riders from Broadlands managed to get away. The rest of them were lying on the ground when Tanner Biggs and his men stopped shooting.

"Maybe that'll teach'm a little lesson," Tanner Biggs said. "If not, there's more where that came from."

As he looked at the fallen riders, Tanner Biggs was upset that John Demsond wasn't among them. He shook his head in disbelief.

He pulled his knife from his boot, hoping to get a few scalps. Then he changed his mind and put it away. He flashed a toothless smile and let out a shrill Rebel yell as he rode off with the others.

"No killing."

CHAPTER FORTY-ONE

Broadlands Farm
July 6, 1868

I stayed close to the Broadlands Farm after the shooting. Four men died in the ambush, and three were seriously wounded, including Jerome Alexander. More troops were brought into the area, and things calmed down somewhat. No one saw the shooters, so no arrests followed.

On Monday morning, ten days after the shooting, several of us were in Jerome's bedroom. Mary Alexander sat in a chair, holding his hand. Jerome was in bad shape, but the doctor thought he would recover with only a slight limp. Jason returned from Washington to be at his brother's side along with the rest of the family. I could tell that he was very worried about Jerome's leg.

There were other problems as well. Some of the animals at Broadlands were sick.

Ten of the oxen that were used for many of the heavy tasks on the farm were downers, unable to get up from the ground. Their tongues were swollen, and they wouldn't drink or eat. Everyone knew that they were going to die.

Some of the shorthorn cattle were showing signs that they were about to become sick as well. They were standing in one place with their heads hanging down in a foreboding manner, looking like they were ready to drop to their knees at any moment. "I've counted about fifty of them looking that way," Rand Eaton reported to John T. Alexander. "They are all glassy-eyed...that was the first thing I noticed before they dropped their heads.

"We can't get Dr. Lawrence over here," Eaton continued. "He's too damn busy right now—he's got too many longtime friends in the area who're losing animals—and we can't count on him much at all for a while. I think we should separate the healthy animals from the sick ones as much as possible."

"Yes, let's do that right away," John T. Alexander muttered. He was sitting in a chair in the corner of the room. "I'll see if I can get some help from elsewhere."

Jason stepped back from his brother's bedside and walked over to join the rest of us. "Let me send a wire to Washington. Last week, I met Horace Capron, a commissioner in the Department of Agriculture. I'm sure he knows someone who could help us with this."

"It could be some kind of poison that Tanner Biggs is spreading around," I said.

"In addition to the *lead* poison?" Rand Eaton added bitterly.

Just then, Jeanine walked into the room. "I'm still missing one of my mares."

"We'll find her," Rand Eaton said. "I've got several of the boys out looking." I very much admired this man's energy, but even Rand Eaton was beginning to show signs of wearing down.

He wasn't alone. The general level of tension in the area was very high. Jason Alexander and I were most familiar with the condition, having experienced the stress on almost a daily basis during the war. Something little could turn into something big without any warning. In one moment, you were sharing pleasantries with a friend, and in the next moment, you were burying him.

⌘　⌘　⌘

I didn't want Jason to ride into town alone, and Jeanine hoped to spend some time with her brother, who had been away for a while, so the two of us joined him on the ride to Tolono.

It was another hot day, so we chose the carriage with the nice cover to protect us from the sun. "How's your friend in Washington?" I called back to Jason, who sat with Jeanine in the backseat.

"Keep your eye on the road," Jeanine said.

I turned my head even more. "Was Miss Anna Carroll able to get paid?"

"She has a lot of problems," Jason said. "I need to go back as soon as things settle down here." He paused for a bit. "Some of her friends have failed to support her request to be paid for the extensive work that she's done in Washington…and to make matters worse, she's starting to lose her hearing.

"She needs the money to help take care of her family. Like you, John, they lost everything in the war. Maryland remained in the Union, thanks to the Carroll family, but both the Union and Confederate soldiers ravaged their property."

"I'm sorry to hear that," I said as we passed the first small group of troops riding on the road to Tolono. I didn't like the way they looked at Jeanine.

She didn't seem to mind. "You'd think there was a war going on here," Jeanine said.

Jason and I answered her at the same time. "There is." We both knew that this thing could get out of hand very easily if the shootings continued.

It seemed as if everyone was carrying a gun now. I was sleeping with one at my side again. Tanner Biggs will do that to you.

I drove the carriage directly to the Western Union office on Reynolds Street, where they had set up a short telegraph line connecting directly to the Illinois Central Railroad Station, where the main wires came in on poles along the rails.

While Jeanine and I sat in the carriage waiting for Jason to return, two men walked out of the telegraph office. They called back to Jason, "You can tell your father that we've contacted the governor."

They didn't wait for a response, stomping past us in a hurry. Moments later, Jason walked out and climbed back into the carriage. "Isaac Larmon and Abe Gaston are escalating this thing. They're getting the governor involved."

"We heard," Jeanine said.

"I don't know what they expect the governor to do," I said.

"Let's get out of here," Jeanine said. "I don't like this town." If she hadn't been with us, I think Jason and I would have liked to walk over to the last place where I saw Tanner Biggs, but that would have to wait for another time. We headed back to Broadlands.

Just as we were about to turn into the gateway to the Broadlands Farm, a Western Union messenger from Tolono rode up alongside us, shouting for me to halt the carriage. "Is one of you an Alexander?"

"Yes," Jason and Jeanine answered.

"I've got a message for John T. Alexander," he said. "I'm allowed to deliver this to a family member. If one of you will sign for the message, I'll be on my way."

Jason signed, and the rider turned and rode off. Jason took the liberty to read the message when he saw that it was from Edward Hinrichsen.

Jason folded the message and placed it in his shirt pocket. "This isn't good," he said.

"What's wrong?" Jeanine said.

"Mr. H. says there's trouble in New York. Some of the dairy cattle are getting sick and dying...some *people*, too. They're blaming the Texas cattle that were shipped from the Broadlands Farm."

Jeanine gasped.

I hurried the horses along.

CHAPTER FORTY-TWO

—+—◄►—+—

Albany, New York
July 13, 1868

Early on Monday morning, the capital of the prosperous state was alive with the news that was coming out of its largest city. Efforts were made by the city's leaders to avoid a panic, but the *New York Times* and the *New York Herald* recognized a headline story. They reported that eight hundred people had died in the past week.

Raven and Badger stood among the throng of people in the capitol rotunda. The two men were not strangers to this place. Passersby paid respect to them by tipping their hats. Badger was neatly dressed in a suit that was perfectly tailored to his long, thin frame. His hair was cut short, and he bore no facial hair. In stark contrast, the tall and burly Raven was a mountain of a man. He wore a crumpled suit that was much too tight for his broad shoulders. His uncombed curly hair was long and seemingly flowed right into his unkempt beard.

They soaked up the content of the discussions all around them. The other issues of the day had quickly been forgotten. Rumors of all sorts quickly began to spread like a wildfire in the dry winds.

Raven and Badger were all smiles. The opening afforded by the moment had not gone unnoticed by these opportunists. Neither one of them had said a word since they came together. After quite some time, Badger spoke first. "This is almost too good to be true."

"My thoughts exactly," Raven said. "We couldn't have asked for a better development."

"What do you think is going on?" Badger asked.

"The Texas cattle have brought in their sickness to New York City," Raven said with a laugh. "That's obviously the problem. Dairy cattle are dying all over the state, and the people are dying in the big city where most of the meat is eaten." He neatly folded his newspaper and tucked it under his arm.

"It could be something else that's causing the problem," Badger said, smiling all the while.

"Perish the thought. It's the cattle from that awful state of Texas."

"Of course it is." Badger tossed his paper aside. "The *Times* reporter called it the poison from the south. I know that you really like that."

"I suppose we both know what we need to do," Raven said.

"Of course. I'll organize my forces to fight this terrible menace," Badger said.

"Such a pity," Raven said.

They laughed and parted without a handshake.

CHAPTER FORTY-THREE

―・―=＋≍＋―・―

Broadlands Farm
July 13, 1868

"It's hot there, just like it is here," Jason Alexander said. "The human waste and animal waste smell terrible. The bugs are everywhere. Food spoils right away. People are always getting sick and dying in the large cities in that kind of weather. I saw it in Washington."

John T. Alexander stopped his pacing and stood near his desk. He reached into his back pocket and pulled out his handkerchief to wipe his brow. His haggard look worried us. "If they think it's the Texas cattle that are causing the problem," he said, "it's going to be hard to prove them wrong."

"It may be impossible to prove them wrong," I said. "Animals are still dying here, and there are reports of deaths in Ohio and Pennsylvania. I thought Tanner Biggs was somehow killing the animals, but there's something else going on that needs to be investigated."

John T. Alexander dropped into the leather chair behind his desk. This office in his house at Broadlands Farm looked almost exactly like the one back home. "We've got to get someone in here who can look these animals over and tell us what's wrong with them. I'll send another telegram to Governor Oglesby."

"I haven't received a response from Horace Capron in the Department of Agriculture as yet. Maybe someone at Illinois College can help us," Jason said. "I'll send a message to the president."

"I'll try Doc Durant," I said. "He knows a lot of people."

"I'm going to send a wire to Gustavus," Jeanine said. She had been so quiet that I'd forgotten she was in the room. She looked at me. "He knows a lot of people." She rose from the leather couch that rested against the west wall and left the room in a hurry.

At the same time, someone knocked on the door. I turned just in time to see Jeanine rush by Rand Eaton. He was soaked from the afternoon heat. "Things are getting worse, Mr. Alexander," he said. "I've lost count of how many sick animals we have."

"Is the lard helping?"

"Yes, it seems to help some of the cattle, but they try to rub it off...and we don't have enough of it to go around."

"And you're separating the sick animals from the others?"

"Yes," Rand Eaton said. There was a look of desperation in his eyes. "The whole thing is so strange. The Texas cattle are just fine. I can't figure it out."

"Bury the dead animals deep," John T. Alexander said.

Rand Eaton took a deep breath. "We don't have enough men here to bury them all," he said.

CHAPTER FORTY-FOUR

Illinois Central Railroad Station
Tolono, Illinois
July 20, 1868

Jeanine's telegram to Gustavus Swift yielded the intended results. The Western Union messenger delivered the telegram while he was attending a fair sponsored by the Illinois Agricultural Society in Chicago. Horace Capron, the commissioner of the US Department of Agriculture, had just introduced the guest speaker, Dr. John Gamgee. The doctor had traveled all the way from Great Britain to speak about his experiences as a member of the Royal Cattle Plague Commission.

After reading Jeanine's message, Gustavus Swift looked up at the man standing at center stage—the solution to John T. Alexander's problem. Even before the doctor's speech had ended, Gustavus approached Horace Capron to arrange a meeting with him.

Horace Capron had the same thought, as he was looking for a way to respond to Jason Alexander's recent telegram. The arrangements fell into place very quickly as Dr. Gamgee learned more about the situation that was taking place in several locations, including

New York City. He was eager to get involved. On Monday morning, I waited in the heat at the Illinois Central Railroad Station for his arrival from Chicago.

Jeanine sat with me on the bench located on the station platform in the shade of the roof's overhang. She was there to see Gustavus Swift, who was riding along with Dr. Gamgee. "I just knew that Gustavus would come through for us."

"Yes, he's something all right," I said.

"You don't like him," she said, "and I don't understand why."

It wasn't so much that I didn't like him. Actually, I did like him. It was just that I knew a lot of men like Gustavus Swift. He was in a single-minded pursuit of his dreams—a businessman with a goal that would not be denied. His life would keep him close to the big cities, and all of the associated activities.

Jeanine was a country girl. She would be happy only in the country, around nature and her horses. Her spirit would be destroyed in the big cities. I didn't want to see that happen to her. But there was no way for me to explain that to her without a misunderstanding.

"You're imagining things, Jeanine," I said.

She shrugged.

Soon we could hear the oncoming train's whistle off in the distance. More people began to appear on the platform. Most of them weren't speaking to us.

We were surprised to find that two additional passengers stepped off the train with Gustavus Swift and Dr. John Gamgee. They were Dr. John Billings and Dr. Edward Curtis. They were introduced as Dr. Gamgee's assistant surgeons.

I liked Dr. Gamgee the moment I met him. He was a big man with a bald head and tufts of hair above both ears. His thick moustache ran right into his long beard, giving him the appearance of having no mouth. I guessed that he was about thirty-five years old. His eyes burned with excitement.

Jeanine and I wasted no time in getting our four passengers and their bags into the carriage. Dr. Gamgee kept his medical bag on his lap. It was crowded, but we had only a short distance to go to get to the Broadlands Farm. We learned that Dr. Gamgee was a professor at the Albert Veterinary College in London, along with his father, Joseph.

As soon as he stepped from the carriage, Dr. Gamgee rushed off to inspect the sick animals. His assistants were practically running to keep up with him. I went inside the house to let the Alexanders know that their guests had arrived. Jeanine led Gustavus to the horse barn to show him a couple of new horses.

Mary Alexander had taken up residence at Broadlands to care for Jerome. The meals had improved considerably. She set two additional places for dinner, and shortly after noon, the nine of us gathered in the dining room. After the introductions, John T. Alexander said grace, and we began to enjoy the wonderful food. The green beans and the carrots were fresh from Betty Eaton's large garden nearby.

"This is exquisite," Dr. Gamgee said. "This is the best meal that I've enjoyed in this country, Mrs. Alexander, and as you might gather from my portly form, I've seldom missed a meal." He laughed, and the rest of us joined him.

He knew we were anxious to hear about his brief inspection, so he didn't keep us waiting. "My assistants and I were able to take a close look at several of the sick cattle and oxen. More important, we were able to perform a quick postmortem examination on two of the animals that had just died." He paused for a bit to eat another piece of beef and wipe his mouth and his sweat-beaded brow with a napkin.

"What you have here is a disease that I would classify as *infectious* rather than *contagious*. Let me explain. Only those animals that come in contact with the cause of the infection will become sick, or infected. The sick animal will not cause another animal to become sick. Is that clear?"

There was silence while we all took in what he had said.

"Do you have any idea what the source of the infection is?" Jason Alexander asked.

"Now, that's the question, isn't it?" Dr. Gamgee said. "That will take more time to determine—and I hesitate to jump to any conclusions. That would be unprofessional."

"Is it anything like what you encountered back in Great Britain?" Gustavus Swift asked. "I remember that you talked about something called anthrax fever and black water during your presentation in Chicago."

"It is possible that *spores* are involved here," Dr. Billings said, giving Dr. Gamgee some time to eat. "The spores could be present in the carrier animals, and then they could be passed to the other animals through their excrement."

"Did you look at the Texas longhorns?" I asked.

"The Texas cattle seem to be fine, so they could certainly be the carriers of the spores," Dr. Curtis said. "The cattle and oxen that are native to this area are the ones that seem to be unable to handle the spores. Our experience is that once they drop their head, arch their back, labor in breathing, and run in the nose and eyes, they will die."

"And, certainly, if the bloody discharges occur," Dr. Gamgee said. He paused for a spoonful of carrots. "I am intrigued by the application of the lard that you have used, Mr. Alexander. It seems to be helping some of the animals, and I'm curious about that...most unusual."

John T. Alexander smiled. "I can't take credit for the idea. It came from one of my neighbors, Isaac Larmon." The smile disappeared. "But I don't have enough lard and enough men to put it on all of the cattle."

"What you have here is very serious," Dr. Gamgee said. "I won't say that it is as bad as the rinderpest that was raging in Great Britain in June of 1865, and the only reason I'll say that is because the rinderpest also spread to Holland, Belgium, and France."

A stunned silence filled the room. Our fears had not been put to rest.

"You're welcome to stay as long as you like," John T. Alexander said. "I've got to get this stopped before I'm ruined."

We don't have enough men to bury them all.

CHAPTER FORTY-FIVE

Abilene, Kansas
July 20, 1868

Abilene continued to grow at a rapid pace. Plans were being made to incorporate. There was little doubt that Joseph McCoy would be the first mayor. But at the moment, he had greater concerns.

"I don't know any more about it than the rest of you," Joseph McCoy said. "Oh, sure, some of those longhorns come in here worn down from the trail, but most of them are as healthy as could be. Many actually gain weight on the trail drive—they're built that way. They're not spreading any sickness of any sort. That's all made up by the people who want to keep them out of their markets."

"The no-good Yankees!" someone shouted. Profanities filled the air.

The drovers and their cowboys who sat in the saloon were all upset. The cowboys were a rough bunch. When they reached Abilene after a long trail drive, they collected their pay and proceeded to have a good time.

They meant no harm, but once the liquor took hold, the inhibitions of the young men disappeared. They drank, gambled, and visited the houses of prostitution with regularity…until their money ran out. There was no sheriff in Abilene, so they had the run of the town. That would change as soon as the town incorporated and collected taxes.

Tonight, it was quiet on the streets because of the thunderstorm.

Major Seth Mabry was standing among the drovers who were crowded around Joseph McCoy. "I'm sorry to hear that John Alexander's son was shot," Mabry said. "That's not going to sit well with the Cattle King…that's what they call him, you know."

"I've yet to meet a finer man than John T. Alexander," McCoy said. "George Custer was in town a few days ago, and even if they were to send him to Illinois, they're not going to stop Alexander from moving the Texas longhorns to New York."

"I tend to agree with you, Joseph," Mabry said, "but something is killing the cattle that are native to that area, and as long as that continues, we have a very serious problem on our hands."

"As long as the buyers keep buying and the railroad keeps running, I'm putting the Texas cattle in the cars and moving them eastward," Joseph McCoy said. "I have no choice in the matter."

The others cheered.

CHAPTER FORTY-SIX

Union Stockyards
Chicago, Illinois
July 22, 1868

As soon as Gustavus Swift received the message from his plant superintendent, he boarded a train for Chicago. The stockyards were being overwhelmed with cattle that were being rushed there by the cattlemen in the area to avoid financial loss.

The meat packers had a wonderful opportunity to increase their profits by butchering around the clock. Unlike New York, no serious problems had been reported in the local newspapers, so the general public welcomed the chance to purchase fresh beef at a fair price. Long lines were forming at the butcher shops.

John T. Alexander telegrammed his two largest Texas suppliers, Major Seth Mabry of Austin and J. D. Reed of Goliad, asking them to double the size of the herds that they were transporting to him. As soon as the word got out, he knew that the other Texas ranchers, who occupied a state that was larger than the country of France, would do likewise, overwhelming the railroads.

Like the Alexander family, Gustavus Swift didn't believe that the Texas cattle were the cause of the problems with the native animals; moreover, he had no reason to believe that the meat was harmful in any way. He had eaten it often, and it was just fine.

The general manager of the Union Stockyards pushed his hat to the back of his head and looked Gustavus Swift in the eyes. "The word around town is that the banks won't fund anything that's tied to the Texas cattle. Are you going to be able to handle this?"

"Keep sending cattle to my plant until I tell you to stop," Gustavus exclaimed. "This is my opportunity to put a Swift product on every table in the heart of the country, and I intend to do just that."

Word spread rapidly that Swift and Company was expanding its operation, and the other meat packers did likewise, including the Armour family in Kansas City and St. Louis. Within days, the message would make its way to Texas, causing the drovers to vastly increase the size of their herds heading north to Abilene, northeast to Missouri and Arkansas, and east to the Mississippi River.

An unstoppable surge of Texas longhorns filled every available railroad car, steamboat, and barge, creating an unmistakable opportunity for the largest state in the broken Confederacy to lift itself up out of the depths of despair.

CHAPTER FORTY-SEVEN

Broadlands Farm
July 24, 1868

"I've been summoned to New York, Mr. Alexander. I'm afraid that I'll have to take leave of your wonderful hospitality," Dr. Gamgee said. "You've been most kind, opening up your entire establishment to me and my assistants."

"I have nothing to hide. I want to put this problem behind me," John T. Alexander said. "I hope you've had enough time to figure it out."

"Not quite. But I'm afraid that the Texas cattle are involved somehow."

"But you have said that you believe that all of the cattle are safe to eat," I said.

"Yes," Dr. Gamgee stated, "I have no reason to believe that the meat is bad."

"That's not what it says here," Edward Hinrichsen interrupted, tossing a stack of papers onto the top of John T. Alexander's desk. "I brought these copies of the *New York Times* with me, and they're blaming all of these deaths—well over two thousand people now—on the Texas cattle."

"That's nonsense," Dr. Gamgee said. "My assistants and I have been elbow deep in the bodies of these cattle, and we've eaten the meat all week long, and we're quite healthy. Whatever is killing the cattle is not killing the people."

"We need to get you to New York as soon as possible so you can pass that information along," Edward Hinrichsen said. "I'll accompany you personally."

"I'd like for Jason and John to go along, too," John T. Alexander said. "I need my own sets of eyes and ears in that area to help find out who is stirring up all of this trouble for me. I don't intend to sit back and do nothing about it."

"You don't want to be looking for trouble in New York, J.T.," Edward Hinrichsen said.

John T. Alexander gave his old friend a stern look. "I didn't ask for this."

"John Demsond and I won't cause any trouble, Mr. H.," Jason Alexander said with a smile. "We're peaceful fellows."

Edward Hinrichsen tilted his head downward and peered out above the top of his glasses. He didn't say a word.

"It's settled then," John T. Alexander said. "The six of you will leave immediately."

"It would seem so," Dr. Gamgee said. He rose from his chair and shook the hands of John T. Alexander and Rand Eaton. "I would keep applying the lard. When I get to New York, I intend to try out a few other things that may work better and be more readily available. I will let you know right away if I find something."

Jason and I rushed off to pack our bags because we both knew that the next train on the TW&W line departed for the East in less than an hour. We said good-bye to Jeanine, who was standing just outside her father's office.

Jeanine hurried in and approached Dr. Gamgee. She had been patiently listening to the conversation that had taken place over the past few minutes. "Before you leave, would you come over to the horse barn and take a look at a couple of my Morgans?"

"What's wrong?" Dr. Gamgee said.

"They're not looking well," Jeanine said.

CHAPTER FORTY-EIGHT

Albany, New York
August 3, 1868

It took a while to get all of the right people together in one place, and Jason Alexander and I had to wait for it to materialize because it wasn't going to happen just because we asked. A wire from the governor of Illinois helped. Rafner B. Hale, the lieutenant governor of New York, called a meeting of his state's leaders who were involved in "the cattle plague" on the first Monday in August.

Jason Alexander and I sat outside the meeting room all morning long, having not been invited inside. The group departed for lunch at noon without a word being said to us. Most of them had returned by 2:00 p.m., and shortly thereafter, we were asked to join them in their meeting room.

I counted eleven men and two women as introductions were made very quickly. I was able to write down only a few of the names before we got started.

Lieutenant Governor Rafner B. Hale sat at the head of the table. His dark blue suit was perfectly tailored and completely unwrinkled. A blue silk tie rested against his crisp white shirt. He wanted people to know that he was wealthy. "Gentlemen, you have been invited to our gathering so that we might ask a few questions of you," he said.

"Thank you for inviting us," Jason said. I could tell that he was a bit nervous.

Lieutenant Governor Hale leaned forward in his seat. "You may thank me if you wish," he said, "but you will soon find that this is not a happy group. We're not happy because our people and our animals are dying—dying because of the Texas cattle that your father has sent to our fair state. And if I have to order that every one of them that enters New York be killed and burned at our state's borders, I will not hesitate to do so."

"I understand your concerns, but I would hope that you wouldn't jump to the conclusion that the longhorn cattle from Texas are the cause of these problems," Jason said. "We traveled out here with Dr. John Gamgee, and even though he believes that the Texas cattle may have something to do with the sickness, he hasn't ruled out other possibilities."

"But isn't it true that your Illinois legislature has banned the Texas cattle from the state, and that some of your own people and animals have died?"

"The law was passed when no one in Springfield was paying attention," Jason said, "and it hasn't been enforced. People have died. They've been murdered by outlaws and hoodlums. Some animals have died, but we're certainly not going around killing the Texas cattle as a solution."

"Perhaps you should be." This time it was General Marsena Patrick who spoke up in a loud voice. He was the former provost marshal in the Army of the Potomac, and now he was leading the efforts in the city of Syracuse to stop the problems there.

Jason Alexander knew General Patrick. He also knew that General Patrick had made some comments in the past few days about getting the War Department involved in this issue because he thought it was an attempt on the part of the Confederacy in Texas to poison its former enemies. It was an absurd claim. General Patrick was still fighting the war.

"General," Jason said, "that's the last thing I would do. I've yet to find one of the Texas cattle to be sick. They're just fine. I've been eating the beef for the past few months, and I'm not sick. Dr. Gamgee ate it as well. Killing the Texas cattle makes no sense at all."

"If we kill them all, and the problem goes away, then we've fixed it, haven't we?" General Patrick said, leaning back and sticking his thumbs behind the lapels of his light coat as if he'd made some profound statement.

"General Patrick, I think you'll find that the people of New York want to eat beef," I said, "and Texas cattle are here to feed them."

"That's a fine comment coming from a former Rebel," General Patrick said.

"The war's over, General," Jason said. "The Texas cattle aren't carrying the Rebel flag."

"If they're carrying poison," he said, "they're carrying the Rebel flag."

Mercifully, John Stanton Gould changed the direction of the conversation. He was looking into the cattle problems in the Hudson Bay area of New York for Lieutenant Governor Hale. "Mr. Alexander, we're not going to kill all of the Texas cattle coming into New York—honestly, I don't think we could do it if we wanted to—but we've got to solve this problem very soon."

"That's why we're here," Jason said. "We want to find out what's wrong, just like you do. I'm going to stay here in Albany, and John Demsond is going to New York City with Dr. Gamgee and his assistants. We'll be in constant touch with my father through daily telegrams.

"And as far as the War Department goes, General Patrick, I have
friends in the War Department as well as you do. I suggest that you
think very carefully before you make that move, sir."

General Marsena Patrick grumbled to himself.

Lieutenant Governor Hale asked a few questions about the situation in Tolono, but he didn't seem to be very concerned about our an-
swers. It was obvious that he intended to shut down J. T. Alexander
and Company's business in New York as soon as possible.

⌘　⌘　⌘

Back in Illinois, John T. and Mary Alexander returned home with
Jerome shortly after Jason and I departed Tolono. Jeanine remained
at the Broadlands Farm to tend to her ailing horses. More animals in
the area continued to die from the mysterious sickness, but the Texas
cattle were healthy.

Angry mobs continued to gather at both railroad stations in
Tolono in an attempt to force the railroad cars to move on without unloading the Texas cattle. Often, the soldiers intervened and
allowed the cars to be unloaded. Fences were still pulled down at
night, and Texas cattle were shot. No one was arrested.

The turmoil spread across other parts of the state, but Champaign
County continued to be the most violent area. John T. Alexander was
still looked upon as an outsider there, even though he had hired a
number of people from the local area. Anyone who worked for him
no longer felt entirely safe.

⌘　⌘　⌘

In Chicago, the situation was much different. The interest in
fresh beef drove the meat processing plants to capacity. Three shifts
worked at a feverish pace at every facility to process all sorts of cattle

to meet the growing demand. For many of the immigrants, it was their first opportunity to eat good beef.

Some of the native cattle were already sick or dead when they arrived in the railroad cars. Gustavus Swift estimated that at least three thousand native cattle had died at the Union Stockyards. The deaths went relatively unnoticed because of the high rate of movement through the meatpacking facilities located nearby. Often, the sick and dead cattle were processed along with the others.

The *Chicago Sun Times* reported the animal deaths, but the people were more interested in the opportunity to eat the inexpensive, fresh meat. The people in Chicago were very happy about the current situation, and they weren't interested in any news that threatened to disrupt the supply.

CHAPTER FORTY-NINE

—▪▪◼▪▪—

Communipaw Abattoir
Jersey City, New Jersey
August 5, 1868

New York City was filthy. Human waste, animal waste, and putrid garbage cooked to an indescribable smell in the hot August sun. Many people wore bandanas across their noses, making me feel as if I was in the midst of a bank robbery.

I could tell that Dr. John Gamgee and his assistants were also shocked by what they saw, but Dr. Gamgee had suddenly become very quiet, unwilling to share his thoughts with me. His assistants noticed this change in his behavior as well, and they followed his lead. However, I refused to let their reticence keep me quiet, and I let everyone know what I thought of the dreadful conditions in New York City.

I started my diatribe the moment after we stepped from the train, a day after we left Albany. "It's a wonder that everyone in this city isn't sick," I said. "How can anyone possibly blame the Texas cattle for anything with all of this filth around?"

I remained with Dr. Gamgee and his assistants for two days before we parted company. Everywhere we went, it was the same. It felt as if bugs were crawling all over me, day and night. I was always thirsty because of the heat, but I was afraid to drink the water. I lived on raw vegetables and fruit.

On Friday morning I was meeting with Henry Payson, the president of the Communipaw Abattoir, the primary slaughterhouse for the New York metropolitan area, when we were interrupted by a visit from the members of the New York Metropolitan Board of Health—the MBH, as it was called. The men had just made the same short trip that I'd made an hour earlier, crossing the bay to the New Jersey shore, where the slaughterhouse was located. New York City used New Jersey as its dumping ground for such undesirable facilities.

The group had just come from the smaller Bergen's Stockyards and Slaughterhouses on Forty-Fifth and Forty-Seventh streets in New York City. I visited the place yesterday. It was a rat hole, just like the Bull's Head Stockyards that spanned Ninety-Seventh to One Hundredth streets and Third to Fourth streets, which I visited on the same day. The city had lost control of its infrastructure, and its leaders were looking to take the attention away from the horrid conditions.

George Lincoln was appointed to the position of president of the MBH by his close friend Rafner B. Hale. Lincoln knew who I was. "I'm told that a shipment from your employer is to arrive here at any moment. Perhaps we should go down and take a look." His condescending tone warned me that this wasn't going to be a pleasant experience.

Lincoln seemed to know a lot about this shipment. "Only half of the original conveyance will arrive here today," he said. "About two hundred of the sickened cows—all shorthorns—have already been removed from the railroad cars between Ohio and Pittsburgh. They've been destroyed. We'll quarantine all of the cows on these cars as soon as they arrive here, Mr. Demsond. That will allow us to take a close look at them."

It was obvious that the matter wasn't up for discussion, so I remained quiet. I suspected that the quarantine was going to provide a convenient means to kill the rest of the shipment. Just in case I might object, I noticed that three New York policemen, who had arrived with George Lincoln, were staying close to me.

The train arrived just after 11:00 a.m., and the animals were moved to an area on the far end of the complex. There were no Texas longhorns in this group from Tolono. I did notice a small group of longhorns in one of the holding pens that we passed by as we walked to the area where the native cattle were taken. I suspected that these longhorns had also come from Tolono on earlier shipments, but I wasn't close enough to make out the branding. It was obvious that certain cattle were given special treatment here.

Around noon, the MBH inspection team of doctors reported their results to George Lincoln and his board members. I waited a short distance away until he motioned for me to join them in the scant shade of a nearby building. The heat was overbearing.

George Lincoln waved the report in the air as he spoke. "Abnormal temperatures, rapid pulse, bloody secretions, wobbly demeanor, and so on it goes...these cows are very sick. Their meat cannot be eaten. They must be destroyed. I'll order them to be sent to the fat-rendering tubs immediately."

"They can be saved with a little bit of effort on your part," I said. "I'm sure Dr. Gamgee has told you about the lard. He also believes that other remedies may exist. He can suggest other cures."

I looked to Henry Payson for help. "I'm sorry, Mr. Demsond, but Governor Marcus Ward has already told me to follow the instructions of the New York MBH." New Jersey wouldn't dare stand up to New York.

"So you see," George Lincoln said, "we'll be doing this our way, and you'll not be interfering." The New York policemen shuffled a bit in order to remind me of their presence. I didn't need the reminder.

"Why are we wasting all of the time that the good doctors are putting in," I asked, "if you've already decided what needs to be done?"

The policemen shuffled some more.

I waited for an answer.

George Lincoln smiled. He turned to his assistant who was standing nearby and said, "While you're at it, shoot all of the Texas cattle and drag them to the rendering tubs along with the others. Have a good day, Mr. Demsond." He turned and walked away.

The New York policeman grabbed me and hustled me off the property.

CHAPTER FIFTY

Albany, New York
August 17, 1868

Major headline stories filled the newspapers all along the East Coast. The *New York Times* began to call the cattle sickness a malignant typhus, which essentially branded it as the feared rinderpest. Dr. John Gamgee tried to convince the authorities that this was not the case, but the sensational story was exactly what was needed to justify the severe actions that were being taken by the authorities. Dr. Gamgee's presence in the New York area was cited as further proof that the "ravages of the rinderpest" had made their way here.

On Monday morning, Governor Reuben Fenton formed the State Board of Cattle Commissioners. Their charge was to protect the state's two million cattle from infectious diseases. The annual milk and cheese business alone was valued at over $25 million.

The three commissioners were given unprecedented authority, including control over the railroads, waterways, and roadways. Hours later, *The World* printed a story that claimed "the new commission has more power than the governor himself."

The state was divided into three large districts, with a commissioner in charge of each one. General Marsena Patrick was in charge of the Central District (based in Syracuse), Lewis Allen was in charge of the Western District (based in Buffalo), and John Stanton Gould was in charge of the Eastern District (based in Albany). Lieutenant Governor Rafner B. Hale was the head of the commission.

Their first act was to position armed militia at all points of entry to the state of New York. They were instructed to shoot anyone who disobeyed a direct order. They were also instructed to shoot anyone who tried to smuggle cattle into the state overnight. This act legalized shootings that had already taken place at the borders over the past few days.

All cattle entering the state were to be inspected. If they were found to be "unsatisfactory," the cattle were to be placed in disinfecting stockyards, and any means of transportation, such as railcars, were also to be held and disinfected. The cattle were to be penned up until they were released by an assistant commissioner, or disposed of.

The commissioners also issued warrants for the arrest of "shyster butchers." These people were accused of selling tainted meat to the poor in various cities of the state. The *New York Herald* claimed that it was impossible to keep the cattle out of the state and, consequently, the beef from the tables.

The paper hinted that the commission's actions might be motivated by the desire to maintain high prices. Copies of the *New York Herald* mysteriously disappeared from the newsstands, and the printing presses were ransacked.

Soon after I arrived in Albany from New York City, Jason Alexander and I sat on a bench in the rotunda of the capitol building as the news about the new commission spread like wildfire. The previous evening's papers had predicted the announcements with great accuracy, as the usual leaks had made their way to the pressrooms for the customary payoffs to unsavory politicians.

"John, your description of the situation in New York City gives me little hope that we'll be able to penetrate that market with any consistency, and after hearing today's news, the same situation will exist elsewhere in the state. Perhaps I should recommend that my father stop sending cattle this way."

I waited until a nearby group of bystanders was out of earshot before I replied. "Cattle can still be driven into the state on the trails that bypass the railroad stations, and the slaughterhouses will take them in at night. Since we know that the meat won't make the people sick, I have no problem recommending that your father take this approach until the truth comes out and the market opens up once again. This whole thing is about money and power."

"But what about the native cattle that are getting sick?" Jason asked.

"I spent a lot of time with Dr. Gamgee over the past few days. He's experimented with a number of possible remedies. He suggested we use a product that I'm familiar with from my days in the medical sales business before the war. It's called carbolic acid, and it's plentiful. It sells here in New York for eight cents a gallon. Dr. Gamgee claims that it's likely to kill the minute spores that are harming the native cattle."

I paused to give Jason time to think about what I was saying before I continued, "Dr. Gamgee suggests dousing the cattle with a weak solution of the carbolic acid as soon as they show the first signs of the sickness. He also says that soaked rags should be hung out in all of the barns where the animals are kept for any period of time. I believe it's worth a try."

"What have we got to lose?" Jason asked. "Let's get over to the Western Union office right away. We'll want to get a large supply of this stuff as soon as we can."

As we walked, Jason continued. "I'm going back to Washington to help Miss Carroll with her continuing problems there. I think you've done all that you can here, so I think you should go back to Illinois."

When we reached the Western Union office near the capitol building, the attendant immediately recognized Jason when he approached the window. A message was handed to him.

Jason read it quickly and shook his head.

"Bad news?"

"All of Jeanine's horses at the Broadlands Farm have died," he said.

CHAPTER FIFTY-ONE

Albany, New York
September 1, 1868

I wanted to return to Illinois right away to see if I could help out, but that wasn't to be. Jason and I remained at the Western Union office in Albany as he traded messages with his father for several hours. John T. Alexander had notified all of his buyers that he would make good on any cattle that died from the strange sickness. He asked Jason to meet with officials at the Bank of New York and the Bank of Ontario to secure the loans that he would need to back up his offer.

Mr. Alexander asked me to line up the supplies of carbolic acid and get them shipped to Tolono and Alexander. He also asked me to remain in Albany and meet two special commissioners who had been appointed by Governor Oglesby of Illinois to meet with Governor Fenton regarding New York's ominous health decrees. John T. Alexander had used all of his political might to persuade the Illinois governor to make this overture.

The two special commissioners arrived at the Albany Station on the first day in September, and I greeted Harvey Edwards and Edmund Piper as they stepped onto the platform on this sweltering

Tuesday afternoon. I briefed them on all of the recent developments here in the state of New York as we rode the carriage to their hotel.

"We'll be meeting with Rafner B. Hale and George Lincoln on Friday of this week," Piper said, almost seeming to ignore me as he spoke. "We have been promised a meeting with Governor Fenton before we depart, but that date hasn't been set as yet."

"What is your objective?" I asked.

Edwards cleared his throat. "Objective?" His question floated in the air for quite some time before he continued, "What do you mean?"

"What do you hope to accomplish?" I asked, thinking that my question might just be too complicated for him.

Piper leaned forward in his seat. "We want to get Illinois cattle to the New York market once again."

I felt better. "That will take some doing," I said. "For some reason, Hale and Lincoln have expanded this thing way beyond where it needs to be. I'd like to think that they're just being overprotective, but I believe there's more to it than that. It may be a simple matter of price protection, gentlemen."

They both looked at me as if I'd called their boss a bad name. Piper quickly changed the subject. "I understand that you've spent a good deal of time with Dr. John Gamgee."

"I have certainly done that. He's studied this problem extensively, and he believes that it's not rinderpest and it's not contagious. He also knows that there is no need to kill the Texas cattle as they're doing here."

"We hope to meet the doctor," Piper said.

"That won't happen if Hale and Lincoln have anything to say about it," I said.

"We'll keep that in mind," Edwards said, waving to the doorman as we reached the hotel.

As I watched them walk away, I decided to contact Dr. Gamgee to make sure he knew that these two special commissioners from Governor Oglesby's office were here in New York. I wanted Dr. Gamgee to meet with Harvey Edwards and Edmund Piper *before* they met with Governor Fenton.

I'd read that many other states had created cattle commissioners as the state of New York had done. I also intended to suggest to Dr. Gamgee that a meeting of all of these cattle commissioners together in one place might give him a chance to educate all of them about the innocence of the Texas cattle. I had spent enough time with him to know that he would relish such an opportunity. I would tell him that Springfield, Illinois, would be the perfect place for this grand meeting. All I could do was to plant the seed, and hope.

⌘ ⌘ ⌘

A short distance away in the rotunda of the state capitol building, Raven and Badger watched as New York's three newly appointed cattle commissioners fielded questions from a cluster of newspaper reporters from all over the world.

"It's quite a feeding frenzy, isn't it?" Badger said. "They're following the script to the letter. We want to build up the fear of the Texas cattle to the point that no one will want to touch the stuff."

"My constituents seem to be quite satisfied for the moment," Raven said, "so if they're happy, I'm happy. And you don't need to worry about Washington—everyone there is busy trying to decide President Johnson's fate. They don't care about dead cattle in New York."

"And the banks won't be loaning money to John T. Alexander?" Badger asked.

"Most won't. This should destroy him, and keep him and his friends out of here forever."

Badger laughed. "Such a shame."

"Indeed." Raven checked his watch. "I need to catch a train for Washington. Contact me only if necessary." Raven hustled off without further word.

Raven paused before he reached the exit, waiting for Badger to disappear from his sight. He signaled for Bear to join him. Bear descended from his hiding place on the terrace that overlooked the rotunda. As Raven watched him approach, he was sure that his bearded friend had gained additional weight even though he'd been quite active in the past months, traveling back and forth between New York and the cattle towns.

"Is Badger satisfied?" Bear said.

"He seems to be," Raven said. "He wants to keep the Texas cattle out of New York. That's all he's concerned about."

"But we both know that can't be done for very long."

"He doesn't seem to realize that," Raven said. "Have you made the arrangements to take the Texas cattle to the shyster slaughter-houses, as they're called?"

"Yes, my men pay the workers at the checkpoints and take the cattle from the holding pens, but instead of shooting and burying them in the deep pits, we take them off to be processed. The meat is very good, you know."

"So I've heard," Raven said. "The restaurant owners say it's *marbled*...layered with fat in the meat."

"I love it," Bear said. "I won't touch the other stuff now. We're going to make some big money if we can corner this market."

"That's precisely what I'm hoping for," Raven said. "I need the money for my campaign. There are a lot of people to pay off."

CHAPTER FIFTY-TWO

—◂═◆═▸—

Alexander, Illinois
September 18, 1868

After leaving the situation in New York, I returned to Illinois. Sheriff Pierce greeted me the moment I stepped from the train at the Tolono TW&W Railway Station on a mild Friday afternoon. The soldiers were gone, and the sheriff and his deputies were maintaining control.

The sheriff told me that things had quieted down considerably, and he wanted to make sure I wasn't going to start any trouble. He said that all of the Alexander family had gone home now, leaving Broadlands Farm in the capable hands of Rand Eaton. Sheriff Pierce was very happy when I stepped back on the crowded train to continue my westward journey.

Things were much more active at the Alexander TW&W Railway Station when I arrived there about three hours later. Many of us left the train. The area was bustling with activity. A large group of men hastily boarded the train. I noticed the banker William Orear among the group. They didn't look happy.

A small scuffle of some sort was taking place at the far end of the platform, and Henry Fitch shuffled off to try to stop it. The

Western Union agent was calling out several names, hoping to hand off some telegrams that had arrived. Robert Keenan was holding up some pieces of paper with names scribbled on them, probably people who had arranged for a room at his hotel in advance of their arrival in town.

I also noticed a tall man who was shouting out the directions to nearby McPherson's Tavern. He almost tripped over a dog that was chasing some small children across the station platform. Others were standing around taking in all of the excitement. It was quite a sight. I loved this town. It reminded me of many of the small, prosperous towns in Virginia...before the war...before they were reduced to rubble.

I looked around for someone from J. T. Alexander and Company, but I didn't see anyone. I found myself walking off in the direction of McPherson's Tavern to quench my thirst. The tall man fell in beside me as he continued to lead a few others along the way. He had done a good job striking up some late-afternoon business for the small establishment.

The place was packed, but I managed to worm my way to the bar. As if by magic, an overflowing mug of beer appeared in my hand shortly after I held it out to place my order. I found that I was standing in the midst of a heated discussion about the local cattle problem.

Sebastian Kumle was speaking. "If John Alexander says that he is going to pay everyone back for any purchases of sick cattle, then that's exactly what he's going to do. I've known the man long enough to say that without any hesitation."

"He can't possibly do that," a large man with a tall beaver skin hat said. "He doesn't have that kind of money."

Another voice chimed in. "He'd banked over a million dollars right after the end of the war...that's a lot of money. It can't all be gone."

"A whole bunch of bankers just left town after meeting with the Cattle King all morning long," beaver skin said. "They told him that he can't borrow any more money, and they want his loans paid off."

"How do you know that?" Sebastian Kumle asked.

"One of them is a friend of mine, and he told me before he got on the train. John T. Alexander is done for. He can't possibly survive this mess. He can't even pay his hired help at this point."

"That's an exaggeration," Sebastian Kumle said. "You're getting people all stirred up unnecessarily." I didn't realize that he had noticed that I was standing in the group, but he pointed to me and said, "John Demsond and I will head out there right now and talk to John Alexander. We'll find out what's going on and get the truth out. We don't need these false rumors."

We walked to Marker's Livery and picked up a carriage for the short ride out to Alexander's farm. "Some of my own horses started to get sick, but I brought them inside and used that carbolic acid solution," Sebastian Kumle said. "It snapped them right out of it. That stuff killed whatever it was that was harming those horses."

"I hope it helped the Alexanders," I said.

He just shook his head. I didn't like that response.

I could tell that something was wrong before we reached the place. I'd never seen it this quiet. No horses were tied up in front of the big house. In fact, I didn't see any horses at all. The cattle pens near the house were empty. No one was around.

I turned to look at Sebastian Kumle as we rode up the lane. He was still shaking his head. "It's not good, John, it's not good."

"How bad is it?"

"You'll soon find out." Sebastian made a point of tying his horses to a hitching post that was some distance from the house. I thought this was odd.

Before we started to walk to the house, he said, "I'm sure that you'll find Jeanine in the horse barn." He continued on toward the house, knowing that I wouldn't be following him. "You go ahead," he called back. "I need to tell J.T. about the rumblings in town."

I slowly walked to the horse barn. I didn't want to find out what I was going to find out.

I didn't see the Chief. I smelled the carbolic acid as soon as I walked in. All of the stalls were empty except one. Jeanine was sitting on a chair near that one.

The Black was still alive. Rags soaked in the carbolic acid solution were hanging in the stall. Jeanine looked as if she hadn't slept for days. She looked at me, but she didn't speak.

"I'm sorry to see this," I said. "I thought the longhorns that were coming here from Abilene were all right."

She nodded. "We got some from the barges in Hannibal." After minutes of silence, she said, "I should have listened to you and kept my horses away from the Texas cattle. I let them share adjacent pastures. Some of them mingled together."

"There was nothing you could do to stop that," I said. "It wasn't your fault, Jeanine."

"The Black is the only one I have left. If he makes it, I'll have to sell him to pay off some of what I owe on the other Morgans that died."

She wept.

I put a hand on her shoulder and knelt down next to her. "The Black is a fine Morgan stallion. That's all you need to start over...and Sting is still alive, too. I have some railroad stock that I can sell. It's enough to get you going again."

"I can't take that," she said.

"If you wish, consider it to be a loan, Jeanine. No interest—you know what the Bible says about that."

She nodded. "I don't know what to say."

I stood up. "Go get some sleep," I said. "I'll watch The Black."

She stood up and looked at me with beet-red eyes. She nodded and walked away.

When she reached the barn door opening, she turned and stared at me. We locked eyes for what seemed like minutes. Then she turned away and walked to the house.

CHAPTER FIFTY-THREE

Alexander National Bank
Alexander, Illinois
September 21, 1868

I'd returned to town with Sebastian Kumle on Friday afternoon after he informed me that John T. Alexander had taken ill. I settled in for a long-needed rest over the weekend in the Grande Jeanne Hotel.

After an exceptional breakfast at the hotel on Monday morning, I walked to the Alexander National Bank on the corner of Main Street and Webster Avenue in the warm sunshine. I was determined to make good on my promise to Jeanine. The leather pouch containing all of my stock certificates was neatly tucked under my arm.

William Orear, the bank president, was in his office behind closed doors with visitors when I arrived. I took a seat in the comfortable waiting area across from the teller windows. One of the local merchants appeared to be depositing his weekend's income with one of the tellers as they exchanged pleasantries. Otherwise, it was quiet.

I picked up a copy of the town's *Daily Sentinel* that was sitting on a nearby table. There was nothing about the local cattle problem in this edition, but there was mention that New York City's newly created Society for the Prevention of Cruelty to Animals was adding guidelines for the treatment of livestock transportation. The article noted that the society planned to print thousands of pamphlets to educate the public and gain support for possible prosecution of railroad and meatpacking companies for their wrongdoings. The New Yorkers were relentless.

Just then, the door to William Orear's office opened, and he walked out with his two visitors. One of them was General Murray McConnell from Jacksonville. The other was Red Beard. He noticed me immediately. The barrel-chested bear of a man smiled at me, but he didn't say a word.

I rose up from my chair. "Mr. Demsond, I'll be right with you," William Orear said. "Go on in and have a seat in my office." He walked to the bank's entryway and bid his guests farewell.

I was still standing in the same place when he came back to his office. He motioned for me to follow him inside. I took a seat across from the bank president's dark walnut desk. The office was nicely furnished with family pictures and a number of hand carvings. Thick rugs were scattered about, covering most of the hardwood flooring.

"I know those gentlemen," I said. "One of them was General McConnell, but the name of the other one slips my mind at the moment."

The banker nodded. "A strange fellow that other one is. He calls himself Bob Jones—but I'm not sure that's his real name. How did you come to know him?"

"I travel to Missouri and Kansas, and I've seen him out there on the trail...and other places."

"He's a land buyer for some company out of New York," he said. "I'm not at liberty to say more than that...confidentiality, you know."

"Of course," I said. Now he really had my interest piqued, but I didn't dare to say more because he might become suspicious.

"My assistant said that you had some stock that you wished to sell...is that correct?"

"Yes, I have one thousand shares of Credit Mobilier stock and two hundred shares of Union Pacific stock," I said.

William Orear sat up straight in his chair and pushed his glasses to the back of his nose. "You don't say," he frowned. "How did you come about getting these shares, may I ask?"

"Certainly," I said. "I would be disappointed in you if you didn't ask." I removed the certificates from the pouch and placed them on top of the desk, directly in front of me. I placed my hand on them. "I did a considerable amount of work for a gentleman by the name of Dr. Thomas Durant...you may have heard of him."

William Orear smiled and nodded his head. "I certainly have."

"The Doc was strapped for cash at the time, so he paid me in Credit Mobilier stock certificates. I think he also did it because it annoyed his partners at the same time. They didn't like it when the stock changed hands...unless it was into their hands, of course. Some of the dividend payments that I've received during this past year included some shares in Union Pacific as well as cash."

"Yes," he said, "I'm aware that they mixed the shares in with the cash that way." I had his full attention now. He eyed the items in front of me.

"You may check with the railroad to verify my ownership if you wish."

"Yes, I will have to do that...you would be disappointed in me if I didn't."

I smiled and pushed the stack of certificates across the desk to him. "You may record the registry numbers."

As he proceeded to make note of the necessary details, I probed a bit more about Red Beard. "General McConnell and Bob Jones are good friends, I take it."

William Orear paused and looked up at me over the top of his glasses. "Business associates," he said.

"I see," I said, not wishing to press my luck any further.

After finishing his work, the bank president returned the certificates to me. He leaned back in his chair and took a deep breath. "I will, of course, calculate the value of these certificates to the penny, Mr. Demsond. I'm sure that you're aware that we are looking at something on the order of a quarter of a million dollars. I would be most happy to take your deposit in this bank if you are so inclined."

"I do intend to deposit *some* of my money here, enough to establish a line of credit for Jeanine Alexander. I will provide you with the necessary details when I return to hand over the stock certificates and receive my cash, Mr. Orear. How long will it take to finish things up?"

"You will have your money before the end of the week, Mr. Demsond."

CHAPTER FIFTY-FOUR

——— ❈ ———

State Capitol
Albany, New York
September 24, 1868

On Friday morning, Governor Richard Oglesby's two special commissioners, Harvey Edwards and Edmund Piper, sat with Governor Reuben Fenton of New York and Governor Marcus Ward of New Jersey to discuss the cattle problem. Governor Fenton had also invited Lieutenant Governor Rafner B. Hale as well as his three cattle commissioners, General Marsena Patrick, Lewis Allen, and John Stanton Gould.

The group of men sat around a large oak table that provided the centerpiece for a meeting room that was adjacent to Governor Fenton's plush office in the capitol building. Pictures of all the previous state governors adorned the walls of the large room. The size of the picture seemed to represent someone's view of the significance of the past occupant of the office. Governor Fenton had already made plans for a very large picture of himself.

Lieutenant Governor Hale tried to get in the first word, but Governor Fenton cut him off. "We're gathered here today to discuss the proposal that Governor Oglesby's people brought to me." He paused to make sure that Lieutenant Governor Hale would remain quiet. "The governor wishes to call a meeting of all of the cattle commissioners from the various states that have been impacted by the cattle problem, to use the Illinois governor's words. I would call it the cattle plague."

Governor Fenton rose from his chair and walked to the fireplace to warm himself from the sudden chill that had descended upon the city. After standing close to the fire for a bit, he turned back to his guests. Grabbing the lapels of his coat, he said, "Governor Oglesby has offered to host the meeting in Springfield, and he will provide room and board for the attendees…a most gracious gesture on his part, I must say. I am inclined to take him up on his offer. He has also asked me to help encourage participation from the other governors."

"Are we free to ask questions now?" Rafner Hale asked in a bitter tone of voice.

Others shuffled in their seats. Smiling demurely, the governor said, "Certainly."

"The whole thing seems to be an unnecessary waste of everyone's time," Hale said. "We are capable of handling our state without the assistance of Governor Oglesby."

Reuben Fenton was quick to respond. "Governor Oglesby has no intention of running our affairs. He wants to initiate an open discussion about the matter and reach a common agreement as to how it should be handled. I find this to be a commendable pursuit."

Rafner Hale shrugged. "It's no coincidence that the greatest perpetrator of this menace, John T. Alexander, is a friend of his."

Edmund Piper spoke up. "The governor has many friends, and some of them have taken large losses in livestock, including Mr. Alexander."

"I don't relish the thought of traveling to Illinois in the winter," Lewis Allen said. "How soon could this be set up?"

"As a practical matter, I would say late November or early December," Harvey Edwards said. "As soon as we get your approval, we will notify Governor Oglesby, and that will set things in motion. We intend to seek representatives from all of the impacted states, and Canada, in addition to Illinois and New York, of course."

"We would object to representation from Kansas and Texas," Rafner Hale said.

The special commissioners from Illinois looked to Governor Fenton to see if he disagreed, but he remained quiet. "I suppose we could go along with that," Harvey Edwards said.

"Then it's settled," Governor Fenton said. "We will meet in Springfield as soon as it can be arranged. I'll commit to sending Lieutenant Governor Hale and all three of my cattle commissioners, and Governor Oglesby is free to include that information with any invitation correspondence that he intends to send out to the governors."

Rafner B. Hale grunted his disapproval.

CHAPTER FIFTY-FIVE

The Gavel Inn
Springfield, Illinois
October 22, 1868

After receiving the news about the value of my stock certificates, I set out to meet with John T. Alexander's most loyal bankers—the same ones whom I had met back in December of last year when I traveled with him to discuss his loans. I decided that I would deposit my $285,000 in those five banks, once I was assured that they intended to continue to loan money to John T. Alexander.

I was quite sure that he would not allow me to loan the money to him directly, so this was the best way for me to do it indirectly. William Orear accompanied me on the trips to see Danford Christie at the Bank of Toronto, Christian Hays of St. Louis, George Wilson of Geneseo, and Thomas Condell of Springfield, our last stop. Each one of these men completely trusted John T. Alexander, and they were sure that he was fully capable of getting his feet back on the ground.

While they couldn't share the details with me, they did inform me that Mr. Alexander had not completely depleted his assets. They also volunteered the information that he was in very serious trouble.

William Orear and I finished our meeting with Thomas Condell on Thursday afternoon, and after I said good-bye to William at the train station, I decided to walk over to the Gavel Inn for a drink. It had been quite some time since I'd last set foot in the place.

I had to laugh when I immediately ran into some of the same people whom I'd met when I was here over a year ago. "Don't you guys ever leave this place?" I joked.

"I would be the first to admit that I spend way too much time here," Buck Lathrop said.

"I've contemplated moving the headquarters of McMunn Enterprises to this location," Brock McMunn said as he slapped me on the back. "Where the hell have you been?"

I was really surprised that they remembered me. "I've been busy."

"So we've heard," Buck Lathrop said. "Your name actually comes up around here quite often. Of course, we have eyes and ears everywhere. That's necessary if you want to do business here."

I couldn't tell if he was serious or just joking. "I wouldn't have expected that you've heard anything about me," I said.

"It's well-known that you've taken in with J. T. Alexander and Company," McMunn said, "and the meat packers."

"I don't have anything to do with the meat packers," I said.

"But you do work for Alexander," McMunn said, waving for a round of beers.

"I do—I don't know what you've heard about him, but I can tell you that he's a good man. I can also tell you that there's nothing wrong with the cattle that have come up out of Texas."

They looked at each other. "We've heard that he's going out of business," Lathrop said.

"I think he can still make a go of it," I said.

"They say that he's overextended and he'll have to sell his place in Champaign County."

The beers arrived. I paid for them before the others could reach for their money. "Here's to Texas cattle," I said, waiting for their response.

"To Texas cattle," Lathrop said. McMunn nodded, and we drank up.

"Do you know what's killing the local livestock?" Lathrop asked.

"I have some thoughts, but I can't prove a thing," I said.

"We'll all find out soon enough," McMunn said. "That big cattleman's meeting will be held here on the first of December. The city has already started to buzz about it. They're going to disclose the details of the problem and put some new laws in place."

"It's not that simple," I said. "No one knows what's causing the deaths. There are several theories—but no one knows for sure. I've spent a good deal of time with one of the best doctors, and he's not sure himself."

"And whatever laws they come up with will be worked around, just like always," McMunn said. "You can put the laws on paper, but money in the pockets of the right people will prevail."

I shrugged. "None of us can stop that," I said, "but we are all capable of refusing to take part in it."

"Here, here," Lathrop said, "well put." We finished our beers, and he ordered another round.

While we waited, I decided to take a long shot. "By the way, do either one of you know a big fellow with a red beard...a land speculator, I think?

Both of them nodded. "His name is Bob Jones," McMunn said. "He's from this part of the country, but he buys for somebody out of New York, I'm told. Anything wrong?"

"Not that I know of," I said.

CHAPTER FIFTY-SIX

—— ⋙✦⋘ ——

John T. Alexander Farm
November 17, 1868

I sat next to Jason Alexander in one of the chairs across from his father's desk on a chilly Tuesday morning. The looking glass was placed on the corner of the desk where I'd seen it many times before. We were lamenting yesterday's passing of Captain James N. Brown, the nearby cattleman and longtime friend of the Alexander family. "He's as fine a man as I've ever known," John T. Alexander said. "His father, Colonel William Brown, purchased land in Island Grove in 1833 along the stagecoach route between Springfield and Jacksonville. They've been our neighbors for a long time."

"I understand that he'll be buried with the same sash that he wore three years ago when he was a pallbearer for President Lincoln's burial at Oak Ridge Cemetery in Springfield," Jason said.

Jason had returned from Washington after U.S. Grant defeated Horatio Seymour for president of the United States. Jason's friend Anna Carroll still had problems collecting all of her back pay, but she hoped that having a good friend as president might help her cause.

Jason wasn't so sure. "Grant seemed to be shunning her during his campaign. Miss Carroll was visibly shaken by his behavior toward her. She thinks that he is being manipulated by many others, including a powerful group from New York."

He turned to look at me. "John and I have about had our fill of those New Yorkers."

"Amen," I said.

With the cooler weather setting in, the animal deaths disappeared. Some markets, such as New York, continued to refuse to take the Texas cattle, but many others were more than happy to take them. John T. Alexander continued to move large numbers of Texas cattle where he could, and he also replaced some of his native stock.

I was busy reviewing all of his transactions with the railroad companies. The contracts I had negotiated with them required that they give John T. Alexander their best shipping rate, which meant they were also required to lower that rate even further if another customer negotiated a better deal.

The railroads were supposed to keep track of the accounts and provide a credit to J. T. Alexander and Company in the form of a "drawback" if the rate was lowered. It was very difficult for me to audit the process because the railroad companies didn't disclose their records. Even when we received a drawback credit, I was sure that we were owed more than what we got.

After the holidays, I intended to dig deeply into the railroad's process for establishing rates. I needed to understand how rates were calculated if I had any hope of confronting the railroads with my challenges to their accounts.

I did manage to find a little time to help Jeanine replenish her stable of Morgans. The Black was the only one to survive. I was able to get some horses for a good price from a fellow Confederate cavalryman who still lived in Virginia. A. J. Alexander, her father's cousin from Kentucky, also sold some very fine horses to her.

Jeanine's pretty smile had returned. And she was treating me a whole lot better than before. "You're still playing second fiddle to Gustavus," Jason joked, "but you've gained a lot of ground."

In two weeks, the cattlemen's conference would commence in Springfield, and John T. Alexander was getting nervous. "Richard Oglesby has been sending me the names of the people who have indicated that they will attend. This is going to be a very large meeting—one of a kind—more like a hearing. There will be newspaper reporters from all over the world."

"But representatives from Texas and Kansas haven't been invited," Jason said.

"That's right, but I invited Joseph McCoy anyhow. I'm sure someone will call him to testify about the Texas cattle that were shipped from Abilene."

"And your friend Danford Christie from Ontario is coming," I said.

"Yes, he is one of the three representatives from the province of Ontario," John T. Alexander said. "I've heard that all of the hotel rooms in Springfield are spoken for."

"Even the Grande Jeanne here is to be filled up, taking some of the overflow," I said. "The early-morning train from here will get the delegates to Springfield in plenty of time."

"You don't trust that New York crowd, do you, John?"

"Not one bit," I said. "I can assure you that they will arrive with a plan, and they will bring plenty of people to help make it happen. They have already notified Governor Oglesby that they plan to call Rand Eaton to the stand."

John T. Alexander grunted. "Broadlands Farm belongs to me. They should call me to testify, not Rand."

"I would guess that they think they can get Rand to make some sort of a mistake since he wouldn't be accustomed to anything like this," I said. "Many of these men are lawyers, you know."

"How long will this thing go on?" Jason said.

"Three full days, starting on Tuesday, the first," I said, "and they plan to run three sessions each day. We'll get back here just in time to turn around and head back the next day."

"I've got a bad feeling about this," John T. Alexander said.

After a bit of silence, Jason and I decided that the meeting was over, so we got up and said good-bye to his father. We walked to the foot of the staircase.

"I'll find out where the New York group has reserved its rooms," I said. "It will be interesting to see who takes up residence in the rooms near them."

"Yes, they'll have taken sides with the New Yorkers, and they'll surely vote in favor of whatever it is that they propose to do."

We went upstairs to say hello to Jerome. His recovery was slow, but he was getting stronger each day. He was planning to head back to Broadlands as soon as he was able.

Afterward, I said good-bye to Jason, and when I walked outside, some large flakes of snow were beginning to fill the air. Dark gray clouds hung overhead. I decided to head into town.

By the time I reached the hotel, it was really coming down.

CHAPTER FIFTY-SEVEN

→·—≡+≡—·←

The Gavel Inn
Springfield, Illinois
November 30, 1868

On the eve of the big meeting, I met with my friends Buck Lathrop and Brock McMunn. The capital city came alive, and the newspapers were filled with stories about the "American Convention of Cattle Commissioners." I was sure that my two friends would know a lot more than the reporters.

"The New York people are at the Chenery House on the northeast corner of Fourth and Washington streets," Lathrop said. "The Wisconsin, Michigan, Indiana, and Maryland people are also there. They all came in on Friday, and they've had several meetings since then. They occupy the entire fifth floor, and they've sealed it off for privacy. The housekeeper said they have prepared a number of documents for the convention."

Buck Lathrop shook his head. "You're up against a very well-organized group, John."

"They'll probably sit close together in the Hall of the House of Representatives to help them communicate quickly during the convention," McMunn said. "New York's Lieutenant Governor Hale is pulling the strings. If he has his way, John T. Alexander will never do business in New York again."

I did my best to hide my fears. "I won't let that happen," I said. "I have a little plan of my own. What else can you tell me?"

"They seem to be having a little problem with one of the doctors...a fellow named Gamgee," Lathrop said. "They tried to send him away, but he wouldn't go. He isn't staying at the Chenery House."

"That's good to know," I said. "I'll try to see that he's called to the stand to testify. He must have something to say that they don't want others to hear."

I scribbled some notes on a piece of paper. "I'm sure they'll want to elect one of their own as president of the convention, but I'll suggest that Mr. Alexander encourage Governor Oglesby to occupy a seat next to the appointed president during the entire three days in order to maintain order."

"Good thinking, John," McMunn said.

I rushed off to send a few urgent telegrams.

⌘   ⌘   ⌘

Tanner Biggs had cleaned himself up and donned a new suit of clothing. In the main lobby of the Chenery House, he made sure that the fifth floor was secured by posting two of his men at the head of the stairs on that floor.

He was watching for some of the other cattle commissioners, who had registered here but refused to join the fifth-floor group, to enter the bar next door to the hotel's restaurant.

Tanner Biggs carried a tasteless arsenic mix that he could slip into a drink and put the individual out of the way for at least a day. One of his men was substituting for a bartender who had mysteriously taken sick the day before. His man had a good supply of the mix hidden away behind the bar.

A few men from the Ohio and Missouri delegations caught Tanner Biggs's attention. A smile came across his lips.

He would welcome them to Springfield and buy them a drink.

CHAPTER FIFTY-EIGHT

—⁖—

American Convention of
Cattle Commissioners
(Hall of the House of Representatives
Springfield, Illinois
December 1, 1868
(Morning Session)

Governor Richard J. Oglesby called the convention to order at 9:00 a.m. Father Patrick O'Riordan prayed for success. The governor welcomed his guests, and then he introduced the five delegates who would represent the commission from Illinois: Dr. William Kile, John P. Reynolds, Dr. H. C. Johns, Harvey N. Edwards, and Edmund H. Piper.

A role was taken to account for the delegates who would represent their respective governments. Lieutenant Governor Rafner B. Hale, Dr. Moreau Morris, General Marsena S. Patrick, Lewis F. Allen, and John Stanton Gould represented New York. Other official delegations included the states of Indiana, Maryland, Massachusetts, Michigan,

Missouri, Ohio, Pennsylvania, Rhode Island, and Wisconsin. Danford Christie represented the province of Ontario in Canada.

"I count thirty-three delegates present and three absent because of sickness," Governor Oglesby said. "I suggest that a two-thirds majority of those present be required to enact any guidelines that would be carried forward as suggested legislation by those attending."

General Marsena Patrick immediately rose from his seat. "I object, Governor. I believe that a simple majority will suffice. Perhaps the delegates should select a president and go from there, sir."

Eventually, Lewis F. Allen was elected to be the president of the convention, and he took a seat next to Governor Oglesby on the raised platform at the head of the hall. He promptly accepted his role to preside over the convention from that point forward. The delegates quickly agreed upon a simple-majority voting process. I shared concerned glances with Jason Alexander, Rand Eaton, and Joseph McCoy as we sat in the gallery area that overlooked the seating of the delegates. Newspaper reporters were allowed to occupy the seats on the floor behind the delegates.

As I scanned across the hall and the gallery, I couldn't find an empty seat anywhere. Tanner Biggs taunted me with a smile from the other end of the gallery. I smiled at Dr. John Gamgee, who sat next to Tanner Biggs. The doctor seemed to force a smile in return. I also saw Buck Lathrop and Brock McMunn. I signaled for them to join us for dinner as soon as the morning session was completed. They nodded.

After conducting some minor business, the convention approved a recess until 2:00 p.m.

⌘ ⌘ ⌘

It was warm for December, and the convention's attendees were happy to take advantage of the unusual weather. All of the snow and ice had melted.

We gathered at a small eating establishment away from the crowds. Lathrop and McMunn promised that the home-style cooking at Ma Kettle's was unsurpassed in the city. When they started bringing out large bowls filled to the brim with many of my favorites, I could see that my friends knew what they were talking about.

I think we were all surprised at how hungry we were. Buck Lathrop was the first to find time for a serious matter. "John, that soldier friend of yours, Biggs, was up to some dirty work last night. He was seen hanging around the bar where three of the delegates were hauled back to their rooms after passing out. Several others were very sick this morning, but they made it to the convention floor."

"Tanner Biggs is no friend of mine," I said. "I hope those men are able to make it to the afternoon session. We may need their votes."

"This thing is going to get ugly before it's over," Joseph McCoy said. "If that New York group has their way, they'll shut down my operation in Abilene for good."

"I honestly don't think they can do that," McMunn said. "As long as the railroads are willing to transport the cattle, there will be meat packers ready to process them...and people ready to consume them. The New Yorkers have grossly underestimated the demand."

"I hope you're right," Jason Alexander said.

For his father's sake, they had to be right.

CHAPTER FIFTY-NINE

——◦≡◦——

American Convention of
Cattle Commissioners
(Hall of the House of Representatives
Springfield, Illinois
December 1, 1868
(Afternoon Session)

Procedural matters filled the first ninety minutes of the afternoon. Afterward, the president of the convention gave the floor to his fellow commissioner from New York, John Stanton Gould. A heavy silence fell upon the hall as the man stepped forward to the speaker's podium.

He looked out upon the packed hall and waved his hand across the room as if he was giving a blessing to all of those therein. "We have been brought forth in a noble cause. We face a need to eliminate the alarming and devastating plague that has killed so many. In the state of New York alone, we have seen almost half of our near two million dairy cattle perish at a fever pace. We are spending more money building places to boil diseased cattle than to produce milk and its compounds. Let us make no mistake about it—this situation is dire, and we are the very people who have been called upon to save our nation from this vicious attack upon its future."

Commissioner Gould paused a moment to wipe some sweat from his brow. "In the Civil War, we learned the value of the old American maxim that in union there is strength. What we have today is another attempt to weaken the Union by transporting diseased cattle from a former Confederate state. The condition of this malfeasance has been known for quite some time. Long before the commencement of the war, attempts were made to cruelly move some of these sick animals northward—but intelligent and trustworthy people stopped this madness in its tracks, refusing to let the fever run into the North. Why must we be called upon to revisit the past? It's not accidental, mind you. It's not accidental at all. The perpetrators of this injustice are well aware of their crime."

The crowd in the hall began to stir a bit as Gould's oration irritated some and encouraged others. "Because of the vast array of those impacted, from farmer to drover to butcher to consumer, not to mention our transportation systems, we will need one common system of legislation to end, once and for all, this threat upon the lives of the American people. Our goal should be, as Governor Oglesby stated in his letter of invitation to this convention, to leave this place with draft legislation that we will all carry back to our respective states for immediate passage.

"In that regard, I am providing you with copies of rough-draft guidelines for the eradication of this menace based upon our extensive research in the state of New York over the past several months. I put this in your hands at this early time in our proceedings in order that you may have some time to study the document and consider its implications. Mr. President, I offer this up as our first exhibit, but I ask that any discussion be deferred until a later time, and if you so choose to appoint a drafting committee, as I suspect you will, I offer this document for them to use as a starting point."

The delegates approved the president's immediate motion by a vote of twenty-three to ten. Afterward, Commissioner Gould went on to refer to the symptoms of the disease, including mention of strong evidence that a temperature of 103 degrees or greater marked the point where diseased cattle would not recover. He also laid the groundwork for support of the spore theory regarding the cause of the malady, but he deferred the details of the explanation to Dr. Morris.

"Good afternoon, ladies and gentlemen, my name is Dr. Moreau Morris, and I am the head of the Department of Agriculture in New York, and I am also an officer on the Board of Health. I have gathered an immense quantity of details about the characteristics of the disease under consideration, a disease that goes by many names: Spanish fever, Texas fever, cattle plague, black water of Texas, Texas murrain, and rinderpest, to name just a few. In this country, it is a malady that is carried from the state of Texas and from the nearby Indian Territory by the longhorn cattle. We have not entirely isolated what it is that they carry, but we are quite sure that it is some sort of a minute spore that hides itself within the animal in a dormant or semidormant state, but, when released in the waste of the animal, becomes active and deadly. The spore is a member of the ordian family, the same as that to which the mildew found on a grape belongs."

The doctor was obviously uncomfortable in the heat that was being created by the many bodies that were stuffed into the hall. "I will read from a document that I will offer as the second exhibit to the convention."

I listened as Dr. Morris described the conditions of the sick animals, and his description generally agreed with what I had observed. He noted that the dead animals almost always had an enlarged liver and an enlarged spleen. I tended to favor the tick theory over the spore theory that he espoused. The tick theory maintained that minute ticks buried in the coats of the cattle carried the cause of the sickness. Rand Eaton was sure of it.

The spore theory proponents argued that the spores attached themselves to organs inside the body and tended to root themselves there like a plant, drawing nourishment from the organ to the point of killing it. They claimed that the spores gained entry to the body by hiding in plants that were eaten by the animals. Dr. Morris claimed that he had replicated the disease in laboratory rabbits.

After Dr. Morris completed his lengthy talk, a short intermission was taken before Commissioner Gould resumed his oratory. He gave a detailed account of incidents about human and animal deaths within the state of New York from July through September. Although he did not come right out and say that the people had died because they ate contaminated meat, he strongly implied that this was so. Then he raised the ante.

"The earliest record of diseased Texas cattle arriving in New York is known to be those that arrived in a shipment from John T. Alexander's Broadlands Farm. Within days, people began dying on the streets of New York City—just long enough for the butcher to have done his work and put meat on the tables of our unsuspecting citizens." A noticeable buzz of chatter filled the hall.

Rising quickly from his seat, Jason Alexander said, "I object to this accusation."

Lewis Allen pounded his gavel as more voices filled the air. "There will be no comments from the gallery at this time. An opportunity will be provided later. Failure to comply will result in mandatory removal from the premises. Please proceed, Mr. Gould."

Jason sat down in a huff. I hadn't seen him this way since I'd fought against him in the War Between the States.

"As I was saying, the cattle shipped from the Broadlands Farm were full of the disease," Gould said, shaking his handful of papers in the air. "They shouldn't have been allowed to cross into our state.

Evidence indicates that everywhere they were offloaded for feeding and watering along the way, the disease was spread to the local animals. I have the facts right here."

Someone in the gallery shouted, "Crucify him." Some laughter followed. Lewis Allen pounded the gavel again. A few of the newspaper reporters hustled out of the hall, no doubt running to the local printing presses or the Western Union office.

John Stanton Gould finished his long presentation with a brief description of the discovery of the use of carbolic acid to save animals when the disease is discovered in time. He attributed this remedy to Dr. John Gamgee as a result of his work fighting the catastrophic rinderpest that plagued Europe. "The advantage of the carbolic acid over other substances is that it destroys the cause of the disease...the spores," Gould said. "It is cheap. It is volatile. It attacks the minute spores that are floating in the atmosphere, and it is precisely those spores that are the chief disease-producing agents. Large quantities of this remedy can be purchased directly from Warren Chemical Manufacturing Company at Number Four Cedar Street in New York."

"Thank you, Commissioner Gould and Dr. Morris, for your fine reports," Lewis Allen said. "Before we adjourn, I would like to suggest that one representative from each delegation be assigned to the draft legislation committee. I leave it up to each delegation to select their representative and report to me prior to the commencement of our evening session. I would like that committee to assemble at seven p.m. for a meeting prior to our general assembly at eight p.m. this evening. This session is adjourned."

CHAPTER SIXTY

—➤—≍✦≍—↤—

American Convention of
Cattle Commissioners
(Hall of the House of Representatives
Springfield, Illinois
December 1, 1868
(Evening Session)

Before the evening session began, Rand Eaton and Joseph McCoy were given notice that they might be called upon during this session. Jason Alexander noted that he would like to be called upon. His request was ignored.

A special edition of the *Illinois Daily Journal* carried a front-page headline that read "Cattle Commissioners Seek to Stop the FEVER RUN." All of the copies were sold within minutes of their appearance. An otherwise quiet time in Springfield was filled with concerned cattlemen and farmers from all over the country. The city welcomed them with open arms. People were sleeping on cots in the hotel lobbies, and the local residents were making some extra

Christmas money by taking in boarders. Taverns, restaurants, and shops were staying open all night long.

"At this point, I open the floor to the delegates for questions and comments," the president said. "I reserve the right to terminate discussions that I believe are prohibitive to the fairness and well-being of those present." Lewis Allen paused for just a moment. "I recognize Professor P. A. Chadbourne of Wisconsin."

"Thank you, President Allen. I have some questions and comments, but first I want to thank the delegation from New York for their due diligence in preparing for this convention and providing so much information. I believe that we are off to a fine start because of your efforts. Now I will move to my questions. The colder weather seems to kill the spores. Are we free of the disease in colder weather? If that is so, are the Texas cattle that winter in our states safe to transport in the spring? In warmer weather, are the only animals at risk the ones that pass over the land where the Texas cattle have roamed? And finally, the Texas cattle come to us in many different ways. Are any of these methods of transport more safe than the others?"

Several hands were raised. Lewis Allen took note and directed the order of the responses. Dr. Johns of Illinois spoke first. "Much like the representatives from New York, we have collected a lot of information here in Illinois. We have received comments that would indicate that in some locations, animals that were separated from the Texas cattle by fencing did not take sick, but in other locations, they did...so the testimony appears to be inconsistent on that matter. Likewise, we have heard from those who say that the sickness never goes beyond the colder weather, and we have others who say that the cattle are continuing to die, even now. Again, we have inconsistency. Such is the nature of this problem."

"Speaking to the question of the different means of bringing the cattle up from Texas and the Indian Territory," Professor Spencer Smith of Missouri said, "I know of no incidents in the state of

Missouri where the Texas or Cherokee cattle that were delivered by way of the railroad from Abilene caused any sickness in our native stock."

Danford Christie from Ontario responded, "I'm sorry to say, sir, that I know of some cases in Canada where the Texas cattle from Abilene did, in fact, cause the sickness to occur in our local herds. I do, however, believe that the time that they spend in transport on the railroad cars significantly diminishes the risk because the spores or the ticks, as the case may be, have more time to disappear—perhaps falling through the spaces between the floorboards."

"You raise an interesting point, Mr. Christie," Dr. Johns said. "Relative to the comment about the ticks, I would like to hear from Mr. Rand Eaton, the superintendent of J. T. Alexander and Company's operation in Champaign County of this state."

Rand Eaton came down from the gallery and took his place behind the speaker's podium. "I will be happy to describe the situation that I encountered at the Broadlands Farm near Tolono. I believe that in every case where an animal of our native stock, be it horses, oxen, or cattle, died because of the presence of the Texas longhorn cattle, there were ticks involved. Now before I go any further, let me make it clear that there is nothing new about the presence of ticks. They have been around here for as long as I can remember. But the ticks that I am talking about are *much smaller* than the ticks that I have been accustomed to."

Rand Eaton paused for a moment to take a drink from a glass of water that sat on a table near the podium. "In fact, I will say that the ticks are often not able to be seen at all without the help of a magnifying glass of good strength. I even won a bet from one of my neighbors when he said that there were no ticks present on a sick animal. He had looked before he made the bet, but with the help of the magnifying glass, I was able to show him the ticks. There are certain places where they like to gather."

A murmur of soft talk came from across the room, and Rand Eaton reached for the water again. "The Texas cattle appear with the ticks on them, but I will agree with Professor Smith—the cattle that came from Abilene didn't carry the ticks. I'm talking about the Texas cattle that came up by way of the river. The ticks gorged themselves on the blood of the cattle, and then they fell off onto the ground. About six to eight weeks later, a new hatching yielded millions upon millions of these things on the ground where the others had fallen. It was these ticks—so small that they were nearly invisible—that feasted upon the native animals that had been moved to the locations where the Texas cattle had been. It is a common practice on the part of all farmers to move the animals around from one pasture to another, after letting the grass grow up for them.

"I would also like to say that I know of no situations where the animals in an adjacent location that was separated by fencing were sickened by the Texas cattle next to them. We had our fencing pulled down by criminals at night, allowing the animals to mingle afterward, and that is why so many of our native stock died unnecessarily. They were killed by men, not by the Texas cattle. I believe that some of those men are in this room tonight."

The room erupted into a loud jumble of conversations. I looked over at Tanner Biggs, and he was laughing uncontrollably. He didn't bother hiding the bottle of whiskey in his hand. I was thankful that all guns had been collected at the door, but I was sure he still had his knife.

Rand Eaton walked away from the podium, and Lewis Allen attempted to restore order. After things quieted down, the convention's president said, "I apologize for taking this first day to such a late hour, but we must press forward. I would like to call upon Mr. Joseph McCoy from Abilene to add more to what has been said."

Joseph McCoy passed by Rand Eaton as he made his way from the gallery to the podium. "My name is Joseph McCoy. My brother,

James, and I run the J. G. McCoy and Company enterprise in the state of Kansas...a state that has not been invited to participate in this affair for reasons that are not at all clear to me. The state of Kansas and the city of Abilene are very much involved in the cattle business, if you haven't heard. But putting this oversight aside, I can speak to the differences between the transport of cattle from Abilene by way of the Kansas Pacific Railroad and the conditions associated with various forms of river transport, as I have witnessed them.

"The primary difference that I have seen between railroad transport and river transport is the length of time that the Texas cattle are forced to go without food and water. In both cases, the cattle are driven hard from Texas, perhaps covering as many as ninety miles in two days, with little time for rest. When they arrive at the point where the Red River meets the Mississippi River, they are promptly loaded onto barges or steamboats, and they aren't fed and watered until they reach Cairo, St. Louis, or Hannibal, many days away. They are loaded up on the barges and steamboats in a very crowded condition, but to be fair, we crowd them into the railroad cars at Abilene as well. The difference, however, is that we have regular feeding and watering points along the railroad route where we offload the cattle for a day or so at a time...this makes all the difference in the world, commissioners. Why? Because if they're healthy, they can shake off those ticks or kill those spores, but if they're not healthy, they can't."

The murmur in the room returned. Professor Smith of Missouri rose from his seat. "As I said before, this man's comments confirm my findings...no cattle from Abilene caused the sickness."

"I disagree, sir," Joseph Poole of Indiana said. "To the contrary, we have several cases of sickness and death of native animals due to Texas and Cherokee cattle delivered by way of Abilene. The rest stops that Mr. McCoy speaks of are nothing more than additional opportunities to cause more sickness to animals along the way."

Similar exchanges went back and forth for many minutes. Tempers were getting short. A pushing and shoving incident broke out in the gallery near the area where Tanner Biggs was seated. I rushed over there to see if I could get an opportunity to even the score with him, but he was gone by the time I arrived.

I looked for Dr. John Gamgee, but he was gone as well.

Lewis Allen decided that the first day had gone long enough, and he adjourned until 8:00 a.m. the following morning.

I rode back to the Alexander Farm on the train with Jason Alexander, Rand Eaton, and Joseph McCoy. Before going to bed for a few hours of sleep, we briefed John T. Alexander on the day's events. He wasn't feeling well, and our report didn't help any.

CHAPTER SIXTY-ONE

————— ❤❤❤ —————

American Convention of
Cattle Commissioners
(Hall of the (House of Representatives
Springfield, Illinois
December 2, 1868
(Morning Session)

I was seated in the gallery once again in preparation for the second day. Even at this early hour, the place was packed. The morning newspapers were loaded with stories from yesterday's proceedings. Almost all the people carried one or more with them as they entered the hall. The shuffle of newspapers was constant background noise all morning long.

I noticed that the three delegates who missed the first day of the convention were in their seats this morning. No one seemed to be absent today.

Professor Spencer Smith of Missouri was the first speaker. "I wish to continue with the discussion about Mr. McCoy's wonderful enterprise at Abilene. I understand that he has shipped well over one

hundred thousand cattle from that location in just a few months…
this is remarkable. His astute presentation was cut short by the same
ruffians who have tried to tarnish the good name of the endeavor to
feed the many hungry Americans who have been deprived of beef
because of protective pricing in the industry. It is precisely the work
of people like John T. Alexander, who was mentioned earlier in an
inappropriate way, that will put meat on tables that have seldom seen
it before.

"I submit that the movement of Texas cattle into the northern
states cannot be stopped—to propose such insanity is ludicrous. We
must focus upon getting the cattle to market safely. That is our chal-
lenge. The transport of cattle by way of Abilene is the best way to
handle this. It is certainly much safer than the cattle drives that go
through the eastern counties of Kansas and the western counties of
Missouri, spreading the sickness all along the way during the warm
months of the year…April to October."

I tried to listen to Professor Smith and read the newspapers at the
same time. It was easy to tell which papers were for or against the
cattle feeders like John T. Alexander. There was little or no attempt
at fair journalism. Buck Lathrop told me that the New Yorkers had
set up a hospitality room on the top floor of the Chenery House for
the reporters for the duration of the convention. It was obvious that
some of the reporters from Chicago and Springfield found it.

Professor Smith continued on. He read several letters from those
in his state of Missouri, giving detailed accounts of incidents where
the sickness was passed from the Texas cattle to their native stock.
Armed conflicts were also described in detail, pitting the local residents against the drovers. Some people had been killed in the con-
frontations. He read on for what seemed like hours.

Dr. William Clendennin of Ohio followed Professor Smith. He
called for the formation of a special committee of delegates to prepare

a resolution asking the legislators in Washington to take the lead on this entire issue.

My newspaper reading was interrupted when I heard Lewis Allen call General Marsena Patrick to the podium. He made a big show as he moved very slowly from his seat to the front of the hall. He cleared his throat and dusted off the top of the podium with his hand before he spoke. "Gentlemen...and ladies...I do see a few ladies here...I maintain that the proposed resolution to Congress is completely unnecessary because we already have an organization that is perfectly designed for this sort of work...the War Department."

Mention of the War Department created an instant hum in the hall. "The machinery required to reign in this plague is already owned by the government. The army contains at every post those well versed in all the sciences. I have experience regarding this matter, and I can assure you that the War Department can put this entire issue to rest just as it did with the Confederate vermin of Texas and the other states that, once before, attempted to destroy our great nation." A small cheer went up in the hall.

I wasn't at all happy with this development. Nor was Jason Alexander. He jumped up from his seat. "Mr. President, these comments are out of order. Nothing is to be gained by such disparaging remarks."

Lewis Allen pounded his gavel. "Once again, I will require that the members of the gallery remain silent if they wish to remain in the hall," he said. "Please continue, General Patrick."

"Thank you, President Allen. As I said, before I was so rudely interrupted, the War Department is fully capable of completing any necessary investigations and enforcing whatever legislation might be put in place. This situation requires a heavy hand if it is to be dealt with in a satisfactory manner. We can play games, or we can go to war against this disease, which proposes to wipe out our beef industry. It is up to us to decide. It is time for the hawks, not the doves."

A loud roar filled the hall. Shouts of all sorts rang out. Tanner Biggs was yelling and screaming obscenities. The man who was once quite stoic now reacted strongly at every opportunity. He picked up his chair and threw it in our direction. Other chairs followed, and another scuffle broke out.

The gallery was cleared for the remainder of the morning session.

~~~

Our group of six returned to Ma Kettle's for dinner once again. General Murray McConnell from Jacksonville greeted us shortly after we walked in. He confessed that he had followed us here so that he could talk to Jason Alexander. Jason asked me to join the two of them at a separate table. General McConnell hesitated for a moment, but Jason gave him a firm look.

After placing our orders for food and drink, we waited for General McConnell to begin. He brushed back his thick hair, and then he spoke, slowly and carefully. "Jason, as you know, I worked as an auditor in the United States Treasury under President Franklin Pierce about ten years ago. I met a lot of people...some good, some not so good...but all of them wealthy and powerful. Some of these people were involved with my family in New York, where I was born. My family fell into the debt of some of these people, and I was called upon to help them out. I refused to become involved in anything during my tenure in Washington, but upon returning to Jacksonville, I have helped some of these people with legal and banking problems."

He paused when our drinks arrived. He looked around the room before continuing. "Recently, I discovered that several of these folks are involved in land speculation that has reached this part of the country. The way they get good deals is to help drive the property down in value before they make their purchases. They are ruthless predators— -when they smell blood, they come in for the kill. The

Texas cattle problem will force many feeders to sell their land in order to pay off their debts…people like your father, Jason."

He stopped again when the food arrived. "That's all I'm at liberty to say to you. I just felt that it was important for you to be aware of this because some of them are actively involved in this convention. I thought your father would be here, but in his absence, I've come to you. I know that J.T. hasn't been well lately."

I thought that General McConnell didn't look well. I wondered what he was holding back.

Jason nodded. "Thank you, General McConnell, I will let my father know. Actually, we have suspected something of this sort. John Demsond has discovered some of the New York connections already."

"We know that they have stoked the fire of the fear of the Texas cattle," I said, "and we are aware that they are trying to hold up the price of beef in the New York area. You're telling us that it has to do with the land as well."

General McConnell looked Jason in the eyes and said, "I'm telling you that if your father is forced to sell his land, he will get practically nothing for it—they'll see to that."

CHAPTER SIXTY-TWO

———— ❈ ————

American Convention of
Cattle Commissioners
(Hall of the House of Representatives
Springfield, Illinois
December 2, 1868
(Afternoon Session)

The afternoon session was delayed to allow the legislation-drafting committee to proceed with its work. They were preparing to address the floor later today. "Even though we are getting off to a late start this afternoon," Lewis Allen said, "I intend to shorten this session in order to provide more time for the very important evening session that lies ahead. I must also apologize for the absence of the next scheduled speaker, Dr. John Gamgee. Unfortunately, he was called back to Albert Veterinary College in London late this morning. Our next speaker, Dr. Moreau Morris, assures me that he will include all of Dr. Gamgee's findings in his presentation."

Dr. Moreau Morris picked up right where he had finished on Tuesday afternoon. He provided a detailed description of the activities in the state of New York. The doctor described how many contaminated herds had arrived in New York, specifically naming John T. Alexander on several occasions. He described how the diseased animals were taken apart; the body parts were weighed and examined in great detail using high-powered microscopes of the latest design. Numerous documents were submitted as exhibits.

As I listened to the doctor's presentation, I realized that he was setting the stage for this evening's draft-legislation proposal. It was a perfect setup, well orchestrated by the clever group from New York. He was very specific about the ability of the spores to rapidly spread in warm weather and the need for a lengthy decontamination process when the diseased animals are discovered entering the state.

Mercifully, Dr. Morris finally terminated his oration. I noticed a good number of the delegates nodding off on the floor of the hall below me. Brock McMunn leaned over and whispered in my ear, "Your boss is in some serious trouble."

How well I knew that he was correct. Jason Alexander, Rand Eaton, and Joseph McCoy looked as if they had seen a ghost. We were preparing to depart the hall when Lewis Allen announced that he was opening up the floor to both the delegates and the gallery.

Dr. H. C. Johns of Illinois asked that Henry Brown, the brother of the late Captain James Brown, speak about his extensive knowledge of the cattle business. We sat back down to listen to him. "Thank you, Doctor, I will be brief. As many of you know, my father was Colonel William Brown, one of the early settlers in this area. He owned much of the ground along the stagecoach route between Springfield and Jacksonville for many years. His good friend Henry Clay referred to my father as *the cattleman*. Our family had been bringing Texas cattle and cattle from all over the world to this area for twenty years prior to the war. I'm telling you that there's nothing new about bringing Texas cattle northward. What's new is the large number of cattle involved and the manner in which they're brought here—that's all."

The low hum in the hall returned. "We drove the Texas cattle to Illinois from the northern parts of Texas, and we didn't have any problems with the kind of sickness that has been seen this year. I must be honest and say that we drove only about a hundred head at a time, and we didn't rush them along at the pace that I've heard mentioned in this convention. We took our time getting them here. We gave the cattle plenty of time to drink, eat, and rest along the way. We always used the same trails through Kansas and Missouri. We never encountered any resistance of any sort. In fact, the locals were glad to see the Browns because we traded cattle for the food and water.

"For those who've studied the numbers, you'll know that there's little money to be made by purchasing, feeding, and selling native cattle stock, although the war, of course, provided a short exception to this rule," Henry Brown said. "A feeder like John T. Alexander can pay his bills only by bringing in longhorn cattle from Texas. If this opportunity is denied to him, the business will be forced to sell out. The delegates of this convention need to find a way to bring the cattle into the North as opposed to finding a way to keep them out. The people want the meat at a reasonable price—the Texas cattle cannot be kept out."

A smattering of cheers rose from the hall. "Thank you, Mr. Brown," Lewis Allen said. "I would now like to offer Mr. Hill from Champaign County in Illinois an opportunity to address the convention."

"Thank you, Mr. President. I am Gordon Hill, and I have been asked to speak for the citizens in the township of Tolono, the location from which John T. Alexander transports his cattle to New York on the railroad. You've already heard from Mr. Rand Eaton, the man who supervises Mr. Alexander's Broadlands Farm near Tolono. Mr.

Eaton failed to do justice to the severity of the problem. I have a document that captures the details, and I offer this as an exhibit to these proceedings. You will see that almost all of our native stock has died in the past few months, including milk cows, horses, mules, oxen, sheep, and goats as well as the shorthorn cattle. Most of our people will never recover from this tragedy…and we are hopeful that John T. Alexander will meet a similar fate."

The low hum returned. "Because we have nothing to lose at this point, our citizens have decided to allow no more Texas cattle to be offloaded from the railroad cars at Tolono. If the soldiers appear again, we will fight them, too." A cheer rose up from a small section of the gallery where Tanner Biggs sat. A small bit of pushing and shoving followed. Some of the delegates shouted up at the gallery, making things worse.

After Lewis Allen restored order, Gordon Hill continued. "We've been conservative and law-abiding citizens, and this is what we've got." After waving his document in the air, he threw it on the floor and walked away.

Tanner Biggs and his men rushed over to our area in the gallery and started a fight. I landed a nice punch to his chin. I was watching for his knife, but the police appeared very quickly this time.

Once again, the president cleared the gallery. Unable to restore order, he terminated the afternoon session.

CHAPTER SIXTY-THREE

———— ✦ ————

American Convention of
Cattle Commissioners
(Hall of the House of Representatives
Springfield, Illinois
December 2, 1868
(Evening Session)

John Stanton Gould took the floor and introduced the proposed legislation to the delegates of the convention. A copy of the document was provided to everyone in the hall. One of the local newspapers had loaned the governor the use of its printing press. A glance at the submission indicated that our worst fears had been realized.

"Because the governments of the states represented herein are so different in the ways they submit legislation for enactment, we have provided our report in the form of general propositions," Gould said. "Mr. President, I would like to read through the entire document before entertaining questions, if you please."

Lewis Allen nodded. I studied the document carefully as John Stanton Gould began to slowly read it to the delegates. The first section, which was referred to as the first general division, was titled "Commissioners and Assistant Commissioners," and it contained six propositions. It was suggested that at least three commissioners be assigned for a five-year term to oversee "the general welfare of cattle within the state for the purpose of preventing the spread of dangerous diseases among them."

Assistant commissioners were to be assigned as necessary to aid the commissioners and "to enforce the rules and regulations as may be necessary to accomplish the objects of their appointment." The diseased animals were to be placed in quarantine for an unspecified period or killed as necessary.

I looked at Jason and said, "This is certainly the New York model where the commissioners have complete control." He nodded.

The second general division was titled "Railroad," and it contained eight propositions. The commissioners were given the power to inspect all cattle brought into the state "whether by railroad, vessels, and common roads." All means of transport as well as the cattle could be detained for an unspecified period. If the cattle are believed to be carrying "dangerous diseases," they could be forbidden to enter the state. Once the cattle were inspected and deemed "allowed to proceed," they were to be held for at least twenty-four hours and be "supplied with food, water, and rest."

This process of food, water, and rest must continue once every twenty-four hours. The railroads were required to arrange for all of this at their own expense. This was as much to say that the owners of the cattle must pay whatever the railroads would charge them for these services. John T. Alexander's costs to get cattle to the market were to increase dramatically in the states where these laws would be passed. I was going to be very busy negotiating new contracts with the railroad companies.

It was further proposed that each train carrying the cattle must carry stamped certification to prove that it was in compliance with the law, and failure to be able to present such certification upon inspection would result in immediate seizure. Attempts to resist or bribe the officials would be met with severe penalties.

"I didn't notice any penalties for the commissioners extracting extra payments from the cattlemen," Jason said.

Some of the representatives from the railroad companies had already vacated their seats in the gallery. I was sure that they were sending urgent telegrams to their headquarters. Well-heeled lobbyists would begin to knock on the doors of the state legislators tomorrow.

The third and last general division was titled "Preamble and Resolution." The convention would recommend "the enactment of stringent laws to prevent the transit through these states of Texas or Cherokee cattle, from the first day of April to the last day of October." They also proposed to make any responsible party pay for "all damages that may result from the diffusion of any dangerous disease from animals in his ownership or possession."

I sat in shock among my friends as we contemplated the creation of many more states behaving in the same way as New York. If this legislation was to take hold with any kind of regularity, the cattle business was doomed.

After John Stanton Gould finished, a few minor changes were suggested by some of the delegates. The most significant of these was the approval of a change from "the first of April" to "the first of March" just to be safe…another whole month of isolation. The delegates also changed "the last day of October" to "the first of November" for consistency…another day lost.

When no further suggested changes were proposed, Lewis Allen offered the floor to Dr. William Kile of Illinois. "This proposed legislation may be well suited to a state like New York with its well defined points of ingress, but for a state like Illinois, with its two thousand miles of railroads and four hundred miles of ferry crossings along the Mississippi River, this legislation is preposterous and futile. It is impossible for such legislation to be enacted even if it is approved, which isn't likely. It is a document prepared by bureaucrats for bureaucrats. I strongly oppose it."

I had traveled enough of the state to know that what Dr. Kile was saying was true.

Dr. Mills of Michigan spoke up. "I don't appreciate the point that was just made by the doctor from Illinois. It is important that we stop the spread of the disease."

"I agree with Dr. Kile," Joseph McCoy shouted, standing near me in the gallery. "It is impractical to implement...and far too much power is given to these commissioners. They would have complete control of the state's commerce—not to mention far-reaching control beyond their state borders. For example, they could come into a state like this one and seize control of an entire convention of cattle commissioners!"

The hall erupted into shouting of all sorts. Several empty bottles were tossed from the gallery into the delegates' seating area. Both Lewis Allen and Governor Oglesby rose from their seats. They couldn't restore order.

This evening session was over.

CHAPTER SIXTY-FOUR

--- ✠ ---

M&W Railway Station
Alexander, Illinois
December 3, 1868

A blanket of smoke covered the town that was just beginning to awaken. I was happy to see John T. Alexander join us on the platform in the early-morning darkness as we gathered for the train ride to Springfield. He'd been briefed on the previous evening's events, and he wasn't about to miss the opportunity to say a few words about it today. John T. Alexander wasn't the kind of man who was going to stand by and watch a bunch of bureaucrats take away his business.

We sat in two rows of seats that faced each other in the second passenger car. "I doubt that this thing will be passed in Illinois," John T. Alexander said, "but if it is, we'll have to get one of our people into one of those commissioner positions. Any ideas, Jason?"

"I'll introduce one of John's friends by the name of Buck Lathrop to you today in Springfield," Jason said. "He would be perfect."

"If the wrong people get in there, they will ask for blackmail money to get your cattle through their districts," I said. "This whole thing is a mess."

"It's what you would expect from a convention of commission-ers," Joseph McCoy said. "If they were asked to draw up plans for a barn, you would see a barn like you've never seen before...no doors, no windows, no roof."

We laughed.

We needed that laugh.

"I'm glad you're feeling up to the trip today, Father," Jason said. "Some of these delegates won't be so bold when they have to look you in the eyes."

"You'd best keep me away from that Biggs fellow," John T. Alexander said.

"I'll keep an eye on Tanner Biggs," I said. "He's easy to find right now with that big bandage on his nose."

We laughed some more.

I got serious. "All joking aside, as I've told all of you before, he's an extremely dangerous man...a remorseless killer. He always carries at least one gun and a knife, and he knows how to use them. If he's near you, you never want to take your eyes off him."

"I'll bet that he's the one who shot Jerome," Rand Eaton said.

"Most likely," I said.

CHAPTER SIXTY-FIVE

*American Convention of
Cattle Commissioners
(Hall of the (House of Representatives
Springfield, Illinois
December 3, 1868
(Morning Session)*

People clustered around John T. Alexander when he entered the hall. I was surprised at how many of the delegates knew him. Even Governor Oglesby delayed taking his seat until after he had spoken with him for a few minutes.

Lewis Allen was clearly annoyed. He abruptly terminated all attempts to further amend the legislation that was approved in last evening's session. We knew that he would try to keep John T. Alexander away from the podium, but we had a plan for that. Danford Christie asked to speak.

"Ladies and gentlemen, I have appreciated your invitation to this convention. I am concerned that the restrictions that have been agreed upon may prohibit the growth of a fine industry. The people of Canada intend to continue to eat Texas beef that has been brought to market by good farmers. The gentleman who can best speak to that is my good friend, John T. Alexander, and I yield the remainder of my ten minutes of allocated time to him."

"This is out of order," Lewis Allen said. "Your request is denied."

Governor Oglesby immediately turned to Lewis Allen and whispered with him for a short time. "I have been reminded that I have set a precedent in this proceeding by allowing such procedure earlier,' Lewis Allen said, "so the gentleman may come forward to the podium as Mr. Christie suggested."

Rafner B. Hale stormed out of the hall, rudely brushing people aside.

John T. Alexander came forward from the back of the main floor of the hall, where he had been standing in anticipation of this moment. He shook hands with some of the delegates as he passed by them. He took a drink of water when he reached the speaker's podium.

The hall was silent. "Thank you for yielding your precious time, Mr. Christie. I will be brief. My purpose is to make sure that everyone understands what has occurred here in Springfield. You have attempted to govern over the commerce between states by creating a document that would be approved by each state individually. Each state will make its own changes, and there will be no two identical sets of legislation afterward. Little or no thought has been given to the *implementation* of this legislation. I submit that it is not able to be implemented in the way you so desire. Your actions taken in this convention will do nothing more than extend the 'fever run' that has been identified by the newspapers. Some time ago, I was lectured by a judge about the debilitating nature of too many rules and regulations...I'm sorry to say that he was so right."

John T. Alexander took another drink of water. "This is not to say that your suggestions aren't good. Many of them have already been implemented without the legislation, but the reason is that they are necessary for the cattle industry to continue to grow. Those in the business will see that it is done...that is what businesses do when they want to sell their goods and make a profit. I will pay back all of those who have been harmed in any way by my cattle, and I have been doing that without any law telling me that I had to do so. I also intend to compensate some of my neighbors in Tolono, but some of the trouble was caused by outlaws pulling down my fences...not by me." John T. Alexander made a point of looking up at the gallery before he continued. His eyes searched for Tanner Biggs.

"I will comply with the laws of the state of Illinois, and I will do my best to comply with the many laws of the many states through which my cattle must pass. I'm not a lawyer, and I don't intend to hire an army of lawyers in order to sell cattle. What I will do is bring up longhorn cattle from Texas, fatten them on grass and corn, and send them to market so people in all states can eat beef for a fair price. All the laws in the world aren't going to stop that from happening."

A loud cheer went up from both the main floor and the gallery. I think John T. Alexander had a bit more to say, but he chose to stop on this high note. It was a good decision. He'd made his point, and he'd made it well.

After John T. Alexander walked away from the podium, I noticed a few of the delegates get up and say their good-byes. They were heading for the railroad station to return home.

Joseph McCoy spoke next. "I want to clarify a point that came up briefly during yesterday's session. I think we must leave here with a perfectly clear understanding about it. I want to be certain that the southwestern cattle that have been wintered in the northern states will be considered in the same way as the native cattle when it comes to shipment during the restricted times. That is to say that, just like the native cattle, the Texas cattle that have wintered in the north aren't prohibited in any way by the restrictions."

Lewis Allen said, "That is my understanding, Mr. McCoy."

"It is an important point, Mr. President," McCoy said. "At this very moment, I have ten thousand Texas cattle arriving in Illinois and Indiana, and thousands more to follow. It is December, so those cattle are being transported during the unrestricted time, so they can be fattened during the winter months and sold in the spring or summer during the restricted period."

Lewis Allen said, "That is my understanding, Mr. McCoy. Remember, however, that those cattle must be properly certified as having been brought north during the unrestricted period."

Joseph McCoy seemed to be satisfied, so he left the podium. Jason turned to me and said, "I guess we're not out of business entirely."

"That's true," I said. "But you'll have to find the markets that will play fair."

Lewis Allen took care of a few other questions, and then he proceeded to bring the convention to a close by thanking all of those who had made it possible to bring this group of cattle commissioners together.

He was mildly complimentary to Governor Oglesby, but he lauded the contributions of his fellow commissioners from New York. Lewis Allen also thanked his boss, Rafner B. Hale, for his support, even though he had already departed.

"I have done as well as I know how in attempting to preside over this esteemed body," Lewis Allen said. "I am gratified at the confidence that you placed in me. I believe that we have done great work here and served our nation well by protecting its people and its commerce by suggesting rules and regulations of common sense. As time passes, history will mark this gathering as momentous. The convention now stands adjourned."

CHAPTER SIXTY-SIX

— ≡✦≡ —

John A. Alexander Farm
December 21, 1868

With the approach of Christmas, we tried to think about more pleasant things than the aftermath of the convention, but it was virtually impossible to get it off our minds. Many of the newspapers argued that the railroads were the most likely benefactors from the proceeding because it gave them a perfect opportunity to raise their rates.

I sat with the Alexander family after a fine supper on Monday night. I was leaving for Virginia tomorrow morning to spend the next several weeks with my cousin Stephen, who had moved there this past summer. I'd loaned him some money, and he'd managed to find a small place near where we'd grown up.

Because I was leaving, the Alexanders plucked some nicely wrapped gifts from under the Christmas tree for me. I was prepared for this, so I'd brought a few gifts of my own. They'd made me feel like a part of their family since I'd arrived here about eighteen months ago. They were wonderful people, and I'd already decided to continue to help them get through their challenges. At the same time, I recognized that the urge for me to go off on my own was growing stronger each day.

Jeanine held back her gift to last, and I did likewise. Jeanine's gift was in a small envelope. I was overjoyed when I discovered that she had given me the title to Sting, the Morgan that I'd been riding since I arrived on the place. Her father had passed the title to her after she'd lost her stable of Morgans. I'd managed to keep Sting alive by boarding him in Marker's Stable in town, away from the Texas cattle.

"I don't know what to say," I said. "I know you know this means a lot to me...I've grown attached to Sting." A short time later, I retrieved a package that I'd hidden in her father's study.

It was poorly wrapped, but she didn't seem to mind. She looked at the certificate that was enclosed in a frame with a glass cover. She studied it for quite some time—and then she laughed and cried and hugged me, all at the same time. "You found The Black's dam! He's fully registered now—so The Black is a purebred stallion. I'm speechless. How were you able to do this, John?"

"It took some digging, I must admit. I combed through records in Vermont and Virginia during my trips back east, I wrote a lot of letters, and I had some help from some good friends." I reached in my pocket and pulled out an envelope that contained the titles to the two Brunk Morgans from Kentucky that I'd recently purchased for her. The owner, Hal Price McGrath, had also included a two-year-old racehorse named Obenshain in the deal. The three horses would arrive on the train next week. These horses would be substantial additions to her stable.

"I met McGrath in New York when I saved him from being robbed on the street at night. He said that he ran a gambling house. He thanked me and asked for my name, and that was the end of it until I received a telegram from him about two months ago. He left New York with his profits and purchased a large place in Fayette

County, Kentucky, which he calls the McGrathiana Farm. He's interested in establishing a regular movement of horses between here and there."

She hugged me again, and I don't think either one of us wanted to let go, but her family was in the room...they were all smiling. Something special happened tonight, and everyone in the room knew it.

Later, Mary Alexander brought out a second pot of coffee, and the conversation turned to business. Everyone was fully aware of the financial strain that had resulted from the horrific losses over the past few months. I'd spent a lot of time with Jason and his father since the convention, working on a plan for survival. It was time to explain it to the rest of the family.

John T. Alexander stood in front of the fireplace, warming himself before he turned to face his family. "This state is likely to pass the legislation that has been suggested by the cattle commissioners. I don't think it's prudent to wait on this before acting. We will need to bring in a lot more cattle before the window closes on the first of March."

He walked over to where Jason and I sat before continuing. "You all know that we have a cash and credit problem. The three of us have worked out an arrangement that will transform some of the hired hands into our partners going forward. Part of their pay will be in the form of land, and they will use that land to raise corn and feed the Texas cattle under a contract with us. Under this arrangement, we can handle more cattle, and keep the business going."

"With our help, the men will build homes on their property and move their families there," I said. "They'll be close to the cattle, and they'll be able to watch them closely, keeping the likes of Tanner Biggs away."

"The value of the land has fallen for the moment, but in time, it will rise again," Jason said. "We need to make a big push to handle more cattle over the next several years than we've ever handled before."

John T. Alexander smiled. "It's a bold plan, but I think this arrangement will help to make it work. I'm prepared to start signing over the land right now—if you all agree to it. I need everyone with me on this."

"I hate to part with the land," Mary Alexander said, "but I understand what we're up against. I'll stay here until we are down to our last acre, and then I'll clean other people's houses if that's what it takes."

Mary Alexander's statement captured the essence of the family commitment and closed the deal. Nothing more needed to be said. John T. Alexander walked over and put his hand on her shoulder.

Knowing the family as I did, I'd already drawn up the contracts earlier in the day and placed them on John T. Alexander's desk. Ten men would each get five hundred acres. I was sure that the contracts would all be signed by the time I returned from Virginia.

CHAPTER SIXTY-SEVEN

+—◄◊►—+

Jacksonville, Illinois
February 9, 1869

"This thing has gone far enough," General Murray McConnell said. "What started out simply as land speculation has now turned into something much greater, and I will have no part of it." He wadded up the pieces of paper that rested on top of his desk and tossed them into the nearby fireplace. It was Tuesday night, and it was cold outside.

Red Beard and Tanner Biggs looked at each other and shook their heads. They squirmed in their seats across from McConnell's desk. "I'm afraid that it's a bit too late for that, General," Red Beard said. "A lot of very powerful people are involved in this deal, and they don't take kindly to others dropping out at a critical time...you should understand that."

"Plotting with the railroads to undermine their contracts with John T. Alexander goes way beyond anything that I ever had in mind, Mr. Jones, or whoever you are. I thought it was about a few land deals," General McConnell said. "You're fools to think that

Edward Hinrichsen is going to sit still and let the railroads cheat his good friend."

"You needn't worry about Mr. Hinrichsen," Red Beard said, changing the tone of his voice. "He'll be dealt with as necessary. All obstacles either have been or will be removed. Many millions of dollars are at stake here...you understand that, don't you?"

General Murray McConnell leaned forward in his chair. "I understand perfectly. I understand that you're criminals who are proposing to break the law, and what I'm trying to get you to understand is that I'm not going to break the law for any amount of money. Do you understand that?"

"Unfortunately, I do." Red Beard rose from his chair. He lifted his coat from the rack and slowly put it on. After placing his hat on his head, he touched the brim. "General, Mr. Biggs, I bid you gentlemen a good night."

After Red Beard left the room, Tanner Biggs slipped a knife from his boot and smiled.

CHAPTER SIXTY-EIGHT

— ⚌ —

Springfield, Illinois
February 10, 1869

I met Buck Lathrop and Brock McMunn at the Chenery House for a late breakfast. They had news about legislation that was going to be introduced at the Twenty-Sixth General Assembly. I hadn't seen them since the end of the American Convention of Cattle Commissioners in early December. We socialized until our breakfast was brought to the table.

"We don't know who's going to present the bill, probably Henry Snapp or Edwin Harlan, but we're not sure at this point," Brock McMunn said. "They're keeping their cards close to the vest, but there is likely to be a good deal of support because of all of the bad press that followed the convention."

"Don't remind me," I said. "I was reading about it when I was in Virginia. The people there thought it was pretty funny, but I sure didn't."

"John, they're going to try to ban the Texas cattle from the state…entirely, and this time they have a reason," Buck Lathrop said. "They want to go way beyond what was proposed by the cattle commissioners. By keeping the cattle out of Illinois, they essentially keep the cattle out of the East since almost everything must ride the railroads that pass through this state to get there. Huge sums of money have come in here from New York to buy favors. It's bad legislation, and we'll help you fight it."

"This news comes on top of Joseph McCoy's report that the railroad people are trying to establish their own railhead to the west of Abilene," I said. "They are promising better transport rates to the drovers, and the railroad will own the stockyards there. Joseph says they're also increasing his transport rates and stirring up the local residents in Abilene who've had their fill of the unruly cowboys. It's all so well conceived that I have to believe that it is an organized effort—bankers, railroaders, land speculators, legislators—too much to be a coincidence."

"But...who?"

"That's what I intend to find out, Brock," I said. "John T. Alexander gave me some good advice—he told me to follow the money. That makes a lot of sense. After all, isn't that what this is all about?"

"Yes, no doubt. And I think your boss is right—someone will eventually come forward. And then we'll know who they are and what they're after."

"Maybe not," Buck Lathrop said. "It could just be those New Yorkers protecting their domain. Pretty simple—keep out the Texas cattle so they can keep their prices up."

"I think there's more to it than that," I said.

The three of us spent an hour discussing a strategy for combating the forces that would try to legislate an end to John T. Alexander's livelihood. Because of his ability to provide credible testimony, we felt that it was essential to get Joseph McCoy in front of the legislators. It was going to be very difficult to get him to return to Illinois when his own business in Abilene was being threatened, but it would have to be done.

Just then, a young boy with a bag full of newspapers entered the room. He held the special edition of the *Illinois Daily Journal* in his raised hand and exclaimed, "Paper...paper...read all about it! General Murray McConnell murdered in Jacksonville last night... read all about it!"

I immediately purchased three copies for us. "He's a close friend of Mr. Alexander," I said. "Somehow, General McConnell's death is connected to this whole nightmare."

⌘   ⌘   ⌘

After breakfast, I boarded the train for Tolono. I was supposed to be meeting with Rand Eaton and John T. Alexander's attorney, George McConnell, but I knew that he would be staying in Jacksonville to tend to his father's funeral services as well as the investigation into the killing. I decided to go ahead and meet with Rand Eaton because the lawsuit that had been filed by Isaac Larmon and some of his friends needed immediate attention.

The plaintiffs accused John T. Alexander, Joseph Sullivant, and John Sidell of killing their cattle that had been held in the fenced areas adjacent to the public roadways where the three defendants had driven their Texas cattle to and from the railroad stockyards in Tolono.

Because of George McConnell's situation in Jacksonville, I intended to find a trustworthy attorney from the local area to assist with the case, which was coming to trial very soon. This case was one of about thirty damage suits that had been filed in Champaign County alone. John T. Alexander was involved in some of the others as well; he was going to be spending a good deal of money in legal fees over the next several years.

After taking care of this matter, I wanted to arrange a meeting with Mr. H. to discuss the problems with the railroad contracts. General Stock Agent Hinrichsen could be anywhere between Tolono and Albany, so catching up with him would take some time.

CHAPTER SIXTY-NINE

Fifteen Miles West of Hays City, Kansas
June 22, 1869

I had to look twice to make sure that I wasn't dreaming before I would acknowledge that I was riding a Seventh Cavalry horse provided by General George Custer. Many of the other guests wisely rode in covered wagons that shielded them from the blazing sunshine on this hot Tuesday afternoon. Preferring the attention of the ladies, General Custer also sat in one of the wagons.

After tracking down Mr. H., and dashing back and forth between New York and Illinois, I began to figure out the nebulous process that the railroads utilized to account for their shipping costs. It was no wonder that the business was so profitable.

Much to my surprise, the TW&W's general stock agent also arranged for me to join a prestigious group of travelers on a buffalo-hunting trip to what the newspapers called the Great American Desert. I had somewhat reluctantly agreed to accept the invitation because I didn't want to offend Mr. H. I had no idea what I was getting into.

After a sumptuous breakfast, we departed Hays City, Kansas. Four of the many wagons were filled with newspaper reporters from all over the world. After a few hours, we reached a point where we looked out upon a large herd of buffalo.

Fifty of Custer's cavalry riders were prepared to stop them if they charged in our direction. I doubted that they would be able to do the job, but I was hoping that I wouldn't have to find out if I was right.

New York Senator Roscoe Conkling was mounted on a horse to my right, and the entrepreneur Jay Gould was on my left. Mr. H. had promised me a rare opportunity to meet some very important people, and he hadn't exaggerated.

"Won't they run when we start shooting?" Senator Conkling asked.

"They will," I said, "but there are so many of them that shooting wildly into the herd will still bring some down."

"I'm surprised that they didn't run away as soon as we arrived," Jay Gould said.

I had learned a little bit about the buffalo from conversations with Joseph McCoy. "They're not real smart," I said. "I'm not sure that we're real smart being this close to them, not to mention the thousands of Indians around here."

They both turned and looked at me upon hearing my comment, and they weren't smiling. This was as far away from the large cities that most of the guests had ever been. General Custer was taking a great risk bringing them out here. I was well aware of his brazen reputation because I'd seen him in action during the war.

I chuckled to think that maybe Mr. H. had given me his place on the guest roster for good reason. I hoped that I would have an opportunity to send him a letter of thanks upon my safe return to civilization.

I'd introduced myself to Roscoe Conkling and Jay Gould when we gathered in Kansas City two days ago. I was shocked to find that six railroads now had stations in Kansas City. Both men knew more about me than I knew about them. I realized that it was common practice for people like them to know a lot about others because they were seldom at a disadvantage in anything they did…except when it came to buffalo hunting.

Senator Conkling challenged me. He picked a target. He missed.

I dropped the large bull that the senator had selected with a single shot behind the ear. He killed a small calf with his second shot. "A smaller target requires a better shot," he said. The animals didn't stampede. They just moved around some as we fired away.

Our party of inexperienced shooters dropped only about a dozen buffalo, but I counted about twenty wounded animals that ambled off behind the rest of the herd when they finally moved away from us.

I thought we were going to skin the animals and take the meat, but General Custer said that it was much too hot to take anything back with us, so everything was left to rot in the Kansas sun. After the shoot, we immediately turned around and headed back to Hays City. I was disgusted with the whole thing.

"I read that the Cumberland County Circuit Court ruled in favor of your employer," Roscoe Conkling said, stroking his freshly cut beard. "It was clever of Alexander and his two friends, Sullivant and Sidell, to get the case moved there." That was a compliment, coming from one of the most powerful men in the country who often served as President Grant's spokesperson.

"I think they would've won if the case had stayed in Tolono," I said. "There's no valid evidence that the Texas cattle cause any sickness when they pass by other cattle that are fenced in. This thing has been blown so far out of proportion that it's truly ridiculous."

"Perhaps," he said, "but I doubt that he will win many more of his cases as they move to the East." Senator Conkling smelled blood like a ravenous wolf.

Jay Gould smelled money. He'd already taken control of the Erie Railroad, and he was rapidly taking control of four other railroads in the West, one being the Union Pacific. There was also talk that he was hoarding gold. "I admire men like John T. Alexander," he said. "They keep the railroads busy."

"He's having a lot of trouble with the railroads right now," I said. "They don't do a very good job of honoring their contracts. After he gets his Texas cattle lawsuits taken care of, he'll be coming after the railroads...and he's going to win a lot of those cases, too." I rode on ahead before they had a chance to respond. Perhaps I needed to improve my ability to make friends.

On the night before we departed Hays City, I sat at a large table with Rutherford Hayes, James Fisk, Julian Sturtevant, Porter Alexander, and Henrietta Green. The conversation was fascinating. It's amazing what one can learn by listening to such people.

Henrietta Green particularly intrigued me. She was a self-made success in a world dominated by powerful men. She made a point of noting that she was here only because the trip was free.

⌘   ⌘   ⌘

On Thursday, I sat on the train next to a reporter from the *New York Times*. He asked me a lot of questions about John T. Alexander. I was happy to provide information about a man whom I greatly admired.

Porter Alexander was sitting nearby and overheard part of the conversation. "I'm actually a distant relative of your employer," he said. "You don't recognize me, do you, Captain Demsond?"

I looked at him more closely. "General?"

He smiled. It was then that I truly recognized Porter Alexander. I'd known him as General E. P. Alexander during the war. He was in charge of the Confederacy's artillery. The opportunity to meet him hadn't come about until now. He was highly respected.

"I'm sorry that I didn't recognize you, General Alexander."

"That's not a problem," he said. "I'm out of uniform now." He moved over to take the seat next to me that was just vacated by the newspaperman. He explained that he was working for the railroads now, and he offered to help me understand how the transportation rates were established. "I intend to publish a book about railway practices sometime in the future," he said.

He willingly answered a number of my questions. "The rates are based upon the value of the services rendered. It costs more to haul freight across a mountain, so generally the railroad charges more to do so. However, if another operator, such as a steamship, competes for that same business, the railroad may charge less than its cost in order to secure the future business with that customer. The whole thing is actually quite complex."

We talked all the way to Abilene. I learned a great deal. I remained in Abilene while the others in our group went on to Kansas City. Joseph McCoy told me that he believed he could transport as many as two hundred thousand head of Texas cattle out of Abilene by the end of the year—all of them having been wintered north of Texas and the Indian Territory, certification of that being rather easy to obtain.

His ability to forge a new market out of nowhere had won him the title of the Real McCoy. Nevertheless, he was being pushed out of Abilene by the new mayor and his supporters, which included the railroad. He was forced to sell his ownership in the Drovers' Cottage and the stockyards at ridiculous prices in order to pay off some of his mounting debt. McCoy intended to move to a small place on the Smoky Hill River for the winter and fatten up a herd of one thousand Texas cattle for sale in the spring.

It saddened me to see what had happened to this man whom I believed would be identified in history as a significant contributor to the growth of this great nation, but the lesson educated me. I could see that it wasn't possible to take on issues with the railroad without having strong support from very powerful people. I'd met a number of them on the trip to Hays City, but I presumed that few of them supported John T. Alexander.

CHAPTER SEVENTY

— ≡✦≡ —

John T. Alexander Farm
August 6, 1869

Friends and family gathered in the heat of the late morning to congratulate John T. Alexander. On this very Friday, a lengthy article about John T. Alexander, the Cattle King, appeared in the *New York Times*.

The entire six-hundred-word article was transmitted to the Western Union office in Alexander and rushed out to the farm by the office manager himself, free of charge. Word spread quickly, and others from the town and the nearby area began to appear as the morning wore on.

The article described John T. Alexander as "a plain, homespun farmer—tall, good-looking, free and easy in manners." He was praised for the contributions that he had made to the entire state of Illinois because "his business each and every year amounts to millions of dollars."

His land holdings were described as being "about nine miles square, and all good land." He was said to have "5,000 acres of growing corn," and that he was selling cattle at the rate of "1,000 to 2,000 head each week." He was described as having "risen to this great prominence by his own talent, energy, and integrity."

The article was going to go a long way in improving the Cattle King's reputation in New York. I recognized the author's name right away—it was the man that I'd met on the train. He seemed to be intent upon countering the injustices of the past when John T. Alexander had been blamed for many deaths in New York City.

John T. Alexander was smiling as he stepped forward to say a few words. "I want to thank you all for being here to share this great honor with me at my home. I am proud to be a resident of Morgan County, and I thank God that I'm able to be a cattleman. There's no finer business on the face of the earth."

One by one, his friends and neighbors came forward to congratulate him. Mary made a huge cake and pitchers of lemonade for them.

I hoped that history would be kind to this man, for he was the sort who could easily be overlooked. The nearby town wouldn't have been named after him had it not been established by Edward Hinrichsen, his close friend, who always joked that "if I'd named it *Hinrichsen*, they would have called it something else anyway."

I saw greatness in John T. Alexander...greatness that included humility, but history doesn't always reward humility. All too often, the humble are thought to be weak. This is seldom true. Humility requires courage.

CHAPTER SEVENTY-ONE

McPherson's Tavern
Alexander, Illinois
October 13, 1869

One significant outcome from the convention in Springfield was John T. Alexander's decision to use Abilene as his only source of Texas cattle. The testimony convinced him that the primary source of the problem, whatever it was, had come from the river routes. The remarkable near disappearance of the problems of a year earlier seemed to confirm his decision.

The cases of sickness in the native cattle were not extensive during the entire summer following the outbreak of a year earlier, and John T. Alexander resumed his large weekly shipments of cattle to Chicago and to the East, with the exception of New York. His decision to enlist the assistance of his ten associates and others in the area to help him prepare the cattle for shipment paid off so well that he considered doing the same thing with his Broadlands acres.

His profits went a long way in reducing his debt, but it certainly wasn't eliminated. It would take several good years to accomplish that.

Even though I certainly didn't ask for it, John T. Alexander made sure that the loans from my bank accounts were also being paid off a little at a time. He surprised me by including a nice piece of property that he owned near Jacksonville as part of my pay. Not surprisingly, I allowed him to graze his cattle on my land.

John T. Alexander's resumption of good fortune uplifted the town named after him. More buildings appeared around the square that bordered Central Park, including a land office to the north of McPherson's. A large grain elevator was constructed near the south railroad sidetrack for storage and shipment of excess grain. I questioned the need for this, but it followed the nationwide pattern of overbuilding along the railroads.

The day was filled with surprises. It was late on Wednesday afternoon, and McPherson's was shoulder to shoulder with people who were very excited at the opportunity to meet my special guest, John Mosby, who was chief consul to the American ambassador in Hong Kong. I had served under Colonel Mosby in the Confederacy, and he was now as much a hero to Union supporters as he was in the South.

Shortly after he arrived, we met privately to conduct the business of setting up a means of shipping John T. Alexander's Texas cattle to Hong Kong beginning early next year. All I had to do was find a way to get the cattle to the West Coast, and since the *golden spike* was pounded home in May to connect the Union Pacific Railroad with the Central Pacific Railroad, this task was now feasible. Corn-fed beef in Hong Kong would command top dollar. Colonel Mosby assured me that the people there had read the story in the *New York Times* about John T. Alexander, and they wanted John T. Alexander beef.

Colonel Mosby also passed on some interesting information that he had picked up while spending some time in New York. "You can't imagine the surprise when I heard your name mentioned," he said. "I was so happy to hear that you had disturbed their little haven. Nice work, Captain."

I took him to meet John T. Alexander and showed him around a bit, and then we stopped in at McPherson's. Colonel Mosby, who wasn't a drinker, had more beers than I could count lined up along the bar because everyone wanted to be able to say that they'd bought John Mosby a beer. I started handing out the beers as the chief consul shook hands with everyone, some more than once.

He said some very nice things about me. "Captain John Demsond saved me from the hands of the enemy on more than one occasion." Men were buying beers for me.

The word in town was spreading fast, and a crowd was already forming outside the front entrance.

"Why didn't you tell me about this?" William Orear asked when he finally reached us. "We could have done something special at the bank." William Orear often reached out well beyond the immediate area for new accounts for his Alexander National Bank with notorious special deals. In late June, he had offered a wagonload of fireworks to anyone who signed up for a new savings account with at least $1,000 by the Fourth of July. I shuddered to think of what he might have done with Colonel John Mosby, the legendary *gray ghost*.

"He doesn't disclose his travel plans for obvious reasons," I said. "He came knocking on my hotel room door early this morning. I couldn't believe it was him."

"Will he be here long?"

"Like I said, I don't know. I suspect that he will run off to the train station and hop on the next train back to Springfield when it arrives in about a half hour."

And that's exactly what Colonel Mosby did. He was an expert at making a sudden appearance followed by a sudden disappearance. He did it all the way through the War Between the States.

McPherson's buzzed for hours after Mosby left. They permanent-ly marked the floor where Colonel Mosby had stood at the bar. I was a bit of a special citizen in the town of Alexander from that day forward. They called me Captain Demsond.

⌘ ⌘ ⌘

Jeanine Alexander accepted my invitation for supper at the Grande Jeanne Hotel that same evening. We'd grown closer with time. When I thought about leaving in the future, I had difficulty thinking about leaving without her.

I wasn't sure what to do about that.

The night air was chilling. We arrived just as everyone was being seated for the meal in the large dining room across from the lobby. My mouth dropped open when I saw Red Beard sitting in one of the twelve chairs at the largest table located near the entrance to the kitchen...the same table to which Jeanine and I were directed.

Bob Jones seemed quite pleased when we sat down directly across from him.

I saw that Jeanine recognized him right away. He stood and reached across the table. "Miss Alexander...Mr. Demsond, my pleasure."

"Mr. Jones," I said, shaking his large hand. "What brings you this way?"

He didn't act a bit surprised that I knew his name. "I'm setting up a new land office here in town," he said.

"Are you buying or selling?" Jeanine asked.

"A bit of both. It's a good time to buy with the land values being down right now, but I eventually hope to sell some of the remaining holdings of the late John Grigg from Philadelphia."

"I understand that he owned a lot of the land in this area at one time," I said.

"All of it," he said. "He was the largest landholder in the country for many years."

Bob Jones discovered that Jeanine and I weren't willing to discuss anything about her father's business, so he quickly lost interest in us.

We were fine with that. Nevertheless, the fact that he'd shown up right here in Alexander was more than a coincidence. Jason Alexander always reminded me that he didn't believe in coincidences—and neither did I.

Follow the money.

CHAPTER SEVENTY-TWO

Chicago, Illinois
May 28, 1870

In a matter of a few short years, the population center of the country moved from Philadelphia to Chicago, continuing a westward movement at the rate of a hundred miles every ten years since the national census was first taken in 1790. The center of activity on the railroads moved accordingly. Chicago was the best place for me to go to negotiate a large number of contracts with the railroads in a short time.

In addition to cattle, John T. Alexander was now shipping hogs to market. It was easy to raise the hogs along with the cattle because they required little attention due to their ability to generally take care of themselves by scavenging. I was able to negotiate good deals for both cattle and hogs because of our numbers, but the railroads pushed hard for guarantees that they would be the sole carrier on certain routes. In return, I would push for their lowest price and a credit if another customer negotiated an even lower price after I signed our deal.

With General Stock Agent Hinrichsen's able assistance, along with the knowledge gained from my lengthy conversation with

Porter Alexander a year earlier, I had devised a way to perform an audit to be sure that the railroads adhered to their side of the bargain. But I wasn't about to disclose my methodology to them—as far as they knew, I had no idea about their accounting process.

On this pleasant Saturday morning, I was signing contracts with several railroad companies that terminated in Chicago. I had taken a room at the new Palmer House Hotel located at the corner of State and Quincy because the railroads that passed through Chicago were holding a conference there. The hotel's grand opening was set for September, but it had already started to admit guests to some of the spacious 225 rooms.

By noon, I had a stack of railroad contracts signed by officials from the Chicago & Northwestern; the Chicago, Burlington, & Quincy; the Chicago, Milwaukee, & St. Paul; the Chicago, Rock Island, & Pacific; the Illinois Central; the Chicago, Alton, & St. Louis; the Fort Wayne & Pennsylvania; the New York, Chicago, and St. Louis; and the Lake Shore and Michigan Southern.

I met Gustavus Swift in the magnificent dining room for dinner. The bright sunshine was flowing in through the large windows, but they were all closed up in order to keep out the foul smell of the large city that was carried by the westerly breeze. His trips to Alexander were now quite rare. I didn't pry into his relationship with Jeanine, but I assumed that he'd asked for her hand in marriage, and she'd refused. We avoided the topic entirely.

"I'm happy to see that J.T. is getting back to where he was during the war," Gustavus said. "They shut him down in New York, but that doesn't seem to have hurt his business at all. Rafner Hale is gradually losing his control out there, so I suspect that the New York market will open up very soon."

"A good number of Texas cattle actually get into that market, but only if Hale profits from it," I said. "He doesn't leave much margin for anybody else, so it's not worth it for us at the moment."

"Other markets are the benefactors...we're not complaining," he said. "I've heard that as many as half a million head of Texas cattle will move up from Texas to west Kansas this year. I have to pay more to compete with the other packinghouses, but the large quantity of available cattle still allows me to turn a nice profit."

"I think the demand for beef will hold up," I said. "The railroads are dropping their transport prices because of the competition—that helps Mr. Alexander to maintain his margin—it's still a good business." I didn't share specific numbers with Gustavus Swift, but I was sure that he understood the economics. John T. Alexander was clearing about $25 a head, and he was selling almost two thousand head every week. By my calculations, he should have all of his debt paid off by the end of this year, or early next year at the latest.

I figured that this milestone would mark a good point for me to depart for the West.

⌘　⌘　⌘

At that same moment, four people sat in the Empire State Hotel over eight hundred miles away in Albany, New York. They'd finished their dinner and moved to a quiet corner in the main lobby.

"We almost had him," Raven said, looking at Mink.

Her gaunt features were misleading. "I just couldn't shut down all of the banks," Mink said bitterly. "He had some local friends that kept him going...and that young Confederate officer friend of his by the name of Demsond had some money as well."

"Yes, he's turned out to be a bit of a problem, hasn't he?" Raven said, almost laughing.

"Should I have Biggs remove him?" Bear asked.

"Tanner Biggs has caused us enough trouble," Raven said. "Try to keep him under control, if that's possible."

Bear shrugged. He didn't like Tanner Biggs, but he'd found that he was very useful. He planned to eliminate him when he was no longer needed. He hadn't forgotten that Tanner Biggs was a despised former Rebel.

"The Abilene operation will be shut down by next year when the Atchison, Topeka, & Santa Fe Railroad extends its line to Newton," Badger said. "They will reach Wichita on the Arkansas River shortly afterward. The Kansas Pacific Railroad is setting up their new stockyards at a point just west of Fort Harker, about sixty-five miles from Abilene."

"The Lawrence, Leavenworth, and Galveston Railroad is building stockyards in Coffeyville, just north of the Indian Territory and west of Joplin, Missouri," Bear said. "They just might grab up all of the Cherokee cattle."

"We have our hooks set well into the entire business at this point, so there's no need to worry," Mink said. Badger and Bear didn't like her condescending attitude, but Raven seemed to enjoy it.

"I worry that the railroads are overextended," Raven said. "Their freight agents have told me that they are charging as little as one dollar for an entire carload of cattle. They're losing a bundle if they're doing very much of that. They must be borrowing like crazy."

"They are," Mink said. "That's good for the banks. And don't you go worrying about the railroads—they're doing all right."

Raven winked at Mink. "It's a delicate puzzle with many parts that are loosely fit together," he said. "As long as something doesn't come along and jar it apart, we're fine."

CHAPTER SEVENTY-THREE

--- ⊯ ---

John S. Alexander Farm
October 8, 1871

I'd lost count of how many wonderful meals I'd consumed at the Alexander residence...probably more than any other person who wasn't part of the family. The thought of becoming *part of the family* had entered my mind on more than one occasion. After Jeanine Alexander had lost interest in Gustavus Swift, I was certain that she had turned down his marriage proposal and decided to remain a single woman. I didn't want to ruin our friendship by making my own offer.

As we sat around the fireplace in the expansive room adjacent to the dining room listening to our good friend Joseph McCoy, I found myself fixating on Jeanine and thinking how wonderful it would be to see her beautiful face first thing in the morning...every morning.

"John...John...what do you think?" I wasn't sure who had asked the question, or what the question was.

Jeanine Alexander laughed.

I looked around the room with a plea for help stuck to my face. Mary Alexander chuckled and rescued me. "Joseph's thoughts about Kansas City, John—are you in agreement?"

Joseph McCoy had moved to Kansas City because he was convinced that Kansas City would soon become the center of the cattle business in the entire country. He argued that its location in the geographical center of the country would guarantee its success.

He noted that half of the six hundred thousand Texas cattle that arrived in western Kansas so far this year had also arrived in Kansas City. "That's along with about fifty thousand hogs, five thousand sheep, and one thousand horses," he said. "We formed the Kansas City Stock Yard Company, which has a complete feed and transfer station with yards, lanes, alleys, scales, and barns...even large business offices. We can handle ten thousand head of cattle and ten thousand hogs at the same time and not break a sweat. We'll double its size by the end of next year."

I'd seldom seen Joseph McCoy so excited. "As soon as the railroad forced Edward Hinrichsen into retirement, I invited him to come to Kansas City and help us with the design. He did a great job—there's nothing like it anywhere else in the world."

"But...what about Chicago?" I asked. "That's where the action is today."

Joseph McCoy was quick to reply. "Chicago doesn't have room to expand. It's already overcrowded, and they don't have a good way to remove the waste from the stockyards and the packinghouses. They didn't plan well...we planned well in Kansas City."

"I suppose I could start sending some cattle to the Kansas City packinghouses in addition to Chicago," John T. Alexander said.

"That would be a big help," Joseph McCoy said. "People watch what you do." Joseph McCoy stood up and walked over to the fireplace to warm his hands. He turned and leaned back against the mantel. "More important, what I need you to do, J.T., is to take the leadership role in the new livestock men's association that I'm going to form in Kansas City as soon as possible."

"What's that?" Jerome Alexander asked.

"It's the piece of the puzzle that is missing today. It's the organization that will prevent the railroads and banks from manipulating the stockmen by taking advantage of their lack of knowledge about transport prices and interest rates. It's the direction that all commerce will take in the future—it's organization by association."

"It makes a lot of sense," John T. Alexander said. "Can you pull everyone together?"

"I'm trying to get it formed up by next year," Joseph McCoy said.

"I'm willing to do it," John T. Alexander said. "There'll have to be an election, of course."

"Of course, but you're the best-known cattleman in the country—the Cattle King. You will get voted in without a doubt."

"It's settled then," Jason Alexander said. "We'll slowly start moving some business to Kansas City."

Just then, a Western Union messenger arrived with a telegram. It was late, so we knew that this was probably some bad news. It was from my friend Brock McMunn, who was in Chicago. I read the message and felt my face going pale.

"Brock writes that there's a terrible fire in Chicago. He says that the stockyards are burning up...and everything else."

CHAPTER SEVENTY-FOUR

M&W Railway
September 22, 1872

"That was some mess," Jeanine Alexander said. "I'm glad to get it all sorted out. It was nice to have you there with me."

"It was no trouble," I said. "You knew how to handle the whole thing. I was pretty much along for the ride."

Jeanine had purchased a Morgan stallion named Slasher from David Heustis in Vermont, but she discovered that Slasher's grand-sire was the same as that of The Black, namely Sherman Black Hawk. Jeanine wasn't happy with that, so I'd helped her to arrange a three-way trade that resulted in her receiving a two-year-old Morgan named Aristos from a stable in Vermont. One of the three owners was there to sign the necessary papers. Hal Price McGrath from Kentucky had big plans for the future, and he was happy to make the trade; he would receive Slasher in the deal and send one of his horses to Vermont.

It was Sunday, and we were due to arrive in Alexander with the horse by late afternoon. He was brown and stood sixteen hands tall with a wonderful depth of body. Jeanine and I could both see that he was going to be fast.

"You're too humble, John," she said. "The contracts that you have encouraged me to use have been a great protection for me. They've saved me more than once. But don't change—humility is a good quality in a man."

The countryside was painting itself with the colors of the fall in the windows of the train as we moved through Ohio. I had enjoyed these past few days, and I really hadn't spent this kind of time with Jeanine since we went to Texas a few years ago. That was an entirely different situation.

"What are your long-term plans?" I asked.

She smiled. "Tomorrow, I'm going to Jacksonville to go shopping with mother."

"Longer than that," I said, smiling back.

"I don't know," she said. "What about you?"

"I asked you first," I said.

She shrugged.

"I've thought about going west," I said. "It's good horse country, you know."

"I've heard that," she said.

CHAPTER SEVENTY-FIVE

Kansas City, Missouri
September 18, 1873

John T. Alexander sold almost all of his cattle at the stockyards in
Kansas City after the great fire in Chicago. Even though impres-
sive efforts were made to rebuild the city, the progress was slow.
Widespread corruption seemed to infiltrate the new Chicago, and
well-known businesses moved out. Many of them went to Kansas
City, now a city of over forty thousand people.

Joseph McCoy's efforts to establish Kansas City as the livestock
center of the country had begun to pay off well before the fire in
Chicago. And two years later, on a cool Thursday morning, his dream
to organize the livestock men became reality.

Shortly after the meeting opened, the two thousand attendees
voted John T. Alexander to be the first president of the National
Association of Livestock Men. Joseph McCoy was elected secretary,
and W. H. Winants was elected treasurer. The association would
be headquartered in Kansas City, where both McCoy and Winants
resided.

The annual dues were set at one hundred dollars per member in recognition of the large amount of work that needed to be done up front, including hiring a part-time lobbyist in Washington and printing a monthly newsletter. The newsletter would contain the rates of freight, bank loans, stockyard charges, and feed charges in the areas of interest to all of the members of the association.

I watched in awe as Joseph McCoy energized the participants with the possibilities of the association and collected much of the dues immediately. He asked me to stay close to Treasurer W. H. Winants until the man could get the money to the Armour Brothers' Bank, where he was employed. I understood that my role was that of a bodyguard rather than a watchdog because I knew that Winants and McCoy were old friends from back in Abilene.

When the morning session was adjourned for dinner, W. H. Winants and I headed for the bank. We knew that something was wrong as soon as we walked out into the street because we saw a huge crowd gathered in front of the First National Bank of Kansas City, the largest bank west of St. Louis. The bank's president, Howard Holden, was pleading with the people.

W. H. Winants recognized a friend standing nearby and asked, "What's going on?"

"The bank's closed," he said. "There's a sign that says they won't be open again for at least a week."

I saw fear in the eyes of W. H. Winants, and he took off running headlong in the direction of the Armour Brothers' Bank. I stayed with him all the way.

There was a line there, too. The bank was open, and it was still accepting deposits, but it was refusing withdrawals. No one was depositing, and I warned W. H. Winants not to deposit the association's money. "I'll mark it and put it in my safe," he said.

Winants wormed his way inside while I remained outside near the crowd. I saw John T. Alexander and Joseph McCoy hurriedly walking in my direction. We all knew what was happening—it had been predicted for months. The only thing missing had been the trigger.

"Jay Cooke and Company shut its doors in New York this morning," Joseph McCoy said. The prominent financial house had excessively speculated in land and railroads across the entire country. The government had done the same, printing money as if there was no end in sight.

"With the telegraph, news spreads like wildfire, so the panic has come this far already," John T. Alexander said. There was fear in his eyes. "I heard someone say that the stock exchange is shutting down to avoid a run on equities. This thing is massive. I need to get home on the next available train."

"You and everyone else," Joseph McCoy said. "I think our association meeting is ended."

⌘ ⌘ ⌘

We stopped at each town along the way back to Alexander to check up on the latest news. The stories magnified. Great Britain and Germany were pulling back the money that the United States borrowed from them. One of the largest banks in the country, E. W. Clark and Company, closed down for good. People were being killed in riots.

The whole family was waiting for John T. Alexander at the train station. A lot of other people had gathered when they noticed the Alexander family standing there. The station agent, Henry Fitch, grumbled and reluctantly lighted some additional torches for the crowd.

As soon as we stepped onto the platform, the news came at us like a storm.

"President Grant has gone into hiding."

"William Orear has closed up the bank."

"The railroad wants cash up front before they will ship anything."

"Rand Eaton says they're pulling down his fences again."

Some pushing and shoving began. I pulled my pistol and fired a shot into the air. "Let's go home, folks. It's been a long day."

CHAPTER SEVENTY-SIX

The Gavel Inn
Springfield, Illinois
December 1, 1873

Life as we knew it changed drastically. Cash was king—few transactions were conducted anywhere without it. The government printed more money, which served only to require more cash to make a purchase. No one got ahead.

The streets of Springfield, and other large cities across the country, were filled with people seeking a handout in order to stay alive. Most of the destitute were veterans and immigrants.

Tents were visible everywhere as people had been pushed from their homes when they couldn't make their payments. It was very cold. The bodies of the dead were placed in front of the tents, where they would freeze and eventually be picked up by the few city workers who still had a job.

The new mayor of Jacksonville, George McConnell, the son of the murdered General Murray McConnell, established shelters in the city's buildings for the veterans and the others who were homeless. The Harvard Law School graduate continued to assist John T.

Alexander with his legal affairs. Additional attorneys were being retained in anticipation of the coming legal battles.

I sat quietly with Brock McMunn and Buck Lathrop in
Springfield. The Gavel Inn was nearly empty. "How's your boss doing?" Brock McMunn asked.

"He was lucky enough to have some cash on hand, so that's been
getting him by, but he couldn't purchase the cattle that he needed
before the winter set in," I said. "That will make for a rough year
coming up. He's paying off his men in land, promissory notes, and a
little bit of cash, which he'll run out of very soon."

"He'll have to sell some of his land to Bob Jones, like everyone
else," Buck Lathrop said.

"Why'd you have to bring him up?" I asked. "I was enjoying
this beer until you said that. I've never trusted Red Beard since the
moment I saw him with a bunch of hoodlums at the Kansas and
Missouri border."

Buck Lathrop nodded. "Bob Jones, or Red Beard as you call him,
is a strange one, but he's made a lot of money. He sells land until there's
a glut, and then he stops and waits. When the price bottoms out, or a
foreclosure occurs, he crawls in like a snake and buys it back."

"It's hard to quarrel with success," Brock McMunn said. "He's
connected with some serious money in Philadelphia and New York...
political ties, too."

"What are you going to do?" Brock McMunn asked, looking at me.

"My money is tied up in these local banks, so I need to stay
around here until I can take it out," I said. "I've got some contract
work with the railroads to finish up for Mr. Alexander, and then I'm
going to head west, once and for all."

"I've heard that a good number of the railroads are going to close
down," Buck Lathrop said. "I doubt that those contracts will be any
good."

"I don't give up easily," I said. "If I can get something back, I'll stay with it. I'm finding a lot of issues with several of the railroads between Chicago and New York, like the Lake Shore and Michigan Southern Railway. They didn't honor the contracts that Mr. Alexander had with them. I've noticed that Cornelius Vanderbilt is trying to take control of many of the railroads between Chicago and New York now. Something smells funny."

"Be careful with Vanderbilt," Brock McMunn said. "He's ruthless. He has an army of lawyers who attack like a swarm of bees."

"I got quite an earful about Commodore Vanderbilt when I was on the buffalo-hunting trip in Kansas a while back," I said. "James Fisk had nothing nice to say about the man, but Senator Roscoe Conkling kept defending him. Jeanine Alexander told me that she met Vanderbilt once at a horse race. He won a lot of money on one of her horses. She said he came by and thanked her. She liked him."

Buck Lathrop picked up the newspaper and waved it at me. "I bet you're mighty happy that you sold that Credit Mobilier stock when you did. What a mess they're in."

"I knew enough of the players to be able to anticipate the disaster that they were heading for," I said. "They were hoping that they could make the company so big that the government would help to keep it afloat, but they were wrong."

I ordered another round of drinks. "I think you both know that President Grant will never get us out of this financial mess unscathed. The Republicans are going to be soundly defeated in next year's elections."

"There's little doubt about that," Buck Lathrop said. "But the good news is that when the Democrats get in office, they will end the reconstruction programs in the South and free up the people of the Confederacy to go on with their lives."

"Yes, that will be good for the country," I said, "but it will take some time to get all of the Union people out of there...probably five years."

"More like ten," Brock McMunn said. "Grant's people have plundered the South, and there's not much left down there—but enough to keep the bloodsuckers around for a while longer."

"They've ripped out hundreds of thousands of trees and hauled the wood to the North," Buck Lathrop said. "There's nothing left to build with in the South."

"How well I know," I said. "The people are fighting mad, but their ability to fight has been taken away. They don't have any guns either."

"A hundred years from now, the South will still hate the North for what they've done," Brock McMunn said.

CHAPTER SEVENTY-SEVEN

—◦—≡◦≡—◦—

Alexander National Bank
Alexander, Illinois
November 17, 1874

"I'm not going to be able to open up this bank again, John, the Panic of 1873 was too much for me," William Orear said. "I'm meeting with each one of my depositors, like you, and negotiating an arrangement to close out the account. Your options are detailed on this document."

He pushed a single sheet of paper across the top of his dark walnut desk. There were three options, and none of them guaranteed that I would get all of my money back. I'd already decided what I was going to do before the meeting started. "I'll move my account to the Mercantile Bank of Chicago. I'm aware that John T. Alexander has moved his account there."

"Please circle that option and sign the document, John. I believe that you'll be happy with that choice."

Some of the larger banks made loans to the smaller banks to keep them afloat or purchased their accounts to help close them out. In some cases, investors lost everything. William Orear was an honorable man who tried his best to make sure that his customers ended up getting at least half of their money back.

"The election results of two weeks ago will guarantee that Congress will not come to the aid of the banks," William Orear said. "The Republicans lost ninety-six seats in the House of Representatives. The Democrats will place their attention on sending home the Union occupation troops and restoring commerce in the South to their own people."

William Orear was aware that I was from Virginia. "Maybe they'll be able to stop fighting back at night when they try to protect themselves," he said, knowing about the shootings and burnings that had gone on for years. "You know it's quite possible that they'll get their man elected as our next president in two years."

"You can't blame the people for voting this way," I said. "The Republicans have printed money to try to hide the problems that the country is facing. They've created thousands of meaningless government jobs as favors."

As I was rising from my chair to leave, William Orear said, "John, I think you're aware that J.T. has a serious debt problem. All of his progress since that terrible summer of 1868 has been erased. I believe that he will soon be approached by Mr. Jones with an offer to purchase his land in Champaign County."

I sat back down. "I don't believe that Mr. Alexander wishes to sell Broadlands...and I know that he doesn't wish to sell it to Bob Jones."

"This depression, or whatever you want to call it, has put great pressure on those who hold J. T. Alexander and Company's debt," William Orear said. "He has no choice, John—he *must* sell off his assets."

He paused for a moment before continuing. "As far as Mr. Jones is concerned, I understand what you're saying, but I can tell you that other potential buyers are backing off when he makes an offer...I'm not sure why."

I shrugged.

William Orear wrote something on a sheet of paper, and then he pushed it across the desktop to me. "I suggest that J.T. contact Wentworth Buchanan, the general manager of the Bank of Montreal. He will make a fair offer."

⌘ ⌘ ⌘

"Don't you think we've gone on long enough with the use of these silly code names?" Badger asked, looking around at the crowd at the Ebbitt Inn to make sure that no one was paying attention to him.

The people in the nation's capital were paying more attention to the other person sitting at the same table, near the roaring fireplace. "Once I'm elected president, we can dispense with such formalities, but until then, we will be cautious," Raven said, acknowledging a few waves from nearby legislators.

"That prospect looked a lot more promising until the election two weeks ago," Badger said. Some people recognized him as well.

"Admittedly so," Raven said. "I have two years to get that problem fixed, and I certainly intend to do so. The Democrats have no viable candidate...except perhaps Sam Tilden, our esteemed governor, and I'm quite sure that he's not interested in running for the office."

"I'm certainly in a position to keep a close watch on him, and I'll do that." Badger paused for a moment to carefully select his words. "There are others who could be nominated as the Republican candidate instead of you...Elihu Washburne of Illinois, Rutherford Hayes of Ohio, or our own William Wheeler."

"Wheeler!" Raven bristled. Heads turned. "Don't make me laugh. If someone from New York is going to get the nod, it's going to be me, the senator from New York, not a representative!"

Badger decided that it was time to appear more optimistic. "I should soon be in a position to realize more substantial profits in the beef industry in our fair state, adding to your campaign coffers."

"That's the stuff," Raven said excitedly. "And soon, Bear will have secured that piece of property in Illinois that he's been after for so long."

"Good," Badger said. "We've shut down Abilene, and we've almost broken the back of the so-called Cattle King. Others have noticed what we're capable of doing if they don't join us."

CHAPTER SEVENTY-EIGHT

— ≡✦≡ —

Louisville, Kentucky
May 17, 1875

The excitement from the crowd of over ten thousand people filled the air on this sunny Monday afternoon at the new racetrack at the south end of the city of Louisville, Kentucky. The 320 members of the Louisville Jockey Club had each contributed one hundred dollars to scrape out a 1½-mile racetrack and construct a grandstand for two thousand onlookers. Their idea was to shape their Kentucky Derby after England's world-famous Epsom Derby, an annual event.

Jason and Jeanine Alexander and I were fortunate enough to have seats in the grandstand, compliments of Hal Price McGrath, who had two horses in the big race, including the favorite, an unruly stallion named Chesapeake. McGrath had assured us that none of the entrants could beat him, and he encouraged us to bet on his stallion as he had done. "Chesapeake is a come-from-behinder," Jeanine said, "and that's pretty risky in my mind. There are fourteen more three-year-olds out there, and it's easy for somebody in the back to get blocked."

"But the track is eighty feet wide in the stretches and sixty feet wide in the turns," Jason said. "If he can't go through them, he may be fast enough to go around them."

"They'll only be out there for less than three minutes," Jeanine said. "That's a lot of work for any horse to accomplish in such a short time. I put a few dollars on a different horse."

Jason nodded. "Which one is that?"

"That's my secret—I'll let you know if I win. What do you think, John?"

"What?" I asked. "I'm sorry...I'm distracted."

"What's wrong?" Jeanine asked.

"I see Rafner B. Hale and Senator Roscoe Conkling sitting together down there...about ten rows in front of us," I said. "I was watching them."

"I didn't know that they were friends," Jason said.

"Colonel Mosby told me a lot about them," I said. "They're not exactly friends...I would call them business associates. They're like two wolves feeding on the same carcass—as long as there's enough for both, they get along just fine."

I turned to look at Jeanine. "You were talking about picking the winner. I certainly wouldn't bet against McGrath—and he has *two* horses in the race."

"Yes," she said, "but the other one is just a rabbit for the others to chase until Chesapeake wishes to overtake him." She sounded as if she knew what she was talking about. "You didn't bet on a rabbit did you, John?"

The handlers were busy trying to get the horses to the line that had been drawn across the track in the dirt. Chesapeake's jockey, Bobby Swim, was having a terrible time controlling the big bay stallion as he bucked like a wild horse. Even after he was finally brought to the line, he lurched forward just as the flag went down to signal the start of the race.

The crowd complained loudly as the judge called for a re-start. Several of the owners shouted at the judge, and one of them threatened to pull his horse from the race. I understood why that man was so upset. His horse, Volcano, had exploded from the starting line as if he'd been shot from a cannon. As he was guided back by the handler, it was obvious that the big horse was confused and disturbed.

Jason looked at me and said, "He won't win...he's done for."

"I agree," I said. "His owner is stalling for time, and I don't blame him."

Minutes later, the flag came down again, and the race began. McGrath's other horse, Aristides, jumped out ahead of the bunched-up group that came off the starting line together in a heap. He was the rabbit—the horse that was accustomed to taking the lead and wearing down the others by setting a fast pace early in the race.

McGrath was stationed at the last turn in order that he might signal the rabbit's jockey, Oliver Lewis, to pull back on Aristides when Chesapeake had rounded the corner at full stride behind him in his explosive run for the finish line.

"Wow!" I exclaimed. "Aristides can run." Only Volcano and one other horse broke away to stay close to Aristides, and at the one-mile marker, the red chestnut stallion was all alone.

His muscles rippled in the Kentucky sunshine as he carried the green-and-orange silks of H. P. McGrath like a Confederate warhorse charging into battle. "There's no horse in the world that can beat him today!" Jeanine shouted.

Oliver Lewis pulled back with all of his might as Aristides came into the last turn. The jockey looked for his boss.

McGrath strained to find Chesapeake. His prize horse was near the rear of the pack. He waved frantically for Lewis to give Aristides his head and let him run to the finish line. Lewis wasn't sure what was happening. What did McGrath want him to do?

Lewis tucked his head under his arm in order to look behind him. Chesapeake, the stablemate of Aristides, wasn't there. Lewis looked up and let the reins slide forward through his fingers. The warhorse surged forward with a jolt that rocked Lewis back in his slim saddle.

McGrath watched in awe as his rabbit won the race in 2:37.75. Chesapeake finally rallied to finish in eighth place. Volcano came in second.

The man sitting behind me laughed. "Chesapeake ran two long races in the past week. That stupid McGrath wore him out. He's damn lucky he had that other little horse out there."

Jason turned to me and smiled. "That horse stands about fifteen hands, just like my horse, Dandy." He pulled his betting slip from his pocket and stood up. "I listened to Jeanine. I've got some money to collect. I'll see you down there at the winner's circle. We will want to congratulate Mr. McGrath."

Jeanine waived her ticket in my face. She smiled and got up to follow her brother to the betting station in order to collect her winnings.

I tore up my ticket.

CHAPTER SEVENTY-NINE

Jacksonville, Illinois
December 25, 1875

Tanner Biggs spent the better part of Christmas Day in the only tavern in town that was open. And it wasn't open to the public on this holiday—just special customers who slipped in through the back door to the place. They were a motley crew of loners who tried their best to forget what day it was.

Some of the poker players grumbled as Tanner Biggs gathered up his winnings and pushed back from the table well into the evening. His toothless smile was unfriendly, and the complaints stopped. "Don't worry," he said. "I'll give all of you bastards a chance to win it back the next time I see your ugly faces."

Even though he had consumed a lot of alcohol during the day, Tanner Biggs stood up straight and walked steadily to the back door. It was cold outside, and it was bitter cold when the strong wind from the northwest had the room to hit you with its punch when a downtown building didn't hinder it. Tanner Biggs put his face right into it as he walked to North Sandy Street. He found it invigorating.

As he neared the Jacksonville Stockyards, he took special care to watch for any others on the street, but it was no surprise to find that he had the whole place to himself. It was Christmas after all. "Only a fool would be out on a night like this," he mumbled to himself.

William Thompson advertised that his Jacksonville Stockyards would easily take in five hundred head of stock, more than any other place in the area except Chicago and St. Louis. He had borrowed heavily from William Orear's Jacksonville National Bank in order to construct the buildings, stalls, and feeding areas that covered an entire city block just north of the downtown square.

About twenty mules were feeding on hay that was stacked in the corner of the stable area. They looked up at him briefly but then returned to their food.

It was a perfect spot on the northwest corner, and the hay bales were stacked together so that they continued on up into the nearby barn. Tanner Biggs stood still, listening and watching for anything other than animal life. Only mules, horses, and cattle were present. There wasn't even a dog.

He put his back to the wind and squatted down. He struck a match and dropped it at the foot of the nearest bale. The dry hay went up quickly. Tanner Biggs enjoyed the warmth of it for just a moment.

In his mind, he could visualize how the wind-driven fire was going to spread across the complex of wooden buildings and hay. He wondered if it might even reach some of the buildings on the square before the firemen could get it stopped.

He laughed and walked away.

CHAPTER EIGHTY

——◆≡◆——

Alexander, Illinois
March 1, 1876

As I headed out to the Alexander's place on Wednesday morning, I passed the sullen Red Beard coming back into town. I knew that he had approached John T. Alexander to make another offer on Broadlands, and I also knew that he was turned down once again.

John T. Alexander wasn't going to sell his property in Champaign County to Bob Jones. Over the past few weeks, we'd worked out an agreement with some investors in Canada to form a partnership that would allow him to continue to operate his cattle business at the Broadlands Farm. The final documents would be signed shortly.

The deal had come just in time, because his creditors were becoming much more demanding. Men like William Orear had suffered greatly when their loans to places like the Jacksonville Stockyards were unable to be paid off. A string of very bad luck seemed to have hit many of the bankers who had loaned money to John T. Alexander.

I waved to Jeanine as I dismounted and tied Sting to the post in front of the house. Jeanine was feeding the horses in the corral that was east of the stable. We were going riding later.

I picked up a cup of coffee in the kitchen before joining John T. Alexander and his sons in the office. They were going over the inventory of stock at the various locations because this was the first of March, the day when all movement from Texas ceased under Illinois law. I took a seat and sipped hot coffee as they tallied the numbers.

"We have enough stock on hand to meet our market obligations for the next eight months, just as we planned," John T. Alexander said. "You boys have done a fine job keeping things moving during the winter while I was ailing."

"We've got an extra five thousand head of Texas cattle at Broadlands for the New York market, Father," Jerome said. "Are you sure it's going to open up this summer like you planned?"

"I've been reading about the meat riots in the papers from the East," Jason said. "Those people aren't willing to tolerate the expensive beef prices any longer...and they're tired of eating horse meat. I think that market will be wide open very soon."

"Jason's right," John T. Alexander said. "The New Yorkers don't believe that the Texas cattle will make them sick—they know they were lied to. Now they're specifically calling for the Texas beef. Even Rafner B. Hale can't keep us out."

Jason and Jerome got up to leave. "Before you fellows head off, you might want to stay a bit longer while I go through these railroad accounts with your father," I said. John T. Alexander motioned for the two of them to sit back down.

I pulled my papers from the leather carrying case that John T. Alexander had given me. I enjoyed showing off the intertwined JTA brand that was emblazoned upon it when I carried it out of town into places like New York.

"I don't have a problem with the numbers that I've received from the Toledo, Wabash, and Western and the Illinois Central," I said, "but I'm suspicious about the railroads between Chicago and New York. It looks to me as if the Lake Shore and Michigan Southern

Railway actually changed the numbers in order to reduce our credit drawbacks."

"Those are pretty strong words, John," Jason said. "How sure are you?"

"I'm sure enough to take on Cornelius Vanderbilt," I said, "because he's about to take the controlling interest in all of the railroads between Chicago and New York."

"Tell me more," John T. Alexander said.

"I've been trading transportation information with all of the members of the cattleman's association," I said. "I have signed documents that prove that others were given a lower price than J. T. Alexander and Company received credit for—a clear violation of the contract. As far as the intentional fraud goes, Mr. H. has talked to a man who said he was ordered to adjust the numbers. We would have to put him on the witness stand, and even then, he might not tell the truth."

"Vanderbilt has one of the best attorneys in the country by the name of John Burrill," Jason said. "We'll not be wanting to take him on. I think we should just push for getting our credits adjusted properly."

John T. Alexander was not convinced. "Maybe so," he said.

⌘　⌘　⌘

Later that same day, Tanner Biggs stopped in to see Bob Jones in his office on the square in Alexander. "You got any more of that good whiskey that you had the last time that I was here?"

Bob Jones thought it might help to hurry his unwanted guest along if he refused to offer him a drink. "No...I'm fresh out," he said. "I thought I told you not to come by here in the daytime."

"You tell me a lot of things, Bob." Tanner Biggs pulled his knife from his boot.

He scraped some dirt from under his fingernails. "You told me that all of those fires would help make John T. Alexander's bankers force him to sell the Broadlands Farm to you. You told me that I would be the superintendent of that place by now."

Tanner Biggs slipped his knife back into his boot. He scooped a wad of tobacco out of his mouth with his finger and tossed it across the floor, making a terrible mess. "Frankly, I'm getting tired of listening to you, Bob."

Bob Jones was a big man. His face reddened to the color of his beard. "You best get your Rebel ass out of my office before I help you out."

Tanner Biggs slowly rose from his chair. He stepped on the tobacco and ground it into the floor with his boots. "You're lucky I chose to come in here during the daylight, Bob. You may not be so lucky next time."

CHAPTER EIGHTY-ONE

Central Park
Alexander, Illinois
July 4, 1876

The celebration had been anticipated for quite some time. Every location in the country was ready for the nation's one-hundredth birthday, and the town of Alexander was no exception. It was a warm day, but not uncomfortable unless you were in the direct sunlight. There was a slight breeze from the west.

I helped Jerome bring a table and chairs to the Central Park in the wagon right after breakfast in order to hold a nice spot for the Alexander family under one of the large shade trees. We weren't the first family to arrive and prepare for the festivities. The Strawns and the Kumleys were already there, staking out their favorite places.

And Tanner Biggs was present as well.

He stood at the south end of the park near Front Street. My former companion pulled off his hat and made a sweeping bow. I didn't return the greeting. It had been a long while since I'd seen him, but I always had the feeling that he wasn't too far off. He had that skill.

Suddenly, the picnic had taken on a different flavor.

"What's he doing here?" Jerome asked.

"Probably more than celebrating," I said. "Let's get back to the farm."

By the time we returned with the others about an hour later, the park was already half-filled with an energetic crowd. Sides of beef and deer were being turned on spits over the fires. Tables were laden with vegetables and fruits, relishes and preserves, and salads. I had some favorites that I would be looking for, recalling previous gatherings in the park.

The clang of the horseshoes signaled the beginning of the games that would go well into the night. McPherson's tapped a keg of beer and placed it on a table in the southeast corner of the park. Everyone knew that this was a bad idea, but I didn't hear anyone complaining too loudly. Justice Owen Luby allowed the keg to remain. Fortunately, we were located on the northwest corner, about as far away from the keg as we could get. I noticed that a couple of families were relocating away from the keg area.

Hartman Zeller, a local farmer from Germany, grabbed his guitar and gathered a few of the local musicians in the southwest corner of the park. All would enjoy their pleasant tunes for hours to come.

Just before noon, Jeanine and I walked over to the railroad station to greet Jason and his friend Meredith Montgomery when they arrived from Jacksonville. Jason had departed early in the morning to take the first train to the city so that he could return with Meredith in time to enjoy the day with the rest of us.

"Jacksonville has quite a party of its own going on," Jason said, looking toward the park. The noisy crowd that was gathered around the beer keg held his eyes for a moment. He looked at me, and I shook my head in dismay.

"The train is full of people heading to Springfield," Meredith said. Her eyes were blue, and her sandy hair danced in the sun. "Thousands of people are gathering there near the capitol building.

My parents went over last night. Our good friend Elihu Washburne is being honored after making a great run for the Republican nomination at the convention in Cincinnati last month." Jason had known Meredith since before the war, and it was nice to see that she was spending the day with him here.

"Did you think Secretary Washburne would get the nod from the party?" I asked.

"Not really," Meredith said. "We thought the nomination would go to Roscoe Conkling from New York. It takes someone who is ruthless like he is to go on and win the whole thing, but one of his primary sources of campaign funds dried up on him. Henrietta Green suddenly withdrew her support for some unknown reason."

"In my opinion, Conkling would have been good for the *Democrats'* cause," I said.

Meredith laughed. "That's exactly what my father said. He doesn't like Conkling at all. I guess it doesn't matter now...Hayes is in."

"Let's not ruin the day by talking politics," Jason said, giving me the eye. Jeanine noticed and pulled me away to help move some food to the center tables.

"I still think you should have entered at least one of the horse races that will take place later today," I said.

She laughed. "John, you know full well that even my slowest horses would outrun anything else that would be entered from around here."

She was probably right about that, but I wasn't going to give up so easily. "Samuel Davis has some good stock, doesn't he?"

"Yes, he does, but I don't think he'll take the chance of getting any of them hurt in these roughhouse races," she said. "There were three horses injured on that bad turn about a mile south of town last year. It's not worth the risk for either one of us."

The noonday meal was a long, drawn-out affair that continued well into the afternoon. People took advantage of the opportunity to sample many different dishes, and when they missed something, its maker often reminded them about it. About an hour after the meal was finished, the desserts were brought out, and the whole process started over again. The pies, cookies, cakes, and cobblers were a second meal.

Things were done much the same way back in Virginia. It even smelled the same. It was times like this when I missed my home the most. I was keeping in touch with my cousin Stephen back there. He was growing grapes now.

The celebration was winding down a little bit by late afternoon, and some of the families with young children were preparing to leave. McPherson's replaced the first keg with a second one. I couldn't understand this line of thinking, and I was surprised that Justice Luby allowed it to continue. The Alexander family and I weren't planning on staying around long enough to find out what the end result might be. "The mosquitoes will feast on the sleeping bodies in the park tonight," Jeanine said. "How much alcohol in the blood can a mosquito handle, John?"

"That's a good question, Jeanine," I said and laughed. "Some will reach their limit tonight."

"Perhaps they'll explode when they get near a fire," she said with a laugh.

Just then, Henry Fitch appeared from the train station and walked to the center of the park, waving a piece of paper in his hand. He stepped on top of one of the tables that had been cleared, and he continued to wave the paper until he gained the attention of much of the crowd. The music stopped.

Jason and I walked over to be closer to him.

"I have just received a wire that is being transmitted along the railroad telegraph system this afternoon." Fitch's hand was shaking as he read from the paper. "The *Helena Herald* has reported that General George Armstrong Custer has been killed along with all of his men of the Seventh Cavalry. They were attacked and massacred by thousands of Indians near the Little Bighorn River not far from Fort Smith."

My mouth went dry. I'd fought against Custer in the war. He was no friend of mine, but I wasn't happy to hear how he'd died. I was aware that Jason knew him quite well.

Menacing shouts rang out. "Now we'll kill those redskins for sure." "Grant will lead the troops himself." "The only good Injun is a dead Injun."

One of the voices was recognizable. Tanner Biggs came forward with pistol raised. "I hate Custer, but I hate the Indians more," he said. He fired two shots into the air.

Others from the keg crowd did likewise. People scattered in all directions. Justice Owen Luby moved swiftly on the lead trouble-maker, but in a flash, a knife appeared in the Rebel fighter's other hand. With a quick and deft move, Tanner Biggs plunged the knife into Justice Luby's side. For a moment, the blood on the extracted blade was the only indication that it had found its objective.

Hand-to-hand combat with Tanner Biggs was a sure ticket to the grave. I'd watched him kill a dozen Bluecoats in a matter of minutes without working up much of a sweat. He pushed aside the crumpled, bloodied body of Justice Luby and continued to move forward. He slashed his way through the screaming crowd. His black eyes were terrifying.

I recognized the determined, battlefield motion. He had a target in mind.

Jason sensed this as well, and the two of us moved to cut off Tanner's advance in the direction of the Alexander family gathered in the far corner of the park. He waved his pistol in one hand and his knife in the other. The people who moved frantically to get out of his way blocked ours, and Tanner arrived at his destination ahead of us.

He went right at the Chief. The skilled horse trainer was un-armed. He stood tall in front of his family, making sure that they were safe. If the Indian had a plan, it was well hidden. It looked to me as if he was just going to stand there and be cut down.

But just as Tanner Biggs raised his knife high above his head to strike the Chief, a loud shot rang out from close range.

The bewildered attacker flew back, taking one quick look with frozen eyes at Jeanine Alexander's smoking gun before he crashed into a table of cakes and pies. Two dogs madly rushed in to lap up the sweets that covered his lifeless body. No one shagged them away.

I gently pried the rifle from Jeanine's shaking hands and helped her to a seat. "Is...is he dead?"

"Yes," I said.

"I killed him." Others gathered around her.

"You saved lives," I said. "You did what you had to do." The others nodded.

Order was restored, and the remaining rowdies, who had quickly backed off, were sent on their way. Dr. Baker tended to Justice Luby and the others who'd been cut.

The day's celebration in Alexander would be long remembered. For years it was known as Custer's Fourth. From that day forward, alcohol was forbidden in the park.

As we headed back to the farm about an hour later, I sat in the wagon with my arms around Jeanine. She was feeling better. I looked up at the stars, wondering what the celebration in this town a hundred years from now would be like. It would really have to be something to upstage this one.

CHAPTER EIGHTY-TWO

❧

Albany, New York
August 17, 1876

John T. Alexander and I arrived in Albany on Thursday morning in preparation for a meeting with Cornelius Vanderbilt. My boss pressed for the meeting for several weeks before Vanderbilt reluctantly agreed. I'd convinced Mr. Alexander that we should try to negotiate a settlement directly with Vanderbilt before seeking relief with each of his railroads in the courts. No attorneys were to be present in our meeting today.

It was hot and humid, so we felt right at home. We stepped from the train at the massive complex of railroad yards in West Albany before going downtown to meet the Commodore. West Albany was a crossroads for the rails that came west from Chicago and north from New York City. The stench was a reminder of the presence of the nearby stockyard and slaughterhouse. The whole area seemed to have doubled in size since my last visit.

Edward Hinrichsen had arranged for us to meet with a friend of his who worked here. David Maywood was a bookkeeper who recorded the freight transactions for many of Vanderbilt's railroads.

A man fitting his description sat alone on a bench in the station's waiting room.

Our instructions were to walk near him and greet him by saying, "Good morning, sir, it's a fine day in Albany," and then walk on. We did so, and the clean-shaven man with the soft black cap got up and followed us out the door.

We continued to walk toward a group of buildings to the south until he said, "This is fine. We can talk here." We sat down on some benches in what looked like a rest area shaded by a small grove of maple trees.

David Maywood never stopped moving his head as he scanned the area looking for those who might see us. "I'm doing this only because I owe a great favor to Edward. I can't stay long."

"What can you tell us?" John T. Alexander asked.

"I told Edward that it must be you, Mr. Alexander, and you alone whom I meet with, but I know who Mr. Demsond is, so his presence is acceptable." David Maywood cleared his throat. "I keep track of the livestock freight transactions from Chicago. I have a record of all of our rates, freight bills, receipts, vouchers, and rebates." He paused when he thought he saw someone approaching, but there was no one in sight. "Don't look at me that way," he said. "Don't you understand that they will kill me if they find out?"

"Please go on," John T. Alexander said. "I know this is difficult for you." John T. Alexander was sympathetic, but his deal to sell Broadlands to the investors in Canada hadn't materialized, and he was desperate. He knew that his business was failing and that this man could help to save it.

"Suffice it to say, Mr. Alexander, that you're being cheated. You aren't getting the deal that Mr. Demsond negotiated on your behalf—you aren't getting the lowest rates. Your drawbacks don't reflect anything close to what you should be getting, and they haven't for a long time. I am aware that Mr. Demsond has made attempts to seek a resolution, but even when he does obtain an adjustment, the records are further manipulated to deny the full recompense."

"So you're saying that it's not an oversight, but a fraudulent act?" I asked. This is what I had repeatedly reported to my boss, but it was good for him to hear it from someone else.

"That's precisely what I'm saying," he said. "Now, I've already said more than I should, and I must keep my job, so I will deny all of this if you try to get me to testify in court, let me warn you. I now consider my debt to Edward Hinrichsen repaid in full, and I bid you gentlemen good day." David Maywood rose from his seat, turned, and walked away.

We sat there and watched him go. When he was out of earshot, I said, "What do you think?"

"I think we'll try to do this without harming the man, but we'll put him on the witness stand if necessary."

I was sure that it would be necessary.

⌘ ⌘ ⌘

Cornelius Vanderbilt was in the process of moving his headquarters to New York City. His office had bare spots where items had already been removed. I tried to guess what might have been there. What remained in his office was impressive in itself. This was a man who wanted everyone to know that he was wealthy.

John T. Alexander wasn't impressed. Vanderbilt's plush office and his obvious attempt to demonstrate a level of annoyance with our presence didn't have the desired impact. I sensed that Vanderbilt noticed this right away. The two men stared at each other in silence before we sat down to talk. I was reminded of two boxers sizing each other up before one of them took the first swing.

We took our seats.

Immediately, there was a short knock on the door. Rafner B. Hale entered the room.

"I've asked my chief operations officer, Rafner Hale, to join us," Vanderbilt said. "I believe you gentlemen have met Mr. Hale in the past, am I not correct?"

We nodded and shook hands. After returning to our seats, John T. Alexander seized the opportunity to open the discussion. "We're partners in free enterprise, Mr. Vanderbilt. I have many ways to get my cattle to New York, but I have an agreement to transport them exclusively on your railroads between Chicago and New York. In return, you have agreed to give me your best rate...always. I am satisfied with this arrangement, and I have not deviated from it."

"I'm satisfied as well," he said, "so why are you here?"

"I think you know why we're here, Mr. Vanderbilt. My chief operations officer, Mr. Demsond, has gathered information that suggests that I have *not* been given the best rate on a significant number of my shipments. I wish to give you the opportunity to correct this mistake in order that we might continue with the mutually acceptable arrangement going forward."

Cornelius Vanderbilt ran his hand through his thinning white hair and stroked his beard, which looked like sheep's wool. "What do you have to say about this, Mr. Hale?"

Rafner B. Hale shrugged. "I'm not aware of any discrepancy."

John T. Alexander smiled and looked in my direction, giving me the floor. "I have the records to back up this claim," I said. "The rates have been obtained from the multitude of livestock men who belong to the association."

"Oh, the wonderful association," Hale exclaimed. "It's just another union that adds to our costs. Your rates would be lower if the association would go away."

"I know better than that," John T. Alexander said, remaining calm.

"I'll ask Mr. Hale here to take another look at our records," Vanderbilt said. "We'll let you know if he finds any errors, and we'll correct them right away." He paused for a moment. "I certainly hope that you don't plan to pursue this matter in the courts if you're not satisfied with our response, Mr. Alexander."

"Frankly, I have no choice in the matter, Mr. Vanderbilt. I think you know that."

"That will be a waste of time, Mr. Alexander, a waste of time—and money, I might add. Let me remind you that I started this business by ferrying passengers and farm produce between Staten Island and New York on a leaky boat. I hold on to what I have by doing whatever it takes."

John T. Alexander was quick to respond. "And I started my business by driving cattle from Ohio to New York when I was six years old. I feed people who are hungry, and I do what it takes to get the livestock there."

After an extended period of silence, during which the boxers just stared at each other, it became obvious that the meeting had ended.

As John T. Alexander and I walked to the door, Hale said, "Albany now has some of the best disease-free Texas beef that the state has to offer. You might want to try it out at Ben's Prime Cut. You can get the address at the desk at the Albany Union Hotel."

As soon as we got outside, I said, "How did they know we were staying at that hotel?"

"It's their town," John T. Alexander said. "It's their business to know what goes on here. I think we'll try out their *best beef* and see if it lives up to their claims."

CHAPTER EIGHTY-THREE

＊＊＋＝＋＊＊

*John T. Alexander Farm
August 21, 1876*

We departed Albany on the morning after our Thursday meeting with Vanderbilt and Hale. We discussed our strategy for filing the lawsuits, knowing we had plenty of evidence to prove that we were being cheated. Even though the legal costs would be high, the potential reward was enough to bring John T. Alexander completely out of debt. There was no choice in the matter.

Our interest in this discussion began to fall off by the time we reached Rochester because of some stomach problems. Both of us were ill. When we reached Buffalo a few hours later, we spent some extra time there, hoping that our situation would improve.

It did not. Nevertheless, John T. Alexander demanded that we press on.

We spent extra time in Erie, Pennsylvania, and Cleveland, Ohio. I started to feel better, but John T. Alexander seemed to be getting worse. He couldn't even stand up straight.

I kept the family informed of our delays with a steady stream of telegraph messages. Every time he felt a little bit better, we boarded the next available train and continued toward Chicago. This routine delayed our arrival there by almost thirty hours.

As soon as we reached Chicago, I contacted Gustavus Swift to obtain the name of his doctor. Gustavus arranged for John T. Alexander to be brought to his home and placed under the direct care of Dr. Raymond Jordan.

Upon close examination of his patient, Dr. Jordan declared that John T. Alexander was a very sick man and made it clear that he should not travel for at least a week. I informed the family and settled in for what looked to be a long stay.

John T. Alexander felt better on Friday. He insisted that we head home, ignoring the doctor's orders. I tried to reason with him, but there was no holding him back. "I'm going home," he said.

He was in terrible shape by the time we arrived at the railroad station in the town named after him. Edward Hinrichsen and I got him home quickly. Dr. Baker tried every remedy that was available.

When I saw John T. Alexander on Sunday, he looked so bad that I thought he was going to die.

On Monday morning, he did.

CHAPTER EIGHTY-FOUR

——— ≡✦≡ ———

John T. Alexander Farm
September 3, 1876

I got through the next several days by not thinking too much about what was going on. The shock of the whole thing didn't wear off easily. Mary Alexander was strong, and she came forward to make it clear what she wanted to be done.

The funeral was quick and quiet. John T. Alexander was in his grave before many found out that he was gone. Newspaper reporters arrived and departed shortly afterward. On the second Sunday after his passing, Edward Hinrichsen and I were the only ones outside of the family who were invited to sit in on a meeting that Mary Alexander requested.

She sat behind the Cattle King's desk. The looking glass was there, right in front of me. I sat next to Jeanine. Jason and Jerome sat in their usual chairs. I wasn't sure that I should be here, but I wanted to help move things forward. Mary Alexander looked at me and began. "John, I want you to continue going after the railroads, but I can't wait for what I know will be a long time and an uncertain outcome. Spend what you need to spend. We're in the right, and we're not backing down from the likes of Cornelius Vanderbilt. Edward, I know you will continue to help out in any way that you can." He nodded, wiping away tears.

"I'm hoping that we will soon get a ruling from the Supreme Court regarding *Munn versus Illinois*," I said. "The case was argued way back in January, and a decision is yet to be rendered. The railroad people are getting nervous, so that tells me that they might lose the case, which means the states will be given the right to regulate the railroad rates. That will force the railroad to explain and publish their rates, and that should help us."

Mary Alexander smiled. "We'll take all the help that we can get."

I was seeing a side of Mary Alexander that had remained subdued in the shadow of her iconic husband for so many years. Had circumstances remained as they were, she would have been quite happy to continue to lead the life that she so loved, but things had changed, so she had changed accordingly.

"Jason, I want to sell Broadlands. See if we can reconstruct that deal with the Bank of Montreal. If not, I want you to sell it piece by piece to pay back our creditors in full—I want us out of debt, once and for all. I'm tired of owing people so much money...I won't live that way any longer. I saw what it did to your father. He kept it all inside—but I lived it with him."

"It's the nature of the business," Jason said, "but I understand what you're saying, Mother." I think Jason wanted to say more, but he refrained.

"Jerome, I want you to begin the transition away from cattle feeding and into crop farming. This soil here is good for farming. I've listened to Edward tell your father about the promising future in grain sales. That's the direction that I want us to move in."

Jerome nodded as his mother described his future. I was quite familiar with the arguments that Mr. H. had put forward about the growing market for grains, and he was very convincing. It was more than just talk because he had a lot of his own money invested in his grain sales business.

Mary Alexander rose from the chair and walked to the window. As she looked out at the farm, a puff of wind blew the curtains across her shoulders, and she stood there like an angel. I marveled at the same scene that I had witnessed years before when John T. Alexander stood in the same place. A chill crawled up the spine of my back.

Without turning, she said, "Jeanine, I want you to keep the horses. You're good with them...very good. That's your calling. The cattle will go, but the horses will stay."

Jeanine smiled but said nothing. Her mother understood, even though she didn't turn to see her daughter's face, which was tracked with tears.

The silence lingered in the room. It was a moment for memories that we shared without the need to talk about them...memories from the heart. It was a moving moment for me to be present in that special room with the Alexander family.

⌘ ⌘ ⌘

At the same time in Washington, Badger tossed his copy of the *New York Times* onto the top of Raven's expensive antique desk. "I met with this guy just a few days ago in the Commodore's office in Albany."

"You don't say," Raven said. "What a coincidence."

"The article calls him the Great Cattle King of the Mississippi Valley. As far as I'm concerned, he's just another insignificant legend who will soon be forgotten. What's more important is that it shouldn't take Bear long to purchase the Broadlands Farm—I'm sure they'll sell it now—and you can close the deal with the Commodore."

"You're wrong. They're not going to sell it to Bob Jones," Raven said. "If you would come down off your pedestal long enough to take a look beyond yourself, you would see that. I was counting on that money to pay back those who supported my *first* campaign for president."

"Rutherford Hayes was a big mistake," Badger said. "He may not be capable of defeating Tilden. We'll get you in next time."

"There will be no *next time*, Hale, you're finished. I've already talked to Vanderbilt and Hetty Green. You need to get out of town right away...heed my warning."

"Hetty Green! She abandoned you! Why would you side with her? You can't do this!"

"It's done—get out."

"You'll be sorry...you'll see," Hale sputtered. "I'll bring down your little fiefdom, Conkling. You're a pompous ass. The new president, whoever it turns out to be, will see that. You're the one who's finished, not me."

When Rafner B. Hale went outside, he saw Bob Jones and three toughs off in the distance. They followed him as he hurried away.

Rafner B. Hale was never seen again. He just disappeared from the face of the earth.

CHAPTER EIGHTY-FIVE

―――・――

La Salle Street Station
Chicago, Illinois
December 29, 1876

The lawsuits were filed against several railroads. J. T. Alexander and Company filed lawsuits in Illinois and New York, and in every state between them. George McConnell and his group of attorneys were very optimistic. In fact, once the deposition from David Maywood was obtained, they expected that Vanderbilt would be forced to agree to a favorable settlement...a settlement that would clear the Alexander family of all its debt and leave a sizable sum for the ongoing operation.

After the sale of the Broadlands Farm to the Bank of Montreal fell through, Jason turned over the management of the disposition of the Champaign County property to a group led by the Ayers family of Jacksonville. Jason told me that he was going to wed Meredith Montgomery, and they were going to move to Washington. No announcement had been made as yet.

Jeanine and I began some serious discussions about the future as well. We talked about a ranch in Colorado. She was willing to take her horses there. I was ready to go as soon as the legal matters with the railroads were finished.

I was sitting in the LaSalle Street Station and waiting for David Maywood to arrive on the late train in the very early hours of the next morning. I arrived early, and I wasn't looking forward to facing him. I was prepared to receive the brunt of his dislike for what we had done by getting him directly involved. I could certainly understand how he felt.

We just couldn't see any way around it. Without his testimony, the attorneys said that we didn't have a case that would stand up in court. With his testimony, we felt that we would win.

After he arrived and calmed down, I was prepared to tell him that he had a good job working for Gustavus Swift here in Chicago. We were sure that he would want to leave the New York area and get away from the vengeful Vanderbilt. He would see to it that David Maywood would never be able to get a job with any railroad company. Sometimes the good guys get treated worse than the bad guys… all too often.

Raising horses in Colorado was looking better all the time. I was ready once and for all to put the War Between the States and all of its ugliness behind me. I was ready to move on past the bad fortune that beset John T. Alexander. I was ready to spend the rest of my days with Jeanine if she would marry me.

As I sat here in the LaSalle Street Station, I decided that I would ask Jeanine to marry me as soon as I returned to Alexander. I couldn't see any reason to hold off any longer. I needed to find out, one way or the other.

I had a long wait, so I started to go through my stack of newspapers. Story after story described the vicious battle over the outcome of the November election. Rutherford Hayes and Samuel Tilden both claimed victory. The Electoral Commission was to decide the outcome, but the newspaper reporters told of a compromise that was being worked out between the Republicans and the Democrats.

Roscoe Conkling, the powerful New York senator, was leading the Republican effort, and it was rumored that he had offered to withdraw all federal troops from the South if Tilden would concede. Conkling knew that the South could not turn down such an offer.

My reading was interrupted with a commotion in the vicinity of the station agent's office. I watched as the crowd of railroad personnel grew. Judging from the looks on their faces, something terrible had happened.

Curiosity drove me to rise from my uncomfortable seat and approach them. They quieted as I drew closer. "Is something wrong?" I asked.

They didn't answer. The station agent stepped forward. "Are you waiting for a train, sir?" The others listened carefully.

"Yes," I said. "I'm to meet a gentleman who is arriving on the Lake Shore and Michigan Southern Railway's Pacific Express."

The railroad men looked at each other. The station agent cleared his throat. "Sir, we've received a report that the Pacific Express has fallen into the Ashtabula River as a result of a collapsed bridge."

I froze and swallowed hard. "I'm familiar with that bridge," I said. "That's a seventy-foot fall."

"Yes," the station agent said, "I'm afraid they're all dead."

CHAPTER EIGHTY-SIX

John T. Alexander Farm
August 21, 1879

On the third anniversary of John T. Alexander's death, the family gathered to recall fond memories. I was a true member of the family after Jeanine and I were married in a double ceremony along with Jason Alexander and Meredith Montgomery just over two years ago. We were late getting started with children, and there was a race of sorts. Jeanine loved races. Thus far, it was a tie. There were two young babies, and two more were on the way.

Jason and Meredith moved to Washington shortly after their wedding, and this was the first time that we'd seen the two of them since then. Jason was working for a new agency in the government that collected information, which he called intelligence. "It's a lot like what I was doing during the war, but our whole approach is much more sophisticated. We probably know more about you than you know about yourself." I doubted that he was joking.

Jason and I remained close. We frequently exchanged letters and promised to try and see each other more often in the future. Jason kept me well-informed about the activities in Washington. Senator

Roscoe Conkling had broken ranks with President Rutherford B. Hayes when the president refused to allow the senator to make all of the federal appointments in his home state of New York. President Grant had given Conkling unlimited control for the past eight years.

Conkling threatened that he would oust Hayes and get Grant elected to an unprecedented third term, but the Republican Party was leaning to James A. Garfield. Conkling was furious. Jason feared that the vengeful Conkling would somehow undermine Garfield's presidency if he managed to be elected.

Right after the wedding, Jeanine and I purchased five thousand acres in Colorado just south of Fort Morgan. Interestingly, the property was in Morgan County. We constructed a small house and a large barn and stable complex. We moved the horses there during the past summer. It was peaceful and quiet, and we were very happy. It was a great place to raise a family.

The affairs of J. T. Alexander and Company were in the hands of lawyers as the lawsuits slowly moved through the legal system. George McConnell had handed off the cases to other attorneys in Jacksonville. Even though the star witness was gone, the *Munn* case allowed the lawsuits to be pursued more aggressively in each state because the states now had the power to regulate railroad rates. Unfortunately, few states were willing to take on the railroads, so they allowed them to continue to manipulate their rates to suit their own needs. I tried to stay close to the issues from a distance.

Jerome and his mother continued to live in the Alexander Mansion, as it had come to be known. It was still one of the most prominent homes in the entire area, but the Alexander name wasn't recognized as it was before. The legend had faded, and the cattle were gone. Jerome raised large crops of corn and wheat on the land. Some of the former hired hands who had obtained their land from John T. Alexander had actually become much more productive than Jerome with their crops.

Almost all of the debts had been paid off after the Broadlands property was sold along with some additional acres in Morgan County near the Alexander Farm. Mary Alexander was in the process of sharing the remaining assets with her children. After her husband's passing, she'd slowly lost interest in the farm, but one had to look hard to find any identifiable indication of that. She had recently purchased a house in Jacksonville, and Jeanine thought that she would move there before winter. Mary Alexander was only fifty-two years old and in good health.

"John, would you please give us an update on the remaining legal activities?" Mary Alexander asked. "I hate to mix business with pleasure, but this is important for all of us."

"Certainly," I said. "The attorneys haven't been able to gain access to the railroads' books, so it comes down to our records against their records. Vanderbilt has a cadre of highly skilled attorneys, and they are connected everywhere. Our local attorneys have been unable to get much assistance from the additional attorneys whom they have retained out East. That was probably a waste of money."

I noticed the discouraged faces in the room, so I decided to be a bit more optimistic. I looked at Jason Alexander. "Thanks to Jason's knowledge of Napoleon's Maxims of War, we countered Vanderbilt's defenses with a strategy of our own. We have initiated a discussion in Washington regarding the special nature of the commerce that takes place between states, and we have suggested that that sort of trade be regulated under *federal* law instead of *state* law.

"We've been astonished at how receptive a number of the lawmakers have been, and there is now a very strong movement in this direction, largely fueled by the bullying tactics of Conkling and Vanderbilt and others like them."

"I think we may see some legislation for the regulation of *interstate commerce* before much longer," Jason said. "However, it may not come in time to help us out. We find ourselves in a sad situation—the longer we wait, the better our chances are of winning in court as more and more dissatisfaction with the railroads arises within the society at large. But we're all anxious to put this thing to rest and get on with our lives."

"I'm afraid that is true, Jason. The attorneys have consolidated the cases and focused their attention on the New York courts," I said. "We'll lose there, but we'll appeal all the way to the Supreme Court. By that time, we might have enough support to win."

Mary Alexander sighed. "Will I be alive long enough to see this come to fruition?" she asked. We all looked at one another.

Jerome broke the silence. "Realistically, what are our chances there?"

"That's hard to say," I said, "but they're no worse than they are right now...and perhaps better under federal jurisdiction. We don't believe that Vanderbilt's reach extends all the way to the highest court in the country."

I was trying my best to believe that.

CHAPTER EIGHTY-SEVEN

－－ ≡◆≡ －－

United States Supreme Court
Washington, District of Columbia
November 15, 1886

Years passed as the legal cases slowly moved through a system that had become the most complex in the world. Eventually, the lawsuits against the railroads were combined into one case where the defendants were described collectively as *Lake Shore and Michigan Southern Railway Company and others*. After a long wait, the case was finally scheduled to be argued in front of the Supreme Court.

An early snow dusted Washington in the middle of November. Jeanine and I arrived on Friday night after leaving our three sons with her mother in Illinois. Jason and Meredith met us at the train station, and we stayed with them and their sons and daughters. We were anxious to return to Colorado before the bad weather set in out there.

There was little mention of the upcoming case in the newspapers. Jason said that the city was already closing down for the holidays. He also suspected that the railroads had paid the newspapers to keep the case quiet.

Morrison R. Waite was the chief justice of the Supreme Court. His overbearing presence was sure to dominate the proceedings. The Phi Beta Kappa graduate from Yale received his appointment to the court from President Grant in 1874. *The Nation* described him as being at "the front rank of second-rank lawyers." He was famous for his opinion in *Munn versus Illinois* in 1877 when he stated that "when a business is affected with a public interest, it becomes a public utility, making it subject to governmental regulation." He believed in the rights of the states to oversee, as they were so inclined, the activities of the railroads that passed through their boundaries.

The *Munn* case had been weakened by another case decided earlier this year. *Wabash, St. Louis, and Pacific Railway Company versus Illinois* greatly limited the power of the states to control interstate commerce. The *Wabash* case created an uproar, and Congress immediately went to work to hammer out the Interstate Commerce Act. The complex law was expected to be approved early next year. The advantage of the railroads would be diminished.

The new law would create an Interstate Commerce Commission to oversee all commerce between the states. It would instantly become the most powerful commission in the country, and intense lobbying had already begun for its membership. John Mosby had been mentioned as a possibility. "He doesn't have a chance," Jason said.

We knew that our hopes for a favorable decision from the Supreme Court were better if we waited for the new commission to be established, but our luck seemed to have run out a long time ago. The date for J. T. Alexander and Company's case was set, and we would have to live with it.

The trial began on Monday morning. Most of the time was utilized by the railroad attorneys as they described the process that the railroads used to fix rates. They had established a "trunk-line pool" as a depository for transactions crossing state lines. Payments were made from the pool to the railroads in proportion to the extent of their involvement. J. T. Alexander and Company's many shipments to the New York area passed through several states.

One of the railroad attorneys admitted that "the rates were honeycombed with rebates." J. T. Alexander and Company's attorney retorted, "To say that this pooling process is *extremely complex* is tantamount to saying that the Electoral Commission is extremely complex—we all know that. We cannot let it rule the day just because we don't understand it."

John Burrill was Cornelius Vanderbilt's top attorney. He sat quietly for a while, leaning back in his chair with his head resting against his interlaced fingers. He looked up at the ornamental ceiling, seeming to study each of its nooks and crannies. He appeared to be bored.

In the afternoon, John Burrill came forward and argued that the railroad rates had steadily declined for the well-being of the consumer. "The fourth-class rates from Chicago to New York have fallen from forty-five cents per one hundred pounds in 1876 to just twenty-five cents, just ten years later. The process, though complicated, has yielded undeniably positive results for our nation as a whole. Is that not our goal...the common good?" Burrill returned to his seat.

The defense's argument seemed to sit well with the court. Rather than defend the rebate process, the railroads had chosen to defend the process of pooling. The diversion was well crafted. One of the railroad attorneys concluded, "As to the effect of pooling upon rebates, it would be akin to comparing an enormous flock of crows to a few solitary blackbirds."

I wanted to sprout wings and leave town. Their strategy was perfectly directed toward the leanings of Chief Justice Waite and his loyal associates. At the end of the first day, I felt that our case was doomed to fail...but there was a second day to come.

⌘ ⌘ ⌘

Jeanine and I joined Jason and Meredith for supper at the Ebbitt Inn, one of Jason's favorite places. It was a small place with a lot of character. "It hasn't changed much since the war," Jason said. "I ate a lot of meals here and next door at the Ebbitt House, where Miss Carroll stayed. I'm sorry to say that she's no longer in good health."

"From what I read, she still has powerful connections here in Washington," I said.

"That's true," Meredith said. "She convinced President Arthur to deny Roscoe Conkling the secretary of state seat vacated by James Blaine right after the former president took office. Conkling was the leader of the New York machine that spawned Arthur's career. The outraged Conkling fought against Chester Arthur from that moment forward."

"Jason, it was your father who told me to follow the money," I said, "and the money led to Roscoe Conkling. I think he was the leader of the New York group that tried to destroy your father. I can connect him to Rafner B. Hale, Bob Jones, and Henrietta Green, among others."

"His legal firm frequently represents the railroads in front of the Supreme Court," Jason said. "He represented the Southern Pacific Railroad in a big case earlier this year. His picture was on the front page of all of the newspapers. I halfway hoped to see him here during our case."

"I think John might have enjoyed the opportunity to say a few words to him," Jeanine said.

"I would have," I said. "He's a powerful man who thought he could get away with anything, but he was proved wrong. He underestimated the government of his country. Despite its flaws, it's still better than anything that another country has been able to develop. So far, it's been able to stop the likes of Roscoe Conkling."

CHAPTER EIGHTY-EIGHT

—— ▰◆▰ ——

United States Supreme Court
Washington, District of Columbia
November 16, 1886

The presence of Jeanine, Jason, and Meredith in the courtroom helped me to remain calm until I took a seat on the witness stand, where I was viciously and expertly attacked by John Burrill early on Tuesday morning. He emphasized the time that I spent fighting the stalwarts of the Union cause, such as Commodore Cornelius Vanderbilt, when I served as his enemy in the Confederacy. He absurdly implied that I had carried the grudge forward into this case. He belittled the Confederacy and implied that all former Confederates remained enemies of the Union.

I refused to take the bait, and eventually he had to get down to the relevant details of the case. But instead of rebutting our claims, he took another approach. "Isn't it true, Captain Demsond, that your information was gathered considerably after the fact, and that your evidence was submitted after the statute of limitations in New York had expired?"

After an objection by our attorney was denied, I responded, "It was extremely difficult for us to gather the necessary information because the railroads purposely used confusing freight rates, which they frequently changed. It took a long time for us to accurately reconstruct what had taken place."

"It took so long," Burrill said with a laugh, "that one would suspect that your case was fabricated."

His comment was stricken from the record after the immediate objection was sustained.

I seized the opportunity to continue. "And as far as your question about the statute of limitations is concerned, we're not in agreement with regard to when the clock started. We believe it started at the time when we actually *discovered* the discrepancy between our records and those of the railroads with consideration for the death of the plaintiff and the plaintiff's associated bankruptcy."

"My, your attorneys have certainly trained you to use the right words, haven't they?" Burrill snorted. Once again, his caustic comment was removed from the record; nevertheless, Burrill seemed to move through the process with ease, and his experience in front of the high court was evident.

During the breaks, he bantered with the judges as if they were old friends. I expected them to gather for drinks as soon as we were done.

In military parlance, Burrill held the high ground, and he was openly demonstrating that. The battle was finished before it was started. I felt bad for the Alexander family, but I was glad that it was over.

When we departed the courtroom at the end of the day, we were uncomfortable about the proceeding. The eventual outcome was obvious, but not one of us was willing to say that.

Anxious to get out of Washington as soon as possible, Jeanine and I said our good-byes and went right to the train station for the trip to Colorado with a short stopover in Illinois to pick up our children.

"If it wasn't for Jason and Meredith being here, I wouldn't ever return to this horrible place," Jeanine said.

CHAPTER EIGHTY-NINE

＊━═◆═━＊

The Looking Glass Ranch
Morgan County, Colorado
January 28, 1887

Supreme Court Associate Justice John Marshall Harlan delivered the
opinion of the court on the tenth of January. The stocky Kentuckian
had been appointed by former President Rutherford B. Hayes in
1877 as a reward for handing over the Unionist delegates at the convention in 1876.

Between snowstorms at our ranch in Colorado, I was able to make
my way into town to get supplies and our mail. Jeanine and I read a
copy of the Supreme Court rendering on a cold Friday in January. It
only took sixteen paragraphs to destroy years of effort to right just
some of the wrongs done to John T. Alexander and others like him.

The court had sided with the railroad attorneys, who had identified an administrative oversight that resulted in missing New York's
statute of limitations deadline by a matter of just a few days. Associate
Justice Harlan defended the statute of limitations even though the
time limit had been exceeded only because the railroads had hidden
the facts just long enough to cause the delay.

I'd hoped that the court might be able to see through the smoke screen that the defense had put in front of it and get to the heart of the matter, but I was wrong. I couldn't help but recall the time when I'd sat with John T. Alexander in Judge Charles Constable's office in Jacksonville, listening to him lecture us about *the letter of the law*, warning that the handshake between gentlemen that had been used as a foundation to build this fine country was meaningless after the War Between the States. The judge had been absolutely correct, and it made me sick.

I could still see the look on John T. Alexander's face when he knew that, in his heart, Judge Constable was wrong—but he realized, in his mind, that the judge was right. He was right that our nation had substituted paper for the truth of a man's word.

Perhaps it was necessary...perhaps not. It didn't really matter.

"I guess that closes out the last chapter of my father's life," Jeanine said with tears in her eyes.

I held Jeanine close. "The good in him will live on much longer," I said. "There will always be people like your father who will step forward against overwhelming odds in order to do what is right. When *that* stops happening, it is *then*, and only then, that we close the final chapter for good."

Made in the USA
Charleston, SC
05 January 2014